KATHERINE HASTINGS

Vinci Books

vinci-books.com

Published by Vinci Books Ltd in 2026

1


A CIP catalogue record for this book is available from the British Library.
Paperback ISBN: 9781036715861
The EU GPSR authorised representative is Logos Europe, 9 rue Nicolas Poussion, 17000 La Rochelle, France contact@logoseurope.eu

## By Katherine Hastings

Immortal Hearts

*Into the Light*

*Awakened Light*

*Eternal Light*

The Wilder Widows

*The Wilder Widows*

*The Wilder Widows: Wilder Ever After*

*The Wilder Widows: Walk on the Wilder Side*

Door Peninsula Passions

*The Other Half*

*The Other Room*

*The Other Plan*

Rescue Ops Romance

*Colombian Chemistry*

*Sicilian Savior*

*Russian Rescue*

Daggers of Desire

*In the Assassin's Arms*

*Beneath the Assassin's Touch*

*By the Assassin's Side*

Also by Katherine Hastings

*Riches to Ruinville*

*The Big One*

*The Arch Pirate*

*A War Within*

Spectral Sleuths

*Millie and Mabel's Afterlife Adventures*

## Immortal Hearts Series

Though each book can be read as a standalone, this series is meant to be read in order. While each book features its own love story and HEA, the books follow a continued timeline and pick up where the last one left off without an extensive history, as well as feature reoccurring characters.

# Chapter One

## ANNELLA

The speakers pumped out the music from the band, flooding the club with sounds that made everybody on the dance floor pulse and move to the beat. Normally, I'd have been out dancing in the center of them, but dancing hadn't brought me to the club tonight.

I placed my chin on my hand and tracked the gorgeous bartender with my eyes. When he picked up the whiskey bottle from the drink well, his inked forearm swelled, and with it my desire to have it wrapped around me.

He lifted his head as he poured the liquor into the shot glass, and those emerald green eyes collided with mine. The look inside them sent my stomach into its own kind of dance routine.

A dance routine only Owen could inspire.

After over six hundred years on this planet, I'd never met a man that made me feel the way he did. The feelings he created in me felt primal and raw… not unlike the way he looked.

Owen towered over everyone with his incredible height,

and tattoos covered the massive muscles on his arms. I could only imagine where else on his impressive body they traveled. Paired with his dark wavy hair and rugged beard, he looked dangerous.

Primitive.

Wild.

He looked like a man I wanted to tame, but a man I knew I never could.

No. I hadn't come to the club tonight for dancing. I'd come for Owen.

He gestured to my Blood Mary… because I'd influenced him into thinking liquor filled my glass instead of blood.

"You need another?" he asked, his deep gravelly voice rolling over the words.

Even his voice turned me on–floating over me and leaving every cell crackling with electricity.

"Need another… kiss? Don't mind if I do." I arched an eyebrow, and he matched it.

A smirk lifted his full lips before he angled his ripped body toward me. His substantial height made it easy for him to clear the bar with a slow lean. Each second felt like torture as I waited for his lips to reach mine. When they did, my world flipped upside down as he slid his tongue inside my mouth.

My heart rattled faster against my ribcage while he kissed me slow and sensual. The rough pads of his fingers traced my jawline as he pulled me in even deeper. I relished every second in the ecstasy his kiss and his touch brought me, but before I'd had my fill, he pulled away. I almost jumped the bar and launched into his arms, desperate for a little more.

"Miss me while I was gone?" he asked as he held my hungry gaze and slid the shot glass he'd filled down the bar. It landed directly in front of the man who'd ordered it.

"Cool trick! Thanks, man!" the guy called to Owen before downing his shot.

"Maybe," I answered as I twirled a piece of my long, auburn hair around my finger. "Did you miss me?"

"Maybe." He matched my cool response as his half-smirk grew.

"Just maybe?" I arched an eyebrow.

He leaned forward and brushed another soft kiss against my lips. "Okay. Maybe more than maybe."

I sighed into his kiss and grabbed his t-shirt, knotting it tight into my fist as I deepened it.

I wanted more of him.

*All* of him.

And I was ready to throw our old-fashioned courting out the window and jump his bones right on the bar.

I'd met Owen here a couple months ago on a night out with my family. After a hot make-out session and a few sips of his blood in the stockroom, he'd asked me on a date. I'd accepted, of course, because hello… he's gorgeous. But also, he'd made me laugh and had turned out to be surprisingly sweet for a guy who looked like he could crush a person's skull without breaking a sweat. Instead of just a quickie and a meal, I'd felt something click between us… a connection I'd never felt before.

Though the sexual chemistry between us could burn this entire country down, instead of my usual routine of a quick roll in the sheets and an even quicker goodbye, we'd ended each one of our three dates with only a goodnight kiss.

Long, hot, sensual kisses that left me reeling for days.

After our third date, he'd gone out on tour with his band and left me here for a month with my lust multiplying by the second. Now that he'd returned home and texted me to come see him, I didn't think I could even wait until his shift ended before I unleashed the pent up sexual frustration he'd created in me.

Even though I truly enjoyed this new experience of romance and dating, and dating a *human* no less, the longer I went without feeling him inside me, the more I craved him.

It was intoxicating. A sweet torture—and I savored every second.

A torture that had gone on long enough. A torture I was ready to end.

We continued our silent stare-off as I sucked my lip between my teeth. "What time does your shift end?"

"By the time we're done serving and cleaning up, I won't get out until five in the morning," he answered.

*Fuck.*

Five in the morning meant we wouldn't have time to do much of anything before the sun came up. There were plans to have the Pict witches lift our sunlight curse in the new year, but until then, I'd need to continue avoiding the sun's rays.

"Can you get off early? Like now?" I considered using my powers of influence to make him quit his job so I could have him all to myself tonight if he said no. I'd already been influencing him to not notice me drinking his decadent blood on our dates, but I knew forcing him to quit his job was probably not very good dating behavior.

Another look at those lips, and I still considered it.

"I just got back after a month off. I don't think my co-workers would go for it." He chuckled.

*Double fuck.*

"So, you're saying I just have to sit here and watch you

pour other people's drinks all night?" I stuck out my lower lip in an exaggerated pout.

"Would watching me all night really be the end of the world?"

He walked away, and I soaked in every impressive inch of his massive frame. The broad shoulders and wide back. His perfect round ass I wanted to bounce a quarter off. That face that looked rugged and rough, but beautiful as well.

He glanced over his shoulder and caught me ogling the goods and smiled. "Told you it wouldn't be the end of the world."

I didn't even try to conceal the fact I'd been mentally undressing him. There was no hiding the passion in my eyes, and I loved that he was bold enough to call me out on it.

Hot. As hot as the man himself.

The bar business picked up, and Owen and his two co-bartenders picked up with it. I sat at the bar for the better part of an hour watching him sling drinks with style. Even more than his bartending show, I enjoyed watching him flat-out deny every other woman who came up batting her eyes.

And there were plenty.

Each time a beautiful woman tried to entice him, his eyes drifted to me when he answered her and sent her packing. If there was any way to be more turned on by a guy, I'd never known it.

"You still good over here?" he asked as he took a break from the customers still waving money his way. "Anything I can get you?"

"I think you know damn well what you can get me," I answered unashamedly. I'd given up being prudish centuries ago.

Owen laughed, and it drowned out the din of the crowd. "Damn, Annella. You're killing me, girl."

"Seriously," I said as I leaned closer. "You need to take off the rest of the night. Let's go hang out. You can tell me all about your tour."

When he shook his head, a piece of his dark hair fell in front of his eyes. He tucked it behind his ear. "My tour involved riding on a bus with a bunch of sweaty dudes, playing live music every night, and thinking about you every minute I was gone."

*Thump, thump, thump.*

There went my damn heart again.

"You thought about me?" I tried to keep my voice sexy and cool, but it rose several octaves anyway.

"I haven't stopped thinking about you since I saw you sitting at this bar the night we met."

*Thump, thump, thump, thump.*

There. That was the sweet side of this sexy, powerful man that continued tipping me upside down. For every second I wanted to treat him like a sex toy, I also wanted to get to know the man who could say things that made my six-hundred-year-old heart feel like a teenage girl with a crush the size of Texas.

"Seriously, Annella. I would kill to get off early and spend some time with you. But I'm stuck here all night. How about this? I'll get off at five and take you out for breakfast. There is this twenty-four-hour diner all the late-night servers congregate at, and it's a pretty fun party. We'll have bacon and waffles, drink some coffee while you tell me more about what you were up to all month, then go for a stroll and watch the sun come up. Then maybe we can go back to my place."

The twinkle in his eye almost erased the knowledge that

I couldn't do any of those things. I couldn't eat food, I couldn't drink coffee, and I *definitely* couldn't watch the sun rise.

At least not yet.

Even though I wanted to say yes… God, did I want to say yes… I shook my head.

"I'm afraid I'm not a morning person. How about tomorrow night we go out?"

"I'll take you whenever I can get you," he said. "Tomorrow night it is."

My unnaturally childish smile split my face as I tried to twist it back into the sultry one I'd mastered over the centuries. But as he leaned in for a kiss, I lost the battle and embraced the smitten kitten look he continued coaxing out of me.

After a quick kiss, he leaned back and scanned the bar filled with customers still vying for his attention… the attention he'd given to me and me alone. I caught the glare from the blonde several stools down who'd done her best for the past ten minutes to attract his attention with her over-inflated breasts—and failed. I held her eye contact while I smirked, then took a sip of blood.

*Mine.*

The rock band that had been playing all night came back from their break, but when the lead singer took the mic, it didn't turn a single eye from the show Owen put on behind that bar. Charming, charismatic, and sexy as all hell. He held the attention of everyone in the area.

"We're back from our break," the lead singer said into the microphone. "And we saw that one of our favorite bassists is back from his tour across the pond in Ireland. What do you all say we get Owen Hunter up here to join us for a song?"

The crowd went wild, and all eyes turned toward Owen. Chuckling, he shook his head while he shook a martini shaker. But the crowd urged him on more, and one of the other bartenders gave him a shove. His gaze drifted to me for a moment before he smirked, handed off the shaker, and raised his hands in submission.

Owen walked out from behind the bar and weaved his way through the crowd. The blue lights illuminated his incredible frame as he stepped up onto the stage. When he picked up the bass guitar and took his place in front of the microphone, I was certain I could hear my panties rip.

"Thanks for inviting me up here, guys," Owen said into the microphone. "It's good to be back in Scotland."

The crowd cheered again.

He whispered something to the lead singer, who passed it through the rest of the waiting band.

"This song goes out to a special girl in the crowd tonight."

*Thump, thump, thump, thump, thump.*

His green eyes locked with mine as he lifted his lip in a half-smirk. "This one's for you, Annella."

If I hadn't been dead already, I'd have died again.

When he started plucking the strings on his bass and crooning into the microphone, I nearly melted into a puddle from the heat scorching me from the inside out. The gorgeous man on the stage mesmerized me, commanding the attention of everyone in the building but staring only at me.

While he sang the song about the woman who controlled his heart, those eyes stayed locked onto mine. And I couldn't have looked away even if I'd tried.

Owen commanded me in a way I'd never thought possible.

I'd spent my life as one of the most powerful people on the planet, but underneath his smoldering stare, I felt powerless… an emotion I didn't even recognize.

And one I enjoyed because he made me feel something new and exciting.

After he finished up the song I never wanted to end, the crowd cheered again as he walked off the stage. People clapped him on the back as he made his way back to the bar… and back to me.

Instead of going behind the bar again, Owen walked over to me, stopping in front of my stool. My breath hitched in my chest as I looked up at the beautiful man towering over me.

"You like the song?" he asked as he leaned closer.

Words refused to form on my tongue, the one that wanted to be back in his mouth, so I just nodded my head and bit my lip. I bit it so hard I tasted my own blood.

"Good. I'll give you a private concert later," he whispered as he leaned down and brushed his lips against mine.

I sighed into his mouth as I wrapped my arms around his neck and pulled him in for a kiss so deep I worried I'd hurt him with my vampire strength. But he didn't flinch against the power of my passion, instead sliding his arms around my waist and dipping me backward on my stool. When we finally broke apart, he sat me back upright and gave me one last kiss before heading back behind the bar, leaving me stunned and senseless.

I spent the next two hours watching him like I was the president of his fan club… and I may as well have been.

A sexy rockstar. A sweet romantic. A powerful, primal man who set my soul on fire.

I'd slap on a button with his sexy face on it and wear that shit with pride any damn day.

That realization shocked me.

I was Annella Mackay…

A restless wanderess. A lethal warrior. An immortal vampire. A woman who'd never belonged to a man in her life… and never wanted to.

Owen glanced over at me and smiled.

*Until now.*

# Chapter Two

## ANNELLA

"So then what happened? You just kissed him goodbye and left?" My friend Mark, one of the newest vampire's in our clan, asked from his perch at the foot of my bed.

I rolled onto my stomach and rested my head on my forearms. "Yes. It was torture, but I couldn't stay another minute. I wanted to go back to his place so bad, but it's not light tight. Even going at full vamp speed, I barely made it back here before the sun went up."

"Fucking sunshine getting in the way of a good lay. Been there, sister. It's not fair."

"Not fair at *all.*" I sighed. "I've never wanted anything in my life as much as I want to find out if what those eyes promise is legit… what those *kisses* promise."

"Gah!" He grabbed a handful of his perfectly styled blonde hair. "I can't even imagine!" Mark rolled over and went face to face with me. "*I'm* dying, and it's not even happening to me. On the one hand, it's so freaking hot that you guys are holding out and letting that sexual tension build because the release will be explosive when it happens.

On the other hand, it's like enough already! Jump his freaking bones!"

"My thoughts exactly." I sighed. "And I'm definitely at the jump his freaking bones stage now —enough of the waiting. I can't take it anymore. We're going on our date, and I'm jumping his bones."

"Do it. Jump those freaking bones, sister."

He held out his hand, and I gave it a slap.

"Oh," I added. "I'm gonna stay over at Owen's for the night, then head to our apartment just a few blocks away before the sun comes up. That way, I'll be able to stay in bed with him until the last moment, then just pop down the road to our apartment and get out of the sun. It will only take me a few seconds to get there."

"So, you're saying not to worry, and you aren't kidnapped again if you don't come home tonight."

Until a couple months ago, that would have been a joke. As an immortal vampire, we didn't have to use the buddy system like a normal human woman. I was a vampire… an apex predator. And as one of the original vampires, I was an apex predator *of* the apex predators. We were stronger, faster, and more lethal than any other vampire who came after us. But a couple months ago, Clan Lennox, a clan who wanted to take power from my brother Lothaire, the leader of all the vampires, had got the jump on me and took me prisoner.

Luckily, with the help of Catrain, a Pict witch my friend Thorne went to for help, my family tracked me down and saved me.

*Saved* me. Ugh. Just the thought I'd needed rescuing boiled the blood in my veins. I may be the most petite of my clan, but I'd garnered a reputation for being the deadliest of the originals. My fierce reputation among the vampires only grew each year along with my legend. Then Clan Lennox got ahold of me, and I worried they'd tarnished six hundred years of being the baddest bitch around. I was more determined than ever to remind the rest of the clans just who they'd messed with.

I wanted to make an example of Clan Lennox, but they'd gone into hiding after their plan to kidnap me and kill Lothaire failed. I'd been hunting for Leith Lennox, their leader, and his sister Leeya ever since. If they wanted a war—they'd have one.

And I never lost.

"One of these days those fucking Lennox's will have to rear their heads. And I'll be waiting to lop them off the minute they do."

His brown eyes widened. "Samesies, girl. I'm still pissed off that Gregor seduced me to distract me while they took you. The nerve! I don't care if he's a hot Scot, I'm gonna make him pay for using me."

The night they had taken me, Mark had been out dancing with me, but met a handsome Scottish vampire named Gregor. Mark thought he'd met the perfect man, but it turned out that Gregor had just been keeping him busy while they hit me with a UV light and took me down in the alley.

"Every single member of Clan Lennox is dead. No one comes after Clan Mackay and lives to tell about it. No one." I tightened my eyes into tiny slits.

"I'm new to this whole 'slaughtering our enemies' thing, but I'm right there with you, girl. Those bastards almost killed you. They need to go buh-bye."

When I'd been taken and held in that cage under the UV lights that weakened me to the point of near-death, it had been the first time in centuries I'd actually feared for my life. It wasn't since the werewolf wars six hundred years ago that I'd felt the cold fingers of death scraping against my skin.

Back then, we'd realized the werewolves equaled us in strength and were even stronger under a full moon. We'd also been outnumbered. They'd been created by the same Pict tribe who'd created us, and their one goal in life had been to eradicate us.

And they'd almost succeeded.

But we had one advantage on our side. We could create new vampires.

When we fed someone our blood and killed them, a couple hours later, they would awaken. After enduring a painful few minutes of transformation, they emerged as a vampire. Werewolves could only be born. In a matter of days, we created an army to turn the tables and eradicate the beasts instead.

And I'd led the war against them, slaying countless wolves until we'd destroyed every last one of them.

Well, almost every last one of them. We found out when Thorne met Catrain that a few werewolves still existed on the island where she and her tribe still lived. Since magic protected it, they'd managed to survive there undetected.

But the rest of those fucking wolves? Wiped from this planet.

Just like I planned on doing to Clan Lennox.

No one got to terrorize me and live to tell about it.

No one.

"You guys in there?" Emilia called from the other side of the door.

"Yes! Come in!" I called back.

The door opened, and Emilia flashed to the bed and

landed right next to Mark. Her expectant blue eyes blinked at me. "Well? How was it?"

Mark lifted his hand and stopped me from talking, then rolled over and faced her. "Quick recap. After Owen texted he was back, she went to the bar, they had a super hot greeting kiss, then she had to sit there and watch his rough and rugged sexy ass bartend all night. But lots more kisses between slinging drinks. Then he got up on stage and sang to her—"

Emilia's eyes widened, emphasizing the hopeless romantic my brother Aiden, her fiancé, had turned her into. "He sang to her? He sang to you?" She spun to look at me.

"Yeah. He sang to her. Like a rockstar serenade in front of the entire club," Mark answered and got her attention back. "Long story short, they ended on a hot kiss, and she's seeing him in two hours. And tonight, they are finally doing it. It's business time."

"Oh my God, I'm dying for you!" Emilia squealed and bounced in place. The movement made the long chestnut waves of her hair bounce. "I think it's so romantic that you guys waited, and that he sang to you. He really sang to you? Up on stage?"

With a girlish sigh that never should have come from a woman like me, I rolled onto my back. "You guys. He looked so hot up there. All rockstar shaggy hair, tattooed bad boy… but the way he stared at me while he sang about the girl who controlled his heart..." I drifted off.

"Epic. Oh my God. So freaking epic," Emilia sighed.

"What are you wearing tonight?" Mark asked after a long pause.

"I don't know," I answered, then flashed over to my closet. "It's like nothing is good enough. On the one hand, I'm thinking sexy rocker chick like this." In seconds, I whipped on some torn jeans and a sexy black shirt that dipped to my navel."

"Hot. Very hot," Mark said, and Emilia nodded.

"Or I could go more sexy elegant." I whipped on a black dress that accentuated every one of the admirable curves I'd inherited from my mama.

"Ooh. Pretty." Emilia nodded.

"Another excellent option," Mark agreed.

"Which one? Or should I pick something else? I don't want to look too desperate, but I also want to make sure that there is no way he can make us hold off one more night."

"Oh my God." Mark placed a hand over his mouth. "Our Annella is nervous. *Nervous* about her date with a boy."

"Aww," Emilia crooned as they bumped their shoulders together.

"Shut the fuck up," I snapped but started laughing.

They were right. I *was* nervous. A new emotion I hadn't felt in centuries… just add it to the list of new feelings Owen continued evoking in me.

"Everyone meet me in the family room," my oldest brother Lothaire called from somewhere in the castle, and we all perked an ear toward the sound. "Now."

I switched out of my dress and back into my regular clothes, then flashed down the stairs with Mark and Emilia. Emilia flew to Aiden's side and slid onto his lap. Mark went to his chair nearest Lothaire and his gorgeous raven-haired wife, Grizella, and I sat near Thorne and his new fiancé, the Pict witch, Catrain.

Catrain's tribe had made us immortal over six hundred years ago… and her tribe had cursed us, causing us to survive on blood and hide from the sun. But since we'd found their tribe this year, they'd removed the curse on my brother Aiden, and our friend, and honorary brother, Thorne. Both of them, along with Aiden's fiancé Emilia, enjoyed all the original perks of immortality but could eat food, drink cocktails, and play in the sun.

When Catrain's sister took over for her mother in a couple months, the mother who still hated our kind, she'd promised to remove the sunshine curse on my entire family. I counted the days until I could go in the sun and not have to race back for cover when the sun came up.

It meant more time with Owen.

As excited as I was to have the curse removed, I hoped she'd find a way to do more than just lift the sun curse… I hoped she could return us to our original powers and make us all immortal with all the perks enjoyed by Aiden, Thorne, and Emilia.

"Thanks for coming down," Lothaire started.

"What's up, Lothaire?" Thorne asked as he slid an arm around his little blonde witch. His hand wrapped around her tattooed arm as he squeezed her tight.

Lothaire rubbed a hand down his beard, and his amber eyes narrowed as they swept across us. "Clan Lennox has resurfaced."

Rage pumped through my veins, replacing the lust Owen had filled them with.

"Where?" I growled.

"Leeya was spotted in Glasgow last night."

"Glasgow?" I asked, stuttering over the simple word. "I was in Glasgow last night."

"I know," Lothaire said, concern brewing in his eyes.

"Do you think she was hunting Annella?" Aiden asked. Ice-blue eyes, the same color as mine, flicked to me as they filled with worry.

"Where was she spotted?" Thorne's rugged, shadowed jaw tightened as he waited for the answer.

"Outside the same club."

"Shit," Mark spit. "So, she was hunting Annella."

My eyes narrowed as I digested how close my enemy had been. They narrowed more that she had the audacity to hunt *me.* It was me hunting *her.*

"It seems that way," Lothaire said. "So, until we figure this out, we all need to stick together and stay close to home. We need to work as a clan to find them and get rid of them for good."

It shouldn't have been what popped into my head when our lives were on the line, but a pain of sadness twisted up my gut that I wouldn't be able to see Owen tonight.

After all the waiting and anticipation, it seemed we'd need to hold out even longer.

"No one travels alone right now. They managed to capture Annella with a UV light, and she's far stronger than them," Grizella said, and her emerald green eyes warned each one of us to heed the advice but fixated on me. She knew how much I looked forward to seeing Owen again. "That means none of us can assume we can outfight them. We don't know what they're up to, and we aren't taking any chances. We stick together."

"I understand," I answered as the rest of my family nodded in agreement.

I didn't like it, hell, I hated it. But I understood. And I wouldn't put myself at risk for abduction again, and my family at risk having to rescue me.

"Did anyone get a piece of her clothing, hair, personal effects, anything?" Catrain asked.

As a Pict witch, she could perform locator spells as long

as she had a personal item to track. It was how she'd found me when I'd been taken.

"No. Nothing," Lothaire answered. "A couple vampires loyal to Clan Mackay spotted her, but they didn't approach."

"Damn," Thorne huffed.

"If you can get anything of hers or Leith's, I am happy to run a spell to find them."

"We'll keep trying," Aiden answered. "And in the meantime, we need eyes all over Glasgow. If that psycho Leeya is back, then her brother must be nearby."

Aiden had dated Leeya years ago, and she'd developed an obsession for him that almost took the life of his new love, Emilia. Along with Leeya's brother, who wanted to harvest humans like cattle, the two of them had turned into a massive headache for our family.

A headache it was time we eradicate.

"I've already sent word out to all the vampires in Glasgow to watch for them. In the meantime, we just need to be ready to move out at a moment's notice. Thorne and Aiden, since you can walk in the sun, I think we should plan on having you two do some daytime searches of the city. Just check some of their old haunts."

"I'll help too," Emilia said.

It was easy to forget to include Emilia in these things because until a few months ago, she'd been a human. Now she had the same powers we'd had when we first became immortal… the same powers shared with Aiden and Thorne.

"Thank you, Emilia."

"I'll go too, of course," Catrain said.

She didn't have our immorality or the speed, strength,

and fangs that came with it, but she had some powerful magic that proved very handy in knocking vamps down on their arses. And with her skills with weaponry, she was an incredible asset to our family.

"Let's wait a few days and see what our contacts find out," Lothaire said, "but if they don't locate them, we'll all head to Glasgow and start hunting. Annella, Mark, Grizella, and I can work at night, and the rest of you use your perks of day walking to hunt in the sun. We aren't letting them get away this time."

I'd already been motivated to reap my revenge on them before, but now that they stood between me and Owen, a new fire to kill them all burned inside me.

The knocker on the main castle door slammed against the old wood several times. We all spun toward the sound.

"Are we expecting anyone?" Mark asked.

"No," Lothaire answered as he pushed out of his chair.

We all flashed to the door, and when Lothaire opened it, a body crashed into our foyer.

"What the fuck?" Lothaire said as he sidestepped the body and glanced out at the emptiness outside. "Whoever knocked must have been a vampire because this guy certainly didn't do the knocking. Who the fuck is this?"

Lothaire's massive frame blocked me from seeing the body, so I peeked around him.

When my eyes locked onto the man laying at our feet, my hands flew to my mouth as I gasped.

"Owen!" I cried out, then dropped to my knees and pulled his limp body into my arms.

"Oh my God!" Emilia shrieked, dropping beside me. "Is he dead?"

I pressed my fingers to his neck, then listened for the beat of his heart.

The sound of silence nearly stopped my own.

"He's dead," I whispered, barely able to utter the words I couldn't believe were true. "He can't be dead."

Tears streamed down my face as heartache like I'd never known tore through my soul. I hadn't known him long, but I'd connected with him in a way I'd never connected with anyone in my life. And now he'd been ripped from me before we even had a chance.

"Holy shit." Thorne pushed his hands into his brown hair. "Who in the hell would kill Owen? Wait—"

His voice drifted off as he looked at me.

The agony wracking my body transformed instantly into a rage that burned hotter than the sun.

"Leeya," I ground out. "She saw me at the club last night, which means she saw me with him. Saw us kiss. Saw that he meant something to me. Killing him was a fuck you from that psycho."

Anyone who'd been in that club had seen the connection between Owen and me. Instead of starting a romance, I'd marked him for death. A pawn to be used to cause me pain.

And it had worked.

"Annella, I'm so sorry," Aiden said as he dropped to my side and pulled me into his arms. "We'll get her for this."

I'd already wanted her blood pouring down my face before, but now I wanted to make her suffer long and hard for it. I wanted to hear her screams while I ripped her body apart the way she ripped my heart apart by taking Owen from me.

"I'm going to kill that fucking bitch," I said between sniffles.

"We've got your back, baby." Mark lowered himself to my other side and wrapped his arms around my shoulders.

I couldn't stop staring at Owen. Staring at the gorgeous, powerful man with the beautiful voice now silenced forever. He'd been so full of life, so full of passion and power. Leeya had taken him from me, and I'd never felt the fires of rage and revenge burn hotter.

All the negative emotions in the universe wound through my heart and squeezed the hope right out of it. As Mark and Aiden sandwiched me into a hug, I looked once more at the lips I'd never get to kiss again.

The lips that just… opened?

With a jolt, Owen inhaled a sharp breath, and my shocked gasp inflated my own lungs.

"Jesus, fuck!" Mark shouted as he fell backward.

I struggled to release the breath trapped in my chest as I heard another inhale of air fill his lungs. I looked up to his eyes, and saw them open wide, shocked, and searching his surroundings.

"Where am I? What happened?" he asked as he inhaled another breath.

His confused green eyes searched the faces of my family all hovering over him, then slid to a stop when they landed on me. "Annella?"

"You're alive?" I whispered with a trembling lip.

I didn't wait for his answer or give an answer I didn't have. I just flung myself forward and kissed his lips over and over, then fell forward onto his chest and sobbed into his t-shirt. His arms wrapped around my body as he held me tight.

"What's happening. How did I get here?"

I wanted to answer him, but I still couldn't form words over the lump in my throat.

I'd thought I lost him. I'd thought Leeya had ripped him

from my life forever, but somehow, someway, he came back to me.

"I'm Lothaire, Annella's brother," Lothaire said. "I'm sure you're confused. We are too. What is the last thing you remember happening?"

Wiping the steady stream of tears from my eyes, I sniffled and sat back on my heels. Owen stared at me with the same confusion I shared.

He'd been dead. I was certain of it. Wasn't I? Or maybe Leeya hadn't killed him after all. None of it made sense.

"It's okay," I said to him. "You're safe here. Tell us what happened, and maybe we can help you figure this out."

Owen sat up but still looked dazed and confused. As he opened his mouth to speak, he slammed his eyes shut and fell backward on the floor. His howls of anguish flooded our castle, and his writhing sent me tumbling backward.

Thorne caught me in his arms and pulled me out of the way. Shock mirrored through the faces of my family as we watched Owen writhing in agony at my feet.

An agony I knew well… and one I hadn't felt in six hundred years but had seen many times since.

The agony that came when you awakened from death and transitioned into a vampire.

"Is he… turning?" Aiden asked, confirming my suspicions.

"Yes," I whispered. "I think he's turning into a vampire."

"Why the hell would Leeya turn him into a vampire and send him to us?"

"I don't know," I answered.

After several minutes of agonizing pain, he collapsed into a heap on the floor, his transformation complete.

"Owen, you're okay." I slid to his side now that his thrashing had ended. "Everything will be okay."

"What happened to me? What the fuck is going on?" he grimaced as he rolled up to his knees.

I glanced around at my family and exhaled a sigh. "This will come as a huge shock, and there is no easy way to say it, so I'm just going to rip it off like a band-aid."

"Annella. Tell me what the hell is happening."

"I'm not sure how it happened, but you just transitioned into a vampire."

"What?" he growled.

"I know. It's impossible to think vampires exist, and you think I'm fucking with you, but I'm not. You're a vampire now."

"That's impossible!" Like a wild, confused animal, he launched to his feet and spun around, staring at us.

"It's going to be okay. I promise. I'll show you everything you need to know and explain it to you. Because," I paused and bit my lip, "I'm a vampire too. We all are."

His eyes widened as he looked at me.

"I know this is a shock. First, finding out that vampires exist, second that you're dating one, and third that you've become one. It's a lot to take in."

"I can't be a fucking vampire!" he shouted so loud it forced me back a step.

Lothaire stepped to my side, and it surprised me that even at his impressive height, Owen still had him by a couple inches. It was rare to see Lothaire look small, but Owen managed to pull it off.

"Easy now, Owen. Just take a deep breath and relax," Lothaire said.

Owen grabbed a handful of his hair and shook his head.

"This can't be happening. It's impossible. It can't be possible."

I stepped toward him and touched his shoulder, but he shook my hand off and spun to glare at me. "Don't fucking touch me, *vampire*." His lip curled in contempt.

The response set me back on my heels.

"Hey!" Thorne warned as he stepped to my other side. "Watch it. You're one of us now too. You need to calm the fuck down, big guy."

"I'm *not* one of you," Owen ground out as his furious gaze scanned us all.

"Dude, you're a vampire. And a vampire who is handling this pretty poorly. Being a vamp is actually really cool," Mark started, but Owen just narrowed his eyes.

"You're just in shock learning vampires exist," Emilia said. "I was shocked when I found out too. I was a human when I found out Aiden here is a vampire." She pointed at him. "But it's gonna be okay."

"I *know* vampires exist," Owen spit out. "I fucking hate vampires."

*He knows we exist? What?*

Humans had no idea of our existence… or at least that was what I thought.

"And I can't *be* a fucking vampire!" Owen shouted.

"I'm feeling so judged," Mark whispered.

"Owen," I soothed, trying to push down the anger at his dramatic reaction to me. "You're just really confused right now. It's normal. How about we just sit down and take a breath for a minute? Whether you believe in vampires or hate them because of the things you've seen on TV or whatever, you're one of us now."

"I can't be!" he shouted, and I saw the betrayal flash in his eyes.

The disdain.

The horror.

"And why is that?" Thorne asked.

"Because I'm a fucking werewolf, that's why!"

We all gasped and took a step back.

*What?*

# Chapter Three

## OWEN

A *vampire*?

Me?

No fucking way.

Impossible.

But it was also impossible to ignore the thirst in my mouth that couldn't be quenched with water or the strange feelings in my body I'd never felt before.

I also couldn't ignore the seven sets of eyes staring back at me of the people who'd just told me they were vampires. As I scanned them again, my eyes snapped back to the most beautiful bright blue ones staring back at me with even more shock than I was feeling.

*Annella.*

My beautiful, Annella.

My beautiful Annella, who was… a vampire?

Also impossible.

How had I not noticed? How had I not picked up on the fact that the woman I was falling for harder than I'd ever imagined was the one thing I had been raised to hate with every fiber of my being?

I'd never met a vampire before, or at least not that I knew of, because vampires and werewolves couldn't sense one another as anything other than human. Unless we showed ourselves in true form, we could easily pass by without detection. It's how my kind had stayed hidden from theirs for centuries.

But to think I'd been stupid enough to *date* one? I would've felt like the biggest moron on the planet, except the horrified look on Annella's face confirmed I wasn't the only clueless one in our relationship.

"What the hell do you mean you're a werewolf?" she finally said, her big eyes barely blinking as she stared at me.

"I *mean*, I'm a werewolf."

"How? But… it's…" She shook her head as she stumbled over the words.

"Yeah. So you see. I *can't* be a vampire because I'm already a werewolf." I paused and furrowed my brow. "Can I?"

"Is it possible, Catrain?" the man standing at Annella's right side asked the blonde woman with the black tribal tattoos crawling up her arms.

Her eyebrows rose as she blew out a puff of air. "I don't know, Thorne. I honestly don't know if it's possible."

"Could vampirism override his werewolf gene?" the biggest one asked.

"Maybe? I really don't have an answer, Lothaire," she responded. "It's never been done that I'm aware of."

*Thorne, Lothaire, Aiden, and Catrain.* I made a mental note of which names went with which faces. I remembered Annella mentioning her family on our second date, and I recognized some of them from the first night I'd met her at the club. That must leave Mark, Grizella, and Emilia as the other three faces staring at me like I'd sprouted three heads.

"I thought the only werewolves left were on the Pict island," Aiden said to me. "How are you here?"

"I don't know what the hell the Pict island is, but there are werewolves. We just work really damn hard to make sure vampires never know about us. You already wiped us out once. Now we stay under the radar so you won't do it again. And yeah, I'm one of them." The thirst for blood twisted my guts up into a knot. "Or at least I was. What the hell does this mean? Am I still a werewolf? Or am I seriously a vampire? What the hell is happening?"

Fear and anger churned inside me as I paced in a small circle. Becoming a bloodsucking vampire would be the worst thing in the world in my mind. Their kind had wreaked havoc on us, and on humanity, and the thought I was one of those monsters made me want to puke.

And the fact I'd been dating one?

Holy hell… my father would skin me alive.

"Owen," Annella soothed, and the softness of her voice coaxed me to a stop. "We will figure this all out. I promise."

When I turned and looked at her, the desperate need to pull her into my arms and cover her with kisses almost overpowered the desire for blood I couldn't ignore.

But as much as I wanted to kiss her, I wanted to kill her. She was a vampire, and the hatred for her kind had been drilled into me since birth. It was a dizzying blend of desire and hatred churning inside me.

"Did you do this to me?" I asked her with fury burning in my voice as I realized she may have done it intentionally—turned me into the thing I hate the most.

"No." She shook her head. "I swear I didn't change you. What do you remember?"

Everything seemed so foggy, like blurry puzzle pieces I needed to snap together.

"I remember seeing you last night. I remember closing the bar. Then—"

*The redhead.*

Visions of her luring me outside flooded my mind.

"A red-haired woman. She must have used that mind control shit on me and took me out into the alley. She…"

I drifted off, shocked at the memory that invaded my mind on repeat.

Over and over and over again, I saw it.

"She what?" Annella asked.

"She… she snapped my neck. She killed me."

*Holy shit.*

I died.

I actually fucking died.

I rubbed a hand around my neck, surprised it didn't even ache.

"It was Leeya," Grizella spit out the name like poison.

"Did you drink her blood?" Annella asked. "Think hard."

I closed my eyes and searched my spotty memory.

"No."

"Did she say anything else?" Aiden asked.

I thought harder, and more pieces of the night came back to me. "She tried to kiss me, and when I refused, she started raving like a madwoman. Something about Aiden refusing her and now me, and something about revenge on the entire family. I don't know. I don't know."

"Crazy!" Mark shouted. "I told you guys she's nuts! Owen, this chick is like a bunny-boiling stalker chick. Think *Fatal Attraction* level nuts. I bet she saw you with Annella and wanted to steal you for herself. But then you refused her and…" He made a slicing sound with his mouth as he dragged his finger across his throat. "Donezo."

"Are you saying this bitch killed me because I wouldn't make out with her?"

He pursed his lips and nodded. "Wouldn't put it past her. Coocoo for Cocoa Puffs. Been saying it for years."

"So, she *wasn't* intentionally changing him?" Thorne shook his head. "If she didn't feed him her blood, then how the hell is he still here?"

Looks of confusion passed between all the vampires, but then Annella's eyes slowly widened.

"What?" I asked her as she sucked her lip into her teeth.

"Um," she stalled.

"Um, what?" I growled. "What do you know?"

"Annella? What happened?" Lothaire demanded.

She looked timid as she glanced down at her feet. "I have a habit of chewing on my lip when I'm nervous or anticipating something. Right after you got off stage last night, I bit my lip while you were approaching. I must have bitten it too hard because I tasted a little blood. Then we kissed. I think… I think you may have had some of my blood in your system when Leeya killed you."

"Holy shit," I whispered, remembering the coppery taste of her lips when I'd annihilated her with a kiss. I'd thought maybe it was my blood I'd tasted, or that I'd kissed her so hard I'd nicked her skin. What I didn't know was that I'd let vampire blood past my lips.

And then I fucking died.

Mark lifted a hand. "Hold the freaking phone. Are you saying it was a total coincidence he had your blood in his system? And Leeya seriously killed him out of spite and dropped him on your doorstep as a fuck you? Like leaving a bag of burning dog shit on someone's door? Except that burning bag of dog shit turned out to be a werewolf with vampire blood in his system, so he came back to life, and now we don't know what the hell he is? Is this seriously what happened?"

Annella opened her mouth but just stuttered for a few moments before saying, "I think it is."

A vampire. Me. Owen Hunter. It still seemed impossible to process.

"Wait." I lit up with hope. "Can we undo it? Is there still a way to get rid of this shit?"

They all shook their heads.

"Not that we're aware of," Aiden said. "I tried it, and it didn't end well. Sorry, man."

The doom settled into my gut. "So, I'm really a vampire? Seriously?"

"I don't know," Annella answered. "Considering you started as a werewolf, we're not really sure how this works. It's never happened before. Normally newbie vamps have mouths that feel dry and a burning thirst they can't describe. Do you have that?"

Dry mouth and burning thirst? Check and check.

Fuck.

"Yeah. I've got that."

"It seems like a standard vamp transition to me," Lothaire said.

"And there's no undoing it?" I asked.

"No. Unfortunately not," Thorne responded. "Once you turn, you're kind of stuck for eternity like this. But that's a perk." He grinned. "You can live for centuries now!"

Centuries. *Centuries* as a freaking bloodsucker.

I closed my eyes and exhaled a lengthy breath through my nose.

"So, how does this work? I either off myself or drink some blood or what?"

"You need to feed," Annella said. "You have to absorb some human life force to complete the transformation. If you don't drink human blood, you'll die for real in a day. Two tops."

"Fuck," I grumbled. The thought of drinking blood should have disgusted me, but it was all I could think about.

Well, that and wanting to taste Annella's lips again.

But both things should have caused me to feel appalled.

Yet I craved them both with every ounce of my soul.

Deep down, I knew I should let myself die… again. I'd rather be dead and buried six feet under than become a bloodsucking vampire, yet there was something inside me demanding I submit to the thirst. Demanding I feed even though I knew I shouldn't. Like a drug addict wanting to quit, the power of the drug beckoned me to have it. Only it wasn't drugs… it was blood.

"I can't even believe I'm saying this," I said on a sigh, "but where do I get blood?"

"Normally, you can drink from blood bags, and you never need to feed on a human," Thorne said, "but for your first feed, it has to be fresh off the vein. You need to absorb a life force, and that doesn't come in a bag."

"I'm *not* killing anyone! I'll die before I stoop that low." I iced them all with a glare.

"You don't need to kill to feed," Annella said as she stepped toward me. "You can feed off someone's jugular, stop long before they are in danger, and then we use our mind control, we call it influencing, to erase the experience. They'll never even remember you were there."

I couldn't believe I was even contemplating drinking

someone's blood, but the more she talked about it, the deeper the craving clawed its way into me.

"So, no one gets hurt?"

"No," Grizella answered. "There are rules that prohibit the harming of humans. We can drink their blood, but they must always survive, and never remember."

"It's rule numero uno." Mark lifted a finger.

"I'll show you how to feed and how to erase their memories. After your first feeding, your powers will kick in. I'll teach you about those too." Annella took another step toward me. Even though I wanted to reach out and pull her into my arms, I stepped back.

I saw the pained look on her face at my rejection, and it killed me that I put it there. But she was a *vampire*—my sworn enemy. In fact, my entire species existed only to eliminate their kind. It was part of my heritage to hate her.

But another look in those eyes and I felt my resolve slipping.

Maybe I was overreacting to the news. Maybe she wasn't one of the brutal killers I'd always been led to believe vampires were. It was possible they'd evolved since the first immortals who'd decimated my entire species. They did say they didn't kill humans anymore.

"Wait a minute," Lothaire said. "It was *your* blood that changed him?"

"I think so," Annella answered. "If he doesn't remember Leeya feeding him her blood, then it had to be."

"So, he's a possible original descendent vampire."

*Original descendent vampire?*

"Do I even want to know what the hell that is?" I asked.

Thorne chuckled. "It means that you were turned by one of the original vampires... which means you're far stronger than other vampires. The original vampires are the strongest, fastest, and most lethal. The vampires we make are almost equivalent in those qualities. But with each generation removed from us, the vampires lose a little more of the magic and aren't as powerful. It means you're going to be one badass vampire."

"Like me and Grizella." Mark grinned. "We're both second-generation vamps, so we're pretty much the next best thing to an original. 2.0 vamps."

"Holy shit." I ran a hand through my beard.

But as the information soaked into my shocked brain, I realized what it meant.

If Annella was an original vampire, and this was her family, then this was the Mackay Clan. The *actual* vampires who'd slaughtered my kind. The stars of the stories every werewolf child heard before they went to bed at night.

As I started putting together their names, it all started to click. These weren't descendants of the monsters we'd been created to hunt… it was *them.*

And Annella was one of them.

"Are you… are you the original Clan Mackay vampires?" I asked as I stepped back again.

"Yes," Aiden answered. "We were the first vampires. Catrain's tribe granted us immortality and special powers in exchange for protection. But when the change wiped out over half of our clan, we refused the protection we'd promised them. They tried to remove our immortality, but we found a way around that by consuming blood."

As I looked across their expressions, I started to put together their names. If Mark and Grizella were the new vampires, and Catrain was a witch, then that left the other four as the originals.

Lothaire had kept his name, and if the stories I'd been told were true, he was the leader of the immortals, known for his size and strength. His brother, Aodhagan, would be Aiden, famous for his ice-cold eyes and quick, calculating kills. Teàrlach would have been Thorne… the one known for his skill with a sword and the way he'd laugh into battle. And then that left… *Maighread.*

Maighread Mackay, the famous werewolf slayer.

The name whispered with fear on the tongues of every werewolf ever born.

She'd led the battle against my kind and had earned a reputation for her hatred of us and her skill at dispatching us. Aside from her infamous skills as a werewolf slayer, she'd been known for her undeniable beauty. A beauty that made most men underestimate her—which had been the last thing they'd ever done.

As my eyes slid across their faces, it stopped on the face of the woman I couldn't believe was the greatest enemy my kind had ever known.

I saw it now.

The auburn hair, the full lips, and the fiery blue eyes I'd heard about more times than I could count.

The woman of my dreams was also the one in my nightmares.

The woman who had captivated my mind and soul was the very same one who had sent me screaming under the bed as a little boy each time I heard a bump in the night.

I heard my mother's voice in my head…

*Go to bed, or Maighread will come for you. Brush your teeth, or Maighread will pull them out. Lie to your mother, and Maighread will come pluck out your tongue.*

It seemed impossible that the woman with the radiant smile and the kisses that brought me to my knees was the one with a reputation for unimaginable cruelty, and the one used to scare werewolf children into good behavior for centuries.

"Maighread," I whispered as I stared at her.

"How do you know that name?" She narrowed her eyes. "I haven't gone by that in centuries. I go by my middle name now."

"Because I've heard about you… the werewolf slayer. In fact, I've heard about *all* of you." My lip quivered as I snarled. "Your family killed almost *all* of my ancestors."

"They tried to kill us first," she snapped. Her blue eyes lit up with that famous ferocity.

"You're murderers. Killers. Your family is an abomination."

Her eyes widened. "Us? *We're* the abomination? You turn into a freaking dog."

"We're not dogs," I ground out. "We're wolves. Powerful wolves who can kill your kind."

"Is that so?" she arched an eyebrow.

I lifted my chin and stared down at her. "That's so."

Pursing her lips, she smiled. "If you're so capable of killing us, then why is it that we wiped your kind out?" She stopped and placed a finger on her cheek. "Oops. I guess *almost* wiped you out is more like it. Since you're here, it seems we missed putting down a few rabid dogs."

The passion I'd felt for her transformed into rage as I lowered my head and stepped forward. Annella didn't back up, even though I towered over her. With a *click*, she popped her fangs and stepped toward me.

"Hey now, hey now," Mark said as he stepped between us. "There is no need for a vampire-werewolf boss fight. Or is it vampire on vampire now?" He tipped his head. "Well, whatever. No fighting. Owen, you need to learn how to feed and use your skills. Whether you like it or not, you're one of us now. Deal with it. Annella, it may have been an accident, but it's your blood that turned him. I.e.... he's your responsibility. You both need to put your outdated, discriminatory speciesism crap on the back burner and work this shit out. #vampirelivesmatter #werewolflivesmatter. No one is killing anyone. Capeesh?"

My shoulders lifted with my heavy breaths as I stared into the eyes of Maighread Mackay. A contempt that matched my own replaced the passion as she glared daggers back at me.

"Capeesh," I finally muttered. "Just teach me how to feed, and I'll get the hell out of your life, *Maighread.*"

She lifted her chin. "Just try not to piss on the carpet before you go, *pooch*."

The growl vibrated in my throat as I stared her down.

"You okay, Annella?" Aiden asked.

"I'm just fine, big brother," she answered. "I've handled plenty of werewolves before."

*Handled.* She meant murdered.

I rolled my eyes. "Let's get this over with."

"The sooner, the better," she spit back, then broke apart our stare down to look at Lothaire. "I'll be back in a few hours. Lothaire start hunting Leeya. After I teach this mutt how to hunt, I need to go find that bitch. Dogs for days around here."

"Are you sure you two will be okay alone together?" Emilia asked, and concern weighted her eyes.

"He's a newbie vamp. It's impossible for him to hurt me." Annella rolled her eyes. "We'll be fine."

*Newbie vamp.* I was as infuriated that the term referred to me as I was that I'd kissed the vampire who'd said it... the very same woman who'd torn the throats out of countless ancestors.

*How had I fallen for Maighread Mackay?*

As I stared at her and acknowledged the monster she was, I couldn't help but mourn the loss of the woman I'd fallen for.

Annella.

A woman who made me laugh, made my heart swell each time I looked at her, and a woman who cracked open my heart and made it beat just for her.

But Annella didn't exist... she was a façade for the monster I never wanted to see again.

Her blue eyes locked with mine, and it seemed my heart hadn't gotten the message my head did because it swelled again as I stared at her.

*Fuck.*

# Chapter Four

## ANNELLA

Owen and I stood outside the club in the alley waiting for someone to wander out.

I looked over, and a dizzying mix of emotions swirled inside me as I stared at him.

Just yesterday, I'd have been launching into his arms, covering him with kisses I'd never want to end.

Tonight, I struggled not to part his head from his body.

A werewolf.

A freaking werewolf.

The old saying "he's too good to be true" didn't even begin to cover how I felt. I had fallen for a disgusting, horrific, werewolf.

And no one on the planet hated werewolves more than me.

No one.

They'd hunted us. Terrorized us. Killed us.

A werewolf had killed my best friend, Edine. Ripped her from my arms and from this world.

That devastating loss had fueled a rage inside me for their kind that even today still burned brighter than the sun.

A rage that now ignited every time I looked at the man who'd consumed me with a different fire less than twenty-four hours ago.

"So, we just stand here and wait?" he asked.

A soft gust of wind blew down the alley and tousled his wavy hair. A piece fell in front of his face, so he pushed it out of his eyes and tucked it behind his ear.

He still looked like the same Owen.

Gorgeous. Sexy. A jaw-dropping heartthrob.

But I kept hearing him say it on repeat in my head... *I'm a werewolf.*

A werewolf!

I hadn't been that shocked in six hundred years. Not only did it come as a shock that they still existed out here in the world unbeknownst to us, but Owen was one of them.

*A freaking werewolf.*

Ugh. Talk about bad taste in men.

"Yep. We just stand here and wait. I could use my powers to influence someone to come outside, but I don't want to leave you unattended."

"Why? You think I'm gonna get mugged?" He snorted. "My vampire powers may not have kicked in yet, but I'm six foot seven, and two-hundred-eighty pounds of solid muscle. No one has been stupid enough to hassle me in years."

Didn't I know he was solid muscle. Last night I'd been counting the seconds until I could admire every tattooed and toned inch of him without his clothes on.

But now?

A freaking werewolf.

Ugh!

"No." I rolled my eyes. "I think if a human comes out

while I'm gone, your bloodlust will kick in, and you'll end up killing them. Do you want to shoulder the guilt of murdering someone?"

The cocky grin on his face dropped, then he slowly shook his head.

"Then shut the hell up and do what I tell you."

After a few moments, he quietly said, "Would I really kill someone?"

I scoffed. "Uh, yeah. You're a new vampire. Until you learn to control it, your bloodlust will consume every thought in your head… including the ones that tell you not to kill people."

"Fuck. I do *not* want this. This is the worst thing that could have happened to me. Thanks a *lot* for feeding me your blood."

I scoffed. "Seriously? I'm really super sorry that I didn't know you would get murdered after we kissed. And hey, at least with my blood in your system, you didn't die. Could be worse… you could be *dead*-dead."

"Maybe I should be. Probably better than being a vamp." He pulled a face. "Vampires are vile and disgusting."

Pursing my lips, I tipped my head. "You prefer to be dead? No problem, Owen. All you need to do is refuse to feed, and by this time tomorrow, you'll be history. Or I can speed things up and make it happen easy peasy. Just say the word, and I'll send your pretty head rolling down the alley."

His cocky demeanor dissipated as he shook his head.

"What's that?" I pressed my hand to my ear. "Are you saying you're glad you had my blood in your system, and you're not a rotting corpse in the morgue right now?"

After a long silence between us, he gently shook his

head. “This is just a lot to take in. And I really don’t want to kill anyone.”

“Don’t worry, I have some tips to show you how to get it under control quickly. It’s vampire law that whoever changes someone into a vampire teaches them how to survive… and even though it was an accident you had my blood in your system, it still doesn’t change the fact you’re my responsibility.” I scowled. “Unfortunately.”

“So, you’re stuck with me, huh?”

“Yep. Until we’re sure you’re safe with humans, I’m stuck with you.”

“Well, it’s not like I’m any happier to be stuck with you, *Maighread.*” His lip curled as he snarled the name I hadn’t used in centuries. “What else do I need to know? We’ll do this as fast as we can so we can get the hell away from each other.”

Not only did werewolves still exist, apparently, but they’d also turned me into some kind of werewolf-slaying legend.

Good. Because that’s exactly what I was. It made me smile to know that old folklore of me wreaking revenge on their kind still had them shaking in their fur.

Though I didn’t mind the werewolves feeling like I was the bogeyman, it stung to hear Owen speak with such contempt for me.

Yesterday his eyes had lit up when they’d look into mine, and tonight he looked at me like I was a monster.

And it hurt.

And when I hurt, I lashed out.

“Well, for starters, don’t chase cars. Don’t lick your balls in public. Don’t hump the poodle down the road… oh shit, wait. Those are your werewolf rules, aren’t they?” I tapped my forehead and clucked my cheek. “Sorry, you need the vampire rules.”

His square jaw ticked as he gritted his teeth, and a low growl rumbled through his expansive chest.

"For starters," I said, ignoring his glare, "you can never step foot in the sunlight again. It will incinerate you within seconds."

The scorn in his eyes softened into sadness.

"Oh, shit," he whispered. "I forgot about that. Seriously? I can't ever go in the sun again?"

"Nope. Never. I've got a guy who can make your apartment or any place you live light tight. I'll give you his number."

"I can't believe I'm not going to be able to walk out in the daylight again. What about touring with my band? We usually play at night, but we travel all day. How in the hell is that going to work?"

"My job is to help you understand how not to kill people and the basic rules of being a vampire. Helping you figure out how to be a vampire rockstar is beyond the basic Vampire 101 training I'm required to give you."

"Fine. But what about work? I mean, I guess I can keep bartending nights, but I wasn't planning on doing that forever."

With a snort, I rolled my eyes. "You're a vampire now. You don't need to work. Once I teach you how to influence people, you just make them give you shit. Houses, cars, money… whatever you want."

"You just make people give you their money?" His eyebrows stretched to his hairline.

"Yep. Never the good people, though. Go find some douchey billionaire who's cheating on his wife and treats people like shit. It's really satisfying watching him walk away penniless after signing over everything he owns to you." I snorted and laughed. "Really fun."

Owen chuckled. "That does sound like fun. I actually know exactly who I want to drain dry."

I arched a brow, and he lifted his hands up.

"Bank account. Not blood."

"We don't kill humans. Ever. Rule number one. And that includes killing them to turn them into vampires. It's against vampire law to turn a human without Lothaire's permission, and it's punishable by death to do so. We had some issues a while back with rogue vamps turning humans for fun and letting them loose, and others trying to make their clans more powerful for wars. Now if you want to make a vamp, they need to get vetted. You can feed on humans, but you can't kill them. And never let them remember if you feed on them. Making sure no human discovers us is also up at the top of the rules. You'll be seen from time to time, but you'll use the same influence to erase their memory as you'll use to get rich and eliminate the need for a day job."

"How do I do it?"

"It's easiest if I show you. Once a human comes out here, I'll influence them not to be scared and hold still. Then you can feed on them and complete the transition, and we'll work on influencing them right after. It's one of the most important things you can know as a vampire because you will use it to ensure you're never discovered."

"This is so crazy." He blew out a breath. "Is this really happening?"

"Yep. I still can't believe it, but it's happening."

"So, what else is there I need to know?"

"Hmm. Well, you're immortal, so that's a perk. You can basically only be killed by a vampire or werewolf. Nothing else has the strength to remove your head, and that's the only way you can die. Well, that and the sun, of course. And unless you're threatened and defending your life, there is no killing of vampires allowed. After you feed and complete the transition, you'll also get some other great perks like super speed, hearing, and strength. It takes a few hours to reach full power, but it gives you some time to adjust."

"I've never met a vampire or seen one in the real world… just heard stories. Are you really as fast as they say?"

I shrugged, then flashed up the stairs to the top of the building overlooking the alley. Owen's mouth dropped.

With another flash, I reappeared at his side.

"Yep. We're really that fast."

"Holy shit," he whispered. "I'm gonna be able to do that?"

"Oh yeah. You'll be able to lift cars with a finger, run faster than a bullet, hear a pin drop across a football field, and you'll have perfect vision at night."

"That I do have," he said.

"The night vision?"

"Yeah. Even in human form, we can see at night extremely well. Our hearing and strength are also more powerful than a human. We aren't as strong or fast as a vampire, obviously, but we certainly have an advantage over regular people."

"Hmm. I didn't know that. And what about wolf form?"

"I only transitioned once right after I turned eighteen, but my night vision was even more clear in wolf form. That and I had the super speed and strength. It was incredible what I could do."

"Wait a minute." As I lifted a hand, my mouth dropped open. "Are you saying you've only transitioned one time? *Ever?*"

Crossing his arms, he leaned back against the wall and shrugged. "Yeah. You have your vampire law, and we have werewolf law. Rule number one is after your first transition on the first full moon after your eighteenth birthday, you can never *ever* change again."

"Why?" I asked, shocked to hear that.

"Um, *vampires.* In order to ensure you thought we'd all died, it became law to never use our powers. When we turn eighteen, we can't control it. The moon triggers the genes that cause the transformation. But after that, we can change at will… or not. And we never do again."

"Wow. I guess that explains why we thought werewolves were gone."

"That was the whole point. Over six hundred years of werewolves keeping themselves in hiding, and you assumed we were gone. When a werewolf turns eighteen, they get shipped up to the cabin where all the young werewolves in the area go to transition. They have enormous cages strong enough to hold us until we learn to control the wolf. We're allowed then to run outside through the woods and experience being a free werewolf once. After it's over, we're sent home to never speak of it again."

"Does it hurt? When you change?"

He shook his head. "No. Luckily the witches who made us their werewolf protectors made the transition painless."

"I've never seen a werewolf transition. I've only seen you all in wolf form."

"Yeah, I bet you have. Right before you slaughtered us."

Laughing under my breath, I shook my head. "You know what? Fuck you. Werewolves hunted *us* and killed *us*. I'm so super sorry if we defended ourselves and your kind lost. What is it with people rewriting history to make us out to be the assholes? First, the Picts try to make us out to be monsters after *they* killed half our clan, and now werewolves are all 'woe is me those big meanie vampires' after you literally had one goal, and that was to eradicate us. Just because we *won,* and the werewolves tucked tail and went into hiding, doesn't mean we were in the wrong. You all need to fix your fucking history." I stuck out my lip and rubbed my eyes. "Boo freaking hoo. You started a fight, then you lost. Get the hell over it."

Owen opened his mouth to argue, but the side door of the club opened. An intoxicated man stumbled out and wandered over to the dumpster. Owen and I shared a look as we heard the *zip* of his pants before he started pissing.

"Let's let him finish so he doesn't piss on us," I whispered. "Then, you just wait while I influence him to hold still and not be scared."

Owen nodded his understanding, but as his eyes fixated on the man, bloodlust crept in.

"Wait here," I commanded when I heard the man finish up.

I flashed behind the drunk guy. When he turned around, he stumbled back a step. "Whoa! Where'd you come from, pretty lady?"

The pungent smell of liquor on his breath would have ignited into flames with the tiniest ember—a perfect first feed for Owen.

I looked deep into his eyes and pushed into his mind. "No matter what happens in this alley, you will not feel fear, and you will not run."

The slow, mesmerized nod of his head told me he'd understood me.

"Owen, you can come now," I called to him.

Owen walked over in a daze, the bloodlust pushing him toward a victim.

"Now, you will want to kill him... drain him dry," I started as Owen stopped in front of the man. "But you *must* stop yourself. You can drink for ten seconds from the vein in his neck and then stop."

Even though I knew I'd have to pull him off, like we did with all new vamps on their first feed, I still told him the rules. With my strength, I'd have no problem tossing him aside when the bloodlust took over and forced him to keep feeding.

"How do I make my fangs work?" Owen asked.

"Just lean down near his neck. They'll pop out instinctively. After the first time, you'll be able to control them at will."

In a bloodlust haze, Owen nodded slowly, then leaned down toward the stoic man's neck.

*Click.*

His fangs popped out as he closed in the last few inches.

"Just sink your fangs into his skin. Your body will know what to do."

The man remained calm as Owen sunk his fangs into his neck. My influence held strong as Owen continued feeding.

When ten seconds had passed, I touched Owen on the shoulder. "That's enough. You need to remove your fangs now."

As expected, he clamped down harder, the bloodlust having consumed his mind.

"Owen. Let go. Now," I demanded as I yanked on his shoulder.

Instead of flying backward from the force like any other new vampire would have, Owen just shrugged off my hand.

*What the hell?*

"Owen! Let go!" I shouted and tried to toss him again.

A growl like I hadn't heard in centuries rumbled out of his throat. With a lip-curling snarl, he whipped his head over his shoulder and bared his fangs at me.

It wasn't the blood-dripping fangs that set me stumbling back a step, it was the glowing green eyes.

Vampires didn't have glowing eyes.

Werewolves did.

But Owen was a vampire now.

Or was he?

*What the hell?*

He dove back down into the man's neck, and I saw the life leaving his eyes.

"Owen! You're killing him!" I shouted and dug down into all my strength to try to dislodge him again.

Instead of Owen flying across the alley, with one large swipe of his hand, it was me who slammed against the opposite wall.

Pain seared through my arm, and I glanced down at the deep lacerations sliced into my skin. Another glance to Owen and I saw the cause… he now had long claws instead of fingernails.

*What the hell is he?*

With the man's life slipping away by the second, I didn't have time to process what Owen was. Instead, I leaped back to my feet and shot across the alley, launching myself onto Owen's back.

He roared in pain as I sunk my fangs into his shoulder while I wrapped my body around his back. The attack dislodged him from the man's neck as he swiped his claws at me while trying to get me off. With a flash of movement, he slammed his back against the opposite wall, and the bricks shattered into pieces as I collided with them. Pain seared through my body from the force of the blow, but I refused to let go, digging deeper into his skin while I tightened my grip.

Again, he flashed across the alley and slammed me into the other side. I'd spent my life fighting vampires and werewolves, and never had I felt power or speed like I did from Owen. Even Lothaire, the oldest and strongest vampire, who almost matched Owen in size, was nothing compared to the strength and speed Owen exhibited.

A strength capable of killing me if I wasn't careful.

I pulled my fangs from his shoulder and shouted his name again.

"Owen! Stop! It's Annella! Please, Owen. Stop!"

But my pleas fell on deaf ears, and he reached back and got ahold of my shoulder, tossing me down the alley into a pile of garbage cans. As trash exploded around me, the smell assaulted my nostrils, but I didn't have time to process it before Owen leaped upon me.

With one swipe of his clawed hand, he caught me around the throat and hoisted me into the air. His glowing green eyes bore into mine as he heaved heavy breaths.

"Owen," I choked out the word. "Please. It's me. It's Annella. You have to come back. You have to calm down. I know you. You don't want to hurt anyone. Please, Owen."

His lip twitched as he leaned closer to my face. Hot breath ghosted my lips when he snarled.

I'd been in my share of scraps before, but never had I truly felt outmatched.

Until now.

I had no moves to combat his speed and strength. With one squeeze, he could remove my head and end my immortal life. As I stared into his wild eyes, there was no doubt in my mind that Owen was neither vampire nor werewolf.

He was something else.

And stronger than both.

"Owen, you don't want to hurt me. Please."

As he stared into my eyes, I saw the savage rage start to falter. The intensity of his gaze softened as he looked at me. Slowly the recognition spread across his face, and his grip on my neck loosened.

"What am I doing?" he whispered as he let me go. I dropped to the ground and flashed to the man still standing still.

"Forget what happened here and run home," I said as quickly as I could.

He didn't hesitate and took off down the alley.

I turned my attention back to Owen, who stood hunched over at the end of the alley. After watching him for a few seconds, I approached with careful, concise steps.

"Owen? Is that you?" I asked.

"What the hell happened to me?" He panted. "What the fuck was that?"

"I don't know," I answered as I stepped up behind him. "I've never seen anything like it before."

Owen spun around, and I noticed the glow of his green eyes had faded back to their normal emerald shade. Another glance down showed retracted claws.

"What am I? What the fuck am I?" he rumbled, and it set me back on my heels.

"I think..." I paused as I tried to process what I was about to say. "I think you're a hybrid. A vampire and a werewolf."

"I almost killed him!" Owen roared. "And you! I don't want to be like this. I can't be like this!"

Before I could choke out another word, he was gone.

# Chapter Five

## OWEN

The long horn of the ferry signaled our approach to the Irish dock.

*Home.*

It had been all I could think about since I'd run from Annella tonight. Run from this *thing* I'd become.

All I wanted now was my father's words of wisdom and the support of my three brothers. They'd know what to do.

At least I hoped they would because right now, I couldn't even begin to think straight or see a solution to this problem.

*I'd almost killed a human. And almost killed Annella.*

After running away from Annella, I'd bolted straight to the ferry dock and texted my family while I boarded. Without explaining what had happened, because how could I, I'd used our family S.O.S. with a plea to meet at my father's house in Dublin. Each brother had responded they were on their way.

After how I felt when I drank the man's blood in the alley, I knew if I started to feed again, I wouldn't be able to stop. When my bloodlust had started again on board the ferry, I'd climbed over the edge of the giant ship and hung onto a rope on the side for the entire two-hour duration. It didn't erase the desire to drain every last human on the deck, but it had helped that I couldn't see them.

Now I just had to hope my bloodlust wouldn't put my family in harm's way.

No. It couldn't. My love for my family was far stronger than any desire to drain all the blood from the people around me.

It had to be.

When the ferry docked, I shimmied down the side of the ship and leaped onto the dock. Too scared to get into a cab and be so close to the temptations of human blood, I started sprinting toward my father's house in Dublin. The one time I'd shifted into a wolf, I'd gotten to race through the forest with speeds I'd never imagined I could hit—speeds to rival a vampire. Even though it had been a decade since I'd experienced it, I remembered exactly how it felt.

And I knew that my speeds tonight were even faster than that.

Much faster.

Normally it would take me two hours by car to get from the ferry to my father's place, but at the speeds I hit, I made it there in under fifteen minutes. Annella hadn't been kidding when she'd said I would be fast, and it surprised me to find out that even as a new vamp, I'd been faster than her.

How? Annella was an original. The strongest and fastest vamps on the planet. Yet I'd been able to defeat her with ease. Could she be right? Was I a hybrid? And if so, what the hell did that mean?

I skidded to a stop in front of my father's house. The

small three-bedroom ranch house at the end of the cul-de-sac looked exactly like it did when my brothers and I grew up in it. It wasn't a big house, but it had suited our family fine.

As the oldest brothers, Logan and I had shared one bedroom, while Torin and Colin had shared another. My mother had passed away when I was six, and my father never remarried. Just us five boys living here in the house that still felt like home.

Even though it terrified me to go inside and admit what had happened, I didn't have time to stand outside and gather my nerve. With only an hour until the sun rose, I didn't have much time to fill them in and find a light-tight spot to hide out for the day.

Hoping my father would have a solution for my situation, I took a deep breath and went in.

"Hello? You guys in here?" I called as I pushed open the front door.

"We're in here," my father called.

"Pops?" I said as I walked through the house, pausing to look at the picture in the hallway. It'd been the last one we'd taken as a family before cancer stole my mother from us. She stood next to my father, holding Colin in her arms, with Logan, Torin, and myself grinning widely between them. My mother had been beautiful with her ebony hair and the green eyes inherited by everyone born with the wolf gene. It only took one parent with the gene to pass it on to the children, but in my case, both my parents were werewolves.

"What the hell is going on?" My brother Logan asked as I stepped into the living room. "Are you okay? Your text sounded serious."

My three brothers all rose from their seats. Each one matched me in height, another werewolf trait that went with our green eyes, but all of them had shorter hair. I looked more like my father, who sported the same chin-length messy waves and unshaved facial hair. He stood up slower than my brothers but came over and joined them in greeting me with a brief hug.

"What's up, man?" Colin asked as he released the grip on my shoulders. "I have to be at the fire station for a twenty-four-hour shift in two hours. You're ruining my beauty sleep, so this had better be good."

I exhaled a deep breath. Partly because the bloodlust had risen its head in such close proximity to blood, and partly to stall while I struggled to find the words that seemed impossible to utter out loud.

"I think you all need to sit down. This isn't going to be easy."

They passed sideways glances to one another, but each listened and found their seats.

"Are you in trouble?" Torin asked as he adjusted the gun on his hip. As an officer of the elite tactical force called the ERU, he never went anywhere without it.

I stammered for words as I paced back and forth in the living room.

"You're worrying me, son," my father said. "Just come out and say it. Whatever it is, you know we're all here for you."

"You're damn right we are," Logan answered. "Now, tell us what's happening."

With a deep breath, I found the will to utter the words.

"I, uh… something happened to me. Something I didn't want. I just want you guys to know that I didn't ask for this."

They nodded their heads, but I could see the worry in their eyes.

Blowing out a big breath, I looked down at my feet and dragged out the words I couldn't believe I had to utter.

"I, uh, I… I got turned into a vampire. There. I said it. I'm a fucking vampire."

Silence settled over the room like a heavy blanket. After a few long moments, I finally glanced up from my feet. Four sets of wide eyes stared back at me.

Colin broke the silence first. His deep, hearty laugh echoed around the room, and soon the other three joined him.

"Fuck's sake, man," Logan said between laughter. "I thought you were gonna say you robbed a bank or something. Or killed someone. But a vampire?" He laughed harder. "Okay, then."

"Seriously," Torin said between hysterics. "You're dropping the worst-case scenario on us to soften the blow for the actual news, so it can't be good. We're prepared now. Go on. What is it?"

I looked at my father and swallowed over the lump in my throat.

"I'm serious. I got turned. I didn't realize I was dating a vampire, and I got her blood in my mouth. And last night some crazy vampire chick snapped my neck. She killed me. I woke up as a vampire. A fucking vampire. And it gets worse."

"Worse than a vampire?" Colin's laughter deepened. "Come on, man. It's fucking late, and you dragged us all out of bed for something. You know we've got your back no matter what, so get on with it."

"I'm fucking serious!" I shouted, surprised by the force the words came out.

The laughter around the room halted as my family blinked back at me.

"Dude. Chill out. We're just fucking with you," Logan said.

"Owen," my father said, "you can tell us. We love you, and we'll support you no matter what. What is going on?"

I grabbed my hair and closed my eyes, desperate to make them understand. As anger and frustration boiled up inside me, I felt the *click* of my fangs. Annella had told me I'd be able to trigger them at will, but I wasn't even sure how it'd happened. When I opened my mouth, my brother Logan saw them first.

"Bloody hell!" he shouted as he leaped to his feet with the stealth of not just his werewolf genes, but with the training he'd gotten as a special forces Ranger in the Irish Army. "What the fuck are those?"

I struggled to cover my mouth and get my fangs to retract, but the more upset I got by their reactions, the harder it became to control them.

My father rose from his chair as my brothers hopped up and joined each other in front of the fireplace. A wall of enormous men stood across from me, staring at me like I was a monster.

And I was.

"Your eyes are glowing," Torin whispered as his hand hovered over his gun. "Why are your eyes glowing? Our eyes don't glow unless we're in wolf form."

"I don't know what's happening to me," I said over the lump in my throat. "I don't know what I am. I don't think I'm a werewolf or a vampire anymore. Annella thinks I'm something in between — a hybrid. I'm freaking out, you guys! I don't know what to do! How did this happen to me?"

As panic washed over me in waves, I no longer felt like the powerful man I'd become… or the even more powerful creature who'd manhandled an original vampire. As I stood in my childhood living room, I felt like a small boy who just needed his family to make everything better.

I wanted my mother.

"Hey, hey," Logan said, stepping forward from the group. With careful steps, he approached me. "It's gonna be okay. We've got you, brother. We'll figure this out."

His large hand closed around my shoulder, and for the first time since I'd awaken on the floor of the Mackay's castle, I started to feel like everything really could be okay.

"I don't know what I'm going to do," I said as I got my emotions under control. The fangs retreated into my gums. "I need your help. How do I fix this? What do I do?"

When I turned around, Logan took one look at me and pulled me in for a hug. "You're a Hunter. We always find a way to fix shit. We'll help you through this, okay?"

"Thank you, Logan," I answered. "Thank you. I had no idea she was a vampire. Everything just got so fucked up."

"This is crazy," Colin said as he approached me slowly. "You're not gonna like, kill us, or anything, are you?"

"God, no!" I answered. "I would never harm you guys."

*I hoped…*

I still struggled to suppress the desire to sink my fangs into their skin and devour every last drop of their blood.

But I wouldn't. These were my brothers. My family. I would sooner kill myself before I harmed one hair on their heads.

"Just tell us what happened. Start from the beginning," Torin said.

I was about to start the story when I looked over to the ashen face of my father. He still hadn't responded to my news, and from the frozen look on his face, I worried he'd had a heart attack and died, but just hadn't tipped over yet.

"Pops?" I said as I stepped toward him.

Instead of approaching me and hugging me like my brothers, he took a huge step backward. "Get back," he spat.

"Pops? I won't hurt you. I swear I won't hurt you."

"I said, *get back!*" he shouted as he grabbed a floor lamp and held it like a weapon.

"Whoa, whoa, dad." Torin raised his hands and stepped toward him. "It's Owen. Your son, Owen. He may be a vampire now, but he's still your son… and our brother. He won't hurt us."

"My son died," my father whispered, his lip trembling with his voice.

The words felt like a dagger to my heart.

"He's not dead." Colin stepped to my side. "He's alive, and he needs our help."

"He died!" My father shouted as he burst into tears. "He died! Owen died!"

"Pops, I *did* die… but I came back. I'm back," I said as I fought my own tears.

"No." My father shook his head. "You're not my son. You're not Owen."

"Dad," Logan started, but my father cut him off.

"Get him out of here! Get out! Get out!"

As he swung the lamp at me, I stumbled back toward the door.

"Owen, don't leave." Logan started toward me. "He doesn't know what he's saying. He's just in shock. You know how he feels about vampires." He paused. "How we *all* feel about vampires. Just give him a little time. This is a lot for all of us to process."

I shook my head as I stumbled toward the door. The

pain from my father's rejection hurt worse than the pain I'd endured transitioning on the Mackay's floor last night.

Pure, soul shredding agony.

"I'm so sorry, Pops. I'm so sorry," I whispered as I kept moving toward the door.

Torin moved to me and reached for my arm. "Owen don't go. Not like this."

When his hand closed around my bicep and tugged, the monster inside me surfaced again. My fangs popped out, and I snarled. With lightning-quick reflexes and strength that terrified me, I sent Torin flying backward. He slid across the carpet and came to a stop next to my father.

"Bloody hell, Owen!" he said as he leaped back to his feet.

"I'm sorry!" I covered my fangs again. "I didn't mean to. I can't control it. I can't control it."

"Easy, big guy." Logan lifted his hands as he moved toward me like I was a wild animal. "You're not yourself right now. It's okay."

The heightened emotions inside me started to simmer as I struggled to slow my breathing. "What's happening to me? Why is this happening?"

"Just try to stay calm," Colin said as he stepped forward with Torin at his side.

"I didn't mean to react like that," I said. "It just takes over, and I don't have any control of myself. I'm so sorry I threw you."

"No worries, brother. I'm fine," Torin said. "But we have to figure out what to do with you right now, so you don't accidentally hurt anyone."

"The sun will be up soon, and I can't be in it. I don't know where to go."

"There's a cave by my cabin in the Wicklow Mountains," Logan said. "I can drive you there right now, but I don't know if we'll make it before the sun comes up."

"It will be faster if I run. I'm faster now than I was when I was in wolf form," I said and saw the bulging eyes in response.

"Okay," Logan said. "Just go to my cabin and follow the River Inchavore west. When it makes a sharp left turn, you'll see the entrance of the cave. You should be safe in there."

"Thank you. I'm just so fucking confused and freaked out right now."

"I can only imagine," Torin said. "But we're gonna help you. All of us."

He directed the answer to my father, who still stared at me with horror in his eyes… and it crushed me to see it there.

"Pops. I'm so sorry. I didn't want this. If I had a choice, I would have—"

"You had a choice." He cut me off and tears glistened over his green eyes. "You had a choice when my *son* died last night. In order to become a vampire, you have to feed on a human. Instead of accepting your fate, a fate I will never recover from, you chose to drink blood and complete the transformation into the very creature they created us to destroy. Into a… a vampire."

He closed his eyes as he said the word *vampire,* then took a long pause before starting again.

"My son was a good man, a proud werewolf, and a wonderful… a wonderful son. A son who is now…" He choked out the word. "Dead. Instead of letting him rest in peace, you stole his body and came back as this… abomination."

He waved a hand over me as he spit out the words that tore apart my soul.

Words that weren't wrong.

If it weren't for the bloodlust, I would have chosen death over this.

Death over being the thing I hate most.

The thing that almost killed a human tonight.

The thing that threw my brother across the living room.

The thing that never should have lived.

"You're right," I whispered as I stared into the eyes of the man who'd loved me with all of his heart and soul… a man who now stared at me like the stranger I was. "I should have stayed dead."

"Hey." Logan stepped toward me. "Don't say that."

I shook my head and stepped out of his reach when he stretched an arm out toward me.

"No. He's right. He's right," I repeated. "I'm sorry. I shouldn't be here."

"Owen. Don't say that." Torin started toward me, but I stepped away again as I backed to the door.

When I bumped into the wall, Logan reached out and grabbed me. "You're not leaving. Not until we know you aren't going to do something stupid."

Once again, my primal reaction to the force of his grip resulted in him sailing across the room. A growl rumbled through my chest as I snarled at them.

The shock on my brothers' faces yanked me back into reality. The animal inside retreated as I lifted my hands in submission.

"I didn't mean to do that. Fuck! I'm so sorry, Logan. I… I don't want to hurt any of you. I have to go. I have to end this."

Logan leaped back up. "Don't you dare do anything stupid, Owen!"

"I love you guys," I said as I swept a passing gaze across the faces of the brothers I loved more than anything. My eyes landed on the face of my father, still twisted in pain and anger. "I'm sorry, Pops. You're right. I should have stayed dead. I'm gonna fix that. I love you."

"Ow-!" Torin shouted, but I flashed out of the house before he'd even finished the word.

My legs carried me away from the family I loved, but I didn't even register the scenery flashing by as I ran. Somewhere far away from them so I wouldn't hurt them. I couldn't live with myself if I did.

As I tore out of Dublin, I watched the color of the sky starting to lighten.

The sun would rise soon, and I knew what I had to do.

And where I wanted to go.

I spun south and raced to Killiney Hills. When I reached the top of the hill, I stopped at the base of the obelisk overlooking the bay. It stretched up into the sky and would give me the perfect view while I watched the sunrise... the perfect last view to take in before I left this world.

Using my speed, I scaled up the side of the narrow pillar until I reached the top. When I got there, I sat down on the space just large enough to fit me.

My gaze stretched out across the ocean and the gorgeous countryside surrounding me. Three-hundred-and-sixty degrees of pure beauty would be the last thing I ever saw.

It surprised me how calm I remained as the colors on the horizon glowed with the impending sun. My father was right. I had died… and should have *stayed* dead.

This wasn't a life for me. I wasn't a killer, and I didn't want to spend eternity in the dark with the vile vampires.

But Annella…

Her face flashed into my mind as the colors on the horizon brightened.

I knew I shouldn't care about her anymore, not since I found out what she was… *who* she was.

But deep in my heart, part of me still yearned for her. Part of me mourned that we'd never gotten a chance to see where we could have gone. We'd never been able to explore the deep connection between us.

The orange strip of the sun peeked above the horizon, and I inhaled a deep breath as I waited for the rays to come and the pain to hit me.

My brothers. I hoped they'd be okay. I hoped they'd forgive me for giving up.

The rays crawled across the water, approaching me as they spread.

My father. I hoped he'd forget the monster who'd shown up tonight and remember the son who loved him more than life.

The warm glow illuminated the world surrounding me. As the rays climbed up the sides of the obelisk, I closed my eyes and waited for this nightmare to end.

*Annella…*

Her face popped into my head as the rays caressed my skin.

Her kiss. Her touch. Her laugh. Visions of our short time together flooded my mind as I waited for the pain to start and my body to burst into flames.

A pain that didn't come.

"What the hell?" I whispered as I opened my eyes and stared down at my illuminated skin.

The sun hadn't harmed me. I was still alive.

*Fuck.*

# Chapter Six

## ANNELLA

"Holy shit. Mind. Blown." Mark touched the top of his head and mimicked the explosion, complete with the sound effect.

I'd spent the rest of last night searching for Owen in the city, hoping to find him before he hurt someone. But after hours of searching and no sign of him, I'd stayed at our apartment in the city when I couldn't make it back before sunrise. After sunset tonight, I'd run back to our castle and had just gotten home twenty minutes ago. My family gathered around me while I told them the story about Owen's transformation.

His transformation into something that wasn't a vampire.

"So, he's a hybrid? Is that a thing? What does that mean?" Aiden asked.

"I have no fucking idea," I breathed. "All I know is he is strong as hell and put a beat down on me like I've never known. His eyes glowed green like a werewolf, and he has claws, but other than that, he looked like Owen."

"So, he didn't turn into a wolf?" Thorne rubbed a hand over his scruffy chin. "But he wasn't just a vampire."

"Nope. Something in between."

"This isn't good," Lothaire grumbled. "If he is stronger than you, than he's stronger than all of us. What if he decides to come for us?"

"We have to find him and put him down," Grizella stated matter-of-factly.

Just hearing them talk about killing Owen made my heart stutter to a stop.

But they weren't wrong.

The beast I'd fought in the alley was a danger to every one of my family members, and every human in the vicinity if he didn't get his rage under control.

"Let's not do anything hasty," Catrain said. "Let me go to the island and talk to my family. Maybe Uradech or the other wolves, or my mother, know what is happening to him."

Since Catrain's family had been the ones to cast both spells that created immortals and werewolves, they would certainly be the most likely to know what had happened to Owen.

"That would be great, Catrain. Thank you," I said.

Lothaire nodded his agreement. "The more we understand what he is, the better chance we have of knowing the right thing to do."

I swallowed down my sigh of relief, so I didn't expose how I really felt about killing Owen.

Yes. He was a werewolf—or at least he *used* to be a werewolf—and I *hated* werewolves. The thought of dating one was a notion I'd never even considered entertaining. But even though I tried to erase the feeling of his lips on mine, I couldn't.

He was still Owen.

Still the man that made my heart beat harder than it had in my entire immortal life.

And now he was something different from the beasts I'd hunted to near extinction.

It left me reeling… trying to understand the complexity of my feelings.

"We won't go hunting for him until Catrain gets back from talking to her family," Aiden said, "but if he shows up here and threatens us, we'll have no choice but to put him down. Agreed?"

They all nodded their heads, and I forced mine to nod too.

"He really had claws?" Emilia asked.

"Oh yeah." My eyes widened. "Like five inches long and sharp as all hell. You can't see it now because my healing already repaired it, but my arm looked like a freaking Great White had tried to take it off. Gashes all the way down to the bone."

"I'm just glad you're okay." Emilia slid an arm around my shoulder.

"It was really crazy. He started as a normal bloodlust-fueled newbie vamp, but then something changed. Usually, when you pull them off and the feeding stops, they come back to their right mind in a few moments and have some control again. Not Owen. It was like he was a wild animal, and it wasn't until he almost popped my head off like a dandelion that he came to his senses and stopped."

"But he did come to his senses," Catrain said. "That's a good sign."

"Yeah. He did."

"And then he just ran off?" Thorne asked.

"Yep. I looked everywhere for him but found no signs of

him. The good news is that I didn't find a trail of bodies anywhere, so maybe he didn't hurt anyone."

"Let's hope so. The last thing we need right now with everything going on with Clan Lennox is a vampire on a killing spree."

"Any news on them?" I asked.

Lothaire nodded. "Yes. A report came in that the night Leeya was at the club with you, her brother Leith was spotted in Glasgow as well. That means they're both here."

"So, they are back." I wrinkled my nose. "They must really have a death wish."

"They are up to something," Thorne said. "They wouldn't be stupid enough to come back to the area unless they had to. They could be hiding out in the Caribbean right now, but they came back to our territory. There's a reason for that."

"And we'll find out what it is." Aiden swirled his glass of bourbon around the giant square ice cube in the center.

A loud knock on the door startled us all.

"Annella!" Owen called from the other side.

We all glanced between one another as our fangs popped out.

"Stay here," Lothaire commanded, but I was already on my feet and at the door.

My desire to see him alive overrode any fear I had of the man who'd almost torn me to shreds last night.

The man who had werewolf blood pumping through his veins.

I whipped open the door and saw him standing there, soaked from the rain that poured down behind him.

"Owen," I breathed.

His eyes locked with mine, and I saw the pain and fear

churning beneath the sea of green. "I need help. Please. Help me."

My heart squeezed in my chest as I reached out for his hand, but Lothaire stepped in front of me.

"Wait," he growled and shoved me aside. "We don't know if he's safe."

"Lothaire—" I started, but Owen stopped me by raising his hand.

"He's right." Owen shook his head. "I don't know if I'm safe. I have no fucking idea what is happening to me or how to control it. All I know is that I can't seem to die, hard as I try, and I need one of you to rip off my head. I think that will do the trick."

"What?" I gasped, unable to fully process his admission. "What the hell are you talking about?"

Owen's shoulders slumped in defeat. "I can't live like this. All I want to do is kill people. And this rage inside me… I can't control it. I almost hurt my brothers. Whatever the hell I am can't exist. I've tried frying in the sun, leaping off a cliff headfirst, swallowing enough pills to kill an elephant. Nothing. Nothing kills me. So, I hope that maybe you can at least try."

Lothaire looked at me, and his eyebrows rose almost to his hairline.

Tears burned my eyes as I swallowed over the lump in my throat.

He'd tried to kill himself?

Owen. My beautiful Owen, who sang me love songs and made me laugh harder than I had in centuries, had tried to end his life. A tragedy beyond words.

And a tragedy I had a hand in.

If we'd never met, he'd still be living his life, touring with his band, and not trying to commit suicide in the sun.

Then I processed what he'd said.

"Wait." I lifted a hand. "You went in the sun? And you didn't burn?"

With a heavy sigh, he lifted his hands and shrugged. "Nope. Still here."

"Holy shit," Aiden said behind me. "He really is some sort of hybrid. A vampire would have cooked in the sun."

"That's incredible." Catrain pushed up to my side. "I don't think my ancestors ever would have expected this. You are immortal, but because werewolves can live in the sun, so can you."

As we stared at him like a circus freak, Owen just looked between all of us and shrugged. "I guess so. And because of that inconvenience, I can't kill myself in the sun, so I need some help. So, which one of you wants the honors of trying to rip off my head? Lothaire? You look like a strong chap. Or Annella? You do have a reputation for decapitating a lot of werewolves."

"Is that really what you want?" Lothaire crossed his arms.

"It is," Owen admitted. "My father was right. I should have refused to drink the blood and transitioned. I should have stayed dead."

"Owen," I whispered, "Killing yourself isn't the answer."

"Then what is the answer? Wait until I've murdered a bunch of people, can't live with the guilt, *then* off myself? Huh? No. This isn't right, and I need to remedy my mistake before that happens. I need to die."

Lothaire started to agree, but I spun around and placed my hands on my hips. "That's it! Everyone give Owen and me a minute alone. I'm the one that turned him, so he's my responsibility, and this is *my* decision. Leave us."

Worry lines creased Thorne's forehead. "I don't think it's safe to leave you with him."

Gritting my teeth, I put my hands on my hips. "I will be fine."

"Annella—" Lothaire started, but I stopped him.

"Leave us!"

He recoiled at my words, then lifted his hands and stepped back. "We'll be right in here if you need us."

His lethal glare bore into Owen as a warning before he gestured for everyone to move back. My family walked away, leaving Owen and I standing in the doorway. I stepped outside with him and closed it behind me.

"He's right. It's not safe to be alone with me. I could kill you."

I rolled my eyes. "You won't kill me. And you're not killing yourself."

"What other option do I have?" he shouted, and that deadly rage sprung forth in his eyes again. The soft green flickered with bright green sparks.

"Calm down," I said slowly. "Just take a deep breath and let it out slow."

Even though he practically shook in his skin, he listened to my suggestion. As he exhaled the breath, his eyes softened again, and the glowing flickered out.

"See. You can do this, Owen. You just need to let me help you. All newbie vamps are erratic and easily triggered. If you'd have stuck around to let me teach you, I could have told you that. Now, I will say that you're *more* easily triggered than most vamps, especially since you already fed. It should have calmed you down, at least a little. But maybe that's your werewolf temper coming through. Werewolves are known for being hotheads."

He pursed his lips and gave me a slight nod of agreement.

"But I bet you learned how to control your werewolf temper, didn't you?"

He nodded. "I guess. It's something we all work on hard through our teens before the change."

"Then you can do it again. And once I give you more blood—"

"More blood?" he bellowed. "I'll kill someone if I try to feed again! I don't know how to stop!"

With a heavy sigh, I shook my head. "If you'd let me *finish.* More blood from a *bag.* When a vamp first turns, they need a *lot* of blood to stop the feeding frenzy that takes over. Obviously, we aren't going to kill a bunch of people, and you need to feed on a live human first to complete the transition, so we start with live then finish with *bags*… which you would have known if you hadn't taken off last night."

"So, this frenzy to kill is… normal?"

"Yes." I nodded. "Very normal. I mean, you drank more blood from that man last night than we normally would have, and it hasn't satiated you at all, but maybe because you're a hybrid, you need even more than a regular vamp. But once we get enough blood in you, the frenzy goes away with training and a little time. The frenzy is normal, it's just abnormal that you had the strength to kick my ass and get away before I could help you finish the feed safely."

He rubbed a hand behind his neck as he processed my words.

"How about this? Why don't you feed on some bags and let me work with you to teach you to control your urges and your temper? If it doesn't work, I'll rip your head off myself."

Even though I said it with complete confidence, inside, it killed me to envision ending his life.

Owen paced back and forth, the pounding rain forming a wall behind him.

"What if I hurt someone?"

"We'll go somewhere with no one around. Just you and me."

He stopped pacing and looked deep into my eyes. The eyes staring into mine weren't a werewolves', or a hybrid's… they were Owen's.

*My* Owen's.

"What if I kill you?"

"You won't," I answered confidently, even though I didn't feel as convinced as I sounded.

"You don't know that."

He was right. I didn't know that. In fact, from what I'd seen of him before, he very well could end my existence if he lost control. But I'd gotten him into this situation, and I owed it to him to help him figure out how to survive in these new circumstances.

I kept up the positive tone, hoping to convince myself as much as him. "Yes. I do. If you wanted to kill me, you'd have killed me last night. But you didn't."

"I *wanted* to kill you, Annella. God, did I want to," he said, and I saw the shame in his eyes.

"Exactly. You wanted to, but you stopped yourself. You *can* control it. You just need a little guidance, and I'm going to help you."

Owen paced back and forth, shaking his head.

"I can't risk it. I don't think I should try."

"Did you slaughter any humans since I saw you last?"

He shook his head. "No. I fought it off, but barely."

"See. You can do this. It only gets easier with time. I'm not taking no for an answer."

"Why?" He spun toward me and stared down into my eyes. "Why won't you let me die? You said yourself I'm a werewolf, and my kind disgusts you. Why bother saving me?"

"Because…" I paused.

*Because werewolf or hybrid or not, I'm still crazy about you.*

Instead of blurting out the words that would change everything, I just shrugged.

"Because Clan Lennox is planning something against us, and if we can get you under control, I could really use your help to rid the world of every last one of them. You managed to kick my original vampire ass, so I can only imagine what you can do to a regular vampire."

He stared at me while he twisted his lips.

"And that's it? That's the only reason you want me alive?"

His penetrating gaze pierced into me, but I lifted my chin and hid the feelings for him still trying to claw their way back out.

"Yep. I could use the extra muscle. So what do you say? I'll teach you how to control yourself and live in the world with your new powers, and in exchange, you agree to help me with Clan Lennox. When we get them taken care of, your debt to me will be paid, and you'll be free to go wherever your immortal heart wants."

Owen sucked on his cheek as he continued searching my eyes.

"Do we have a deal?"

"And if you can't teach me how to function like this?"

"Then I promise to kill you. You have my word."

My word was my bond, and I'd never broken it before.

The minute the phrase popped out of my mouth, I wanted to shove it back in. I didn't think I had it in me to end his life, but I'd promised to do it. It meant that I *had* to succeed at training him to resist his urges and control his temper.

Failure wasn't an option.

"Okay. Let's do it," he said as he extended his hand.

I glanced at it before reaching out and taking it. When his enormous hand encased mine, the familiar sparks from his touch traveled through my body like little electric shocks.

The door opened, and Lothaire's frame blocked out the light coming from inside.

"This is a terrible idea," he said.

"Were you eavesdropping?" I arched an eyebrow. "We have rules. No using vamp hearing to eavesdrop on the family."

He furrowed his brow. "I was worried about you, and that's not the point. You can't go off with him alone."

"I can and I will," I said. "I won't take a risk with any of your lives, and until we get Owen under control, I need to be somewhere safe. Somewhere far away from everyone and you guys."

"I don't like it, Nella," Aiden agreed as he stepped to Lothaire's side. "He could hurt you."

I looked over and locked eyes with Owen.

"You all need to trust me on this. I'm taking Owen to the cabin in the mountains, and we'll stay there until he's safe. Could be a couple days or a couple weeks, but I will not give up until we get this under control."

Lothaire grumbled, but he knew better than to argue with me.

"I'll be fine," I said to my family, now gathering at the door. "I promise."

"You'd better not hurt her." Thorne impaled Owen with a glare.

"I don't want to," Owen answered honestly. "I will try my hardest not to. I swear it."

I turned back to Owen and let out a deep breath. "I'd invite you in, but I don't want you going full berserker and killing my family. Just wait here, and I'll go pack a bag and get a bunch of blood bags from the fridge. We'll leave for the cabin now."

He nodded.

"Don't. Move." I held up a finger before flashing past my family, gathering everything I needed, and reappearing a few seconds later.

"I love you guys," I said to the concerned faces staring at me. "I swear I'll be fine. He may be huge and strong, but I'm scrappy."

I grinned, and they all joined me in the gesture, though I could see the unease still tightening their faces.

Unease I secretly still had as I remembered how easily he'd defeated me in the alley.

"Be safe," Lothaire said. "And check in as soon as you can. You won't have good cell service up there, so go at least once a day to somewhere you can check messages and send us one to tell us you're safe. We'll let you know if we hear anything about Clan Lennox. And if you miss a day checking in, we're coming up there."

His intense gaze shifted to Owen.

"All of us."

Owen nodded his understanding, and I joined him.

"I'll check in every day. I promise. Love you guys." With a quick kiss blown off my hand, I grabbed Owen and bolted out into the pouring rain toward our cabin in the mountains.

The one I hoped wouldn't be my tomb if this went badly.

# Chapter Seven

## OWEN

I raced at Annella's side through the pouring rain across the Scottish countryside, slowing down my pace to stay with her.

How was I faster than an original?

Stronger?

Fear drove deeper into my gut as I confirmed my initial thoughts… I *was* more powerful than the originals.

How would she train me without getting herself killed?

And how would I live with myself if I killed Annella?

Then I imagined the pride in my father's eyes if I told him I ended Maighread Mackay. Maybe he'd even forgive me for the abomination I'd become. Pull me into his arms and call me his son again. It was in my blood to kill her and her family, after all… the very reason our kind was created.

The wolf that lived inside me rumbled and begged to take out the vampire it'd been created to kill, but as I glanced over at the incredible beauty racing at my side, I couldn't imagine being the one to take her life.

Not intentionally, anyway. The monster inside me may not heed my choice to let her live, and that terrified me.

Annella skidded to a stop in front of a small, ramshackle cabin deep in the woods.

"We're here. Not a human around to harm for miles and miles."

The broken step bowed under her as she stepped onto the porch and made her way to the front door.

"Come on inside."

The rusty door hinges creaked as Annella pushed open the door. I followed her inside and looked around the one-room dark, dusty cabin.

"What is this place?" I dragged my fingertips through the layers of dust on the small table in the center of the room.

Annella slid her hands down her long hair and rung it out. The wet clothes clinging to her curves, and the sensual movement ignited a different monster inside me scratching to come out. It was the same one that awakened when I first met her. This monster didn't want to kill her… it wanted to rip off her clothes, pull her in its arms and bury itself deep inside her body.

"It's been in the family for centuries. We made this place as a light-tight hideout up here."

Trying to shake off the unquenchable desire for her that coursed through my body, I pulled my eyes away from her. I glanced around at the broken windows and gaps in the wood that didn't look like it would provide any protection from the sun.

"I mean, I know I don't need to worry about the sun, but I don't think you're gonna survive up here when the sun comes up."

Mirth flickered in her eyes as she waggled her eyebrows

and tapped her foot on the floor. When I glanced down, I saw the trapdoor beneath her.

"Follow me," she said as she flipped it open and dropped through the floor.

I peered down the hole, but didn't see her, and was surprised again by how well I could see without a single light on.

"Come on!" she called from somewhere down below.

I jumped through the floor and landed, pausing to take in my surroundings. It wasn't a dark cave or dirt tunnel, but a fully furnished room. Wood lined the walls, floor, and ceiling, and even though dust had accumulated on the surfaces, it looked to be in good condition.

"What is this place?" I asked as I walked around the bunker.

"We have them all over the country. In the event we get stuck close to sunup, we need safe places within a few minutes run all over Scotland."

"That's actually pretty cool," I said as I looked at some of the old antique decorative weapons and art on the walls.

"Nowadays it's pretty easy to find light-tight hiding spots with basements and coolers and stuff, but centuries ago, it was trickier. So, we have these bunkers scattered around to hide out in."

Annella pulled the backpack off her shoulder and dropped it on one of the beds in the corner.

"Now that we're safe from everyone, let's get you filled up on blood and see how you feel." She pulled a bag of blood out of her bag. "This insulated bag is something you'll need as well. These bags hold a couple dozen bags of blood and keep them cool. It's always a good idea to have bags on hand in case you're in a pinch."

Just the sight of it caused my fangs to pop out. The

primal desire to consume every drop of blood sent me to her side in a flash.

"Easy." She placed a hand on my chest. "Just breathe through it."

While I stared at the blood, I focused on taking deep breaths.

"Good," she said as she handed it to me. "Drink this down, and I'll give you more. Five or six bags should be plenty to satiate the bloodlust."

I didn't hesitate and drove my fangs into the side of the bag. As I sucked it down, I felt the bloodlust starting again.

More.

More.

*More.*

All I wanted was to keep going. To consume every drop of blood on this planet.

"Here. Another," Annella said.

I tossed aside the empty bag and ripped the new one from her hands.

*More.*

The need to drink seemed insatiable.

Annella handed me another bag, and then another, and another.

I squeezed each empty bag to get every last drop out of it, then tossed them on the floor and started on another. It didn't matter how many bags I consumed, nothing satiated the need for more blood.

"That's seven bags, Owen. That should be more than enough to quell the bloodlust," Annella said as she zipped up her bag and closed the blood inside.

"*More,*" I ground out and stepped toward the bag.

"Easy, Owen. Just breathe through it. Let the blood work its way into your system, and you'll feel better so—"

"More!" I roared and shoved her out of the way as I launched for the blood.

"No, Owen!" She grabbed my arm and yanked, but it didn't dislodge me.

Instead, I spun around and grabbed her by the neck. A roar reverberated inside my chest as the animal inside me overrode every last one of my senses.

"Owen," she choked out as I slammed her against the wall. "Stop."

All I could focus on was the thrumming of her pulse beneath my fingers.

*Thump, thump, thump.*

The bloodlust drove me down to her neck, and she shrieked as I sunk my fangs into her skin.

The blood coursed through my body, and as it did, power unlike anything I could have imagined awakened inside of me. Every inch of my body ignited with ecstasy as I clamped down harder onto her neck. As I drank even more, the bloodlust inside me eased, and moments later, it faded away, and finally, *finally*, I felt sated.

Then the realization of what I'd done crashed into my mind like a wrecking ball as I snapped back to my senses.

*Annella.*

I retracted my fangs and released my grip on her neck, catching her in my arms before she collapsed to the ground.

"Shit! Oh, shit! Annella! Are you okay? Annella!"

Her limp body folded into my arms as I clutched her to my chest.

*Please don't be dead. Please don't be dead. Please don't be dead.*

"Annella!" I shouted again as I lifted her face. "I'm so sorry! Oh, God. Annella."

Her eyes fluttered open for a moment. "Blood," she whispered. "Need bloo—"

She lost consciousness before she finished.

*Blood!*

I settled her onto the floor and flashed across the room to her bag and grabbed a few bags of blood before rushing back to Annella. I pulled her into my lap and used my fangs to rip open the top. After parting her lips, I poured the red liquid into her mouth while I pleaded with her to stay with me.

"Don't you leave me, Annella. Please don't leave me," I whispered as I rubbed her throat to get the blood into her system.

My heart drummed inside my chest as I held my breath.

*Please be alive. I don't want to lose you. I* can't *lose you.*

After a few moments that may as well have been an eternity, Annella gasped and sat up in my arms.

"Annella!" I slid my hand behind her head and stared into the shocked eyes blinking back at me. "Are you hurt? Are you okay?"

As I stroked her hair, she swallowed hard. After one long inhale, she blew out a deep breath.

"Holy shit. You almost killed me, you arse."

Relief washed over me in waves when I heard her speak. I hadn't permanently harmed her… or killed her.

"I *am* an arse." I smiled down at her. "I'm a really big and very, *very* sorry arse."

As her eyes met mine, the feelings I'd experienced the first time I looked into them ignited inside me again.

A desire so strong it dwarfed the blood lust I'd finally quelled.

I stroked the pad of my thumb across her cheek as my gaze drifted to her lips. They parted in response as her eyes moved to mine.

God, did I want to kiss her.

I wanted to lower myself to her lips and kiss her… again and again and again.

I wanted to kiss her every minute of my immortal life.

But I shouldn't… I couldn't.

My lips didn't get the memo from my mind. As if my lips controlled the rest of my body, they pulled me toward her. Inch by inch, I closed in on her mouth. Inch by inch, I leaned into the thing I wanted more than anything.

When her warm breath dusted my lips, I paused, waiting for her to grant me permission. Waiting for her to lean up and finish the kiss.

Seconds ticked by as we inhaled and exhaled each other's breath… waiting.

Waiting…

When I didn't think I could take another second of the torture, I heard her whisper, "We shouldn't."

My heart sank as I paused, then slowly leaned back. Sad eyes met mine as she took her lower lip between her teeth.

"We shouldn't, Owen. I think we're both really confused right now, and we don't know what you are, or what is happening. Maybe we shouldn't complicate things."

Even though I knew she was right, it still stung like hell hearing the words come out of her mouth.

"You're right. You're absolutely right." I shook my head as I sat back on my heels. "I'm sorry."

"Don't be sorry." She reached out and slid her hand onto mine. "Before this happened, you and I had something really special starting."

I nodded.

God, did we ever. Even though I'd wanted nothing more than to sleep with her, I'd wanted to get to know *her* first. I'd wanted to build something deeper than sex before we went down that road together… something I'd never done before.

Usually, I would meet some girl at the bar or on the road, have a one-night stand, and not think about her again.

But one look into Annella's eyes, and I'd known I didn't want that. There was something connecting us that I didn't want sex to mess up. So we'd waited…

And then, well, everything else happened.

I died.

I turned into a hybrid.

We found out we were mortal enemies.

I almost killed her.

*Twice.*

Now it looked like I'd never find out what promises lay behind those azure eyes.

But she was right. I still didn't understand what was going on with my body. Even worse, I couldn't constrain it yet. For all I knew, sex would turn me into a crazed killer.

As I nodded, she went on. "I just think that until we figure out everything else going on, and get you safe, we should put figuring out you and me on the back burner."

"You're absolutely right. I'm obviously not in control yet, and I don't want to hurt you. I'm so sorry I almost killed you. Are you injured? Do you need more blood?"

Annella reached up and touched her neck. The holes from my feeding had already healed.

"I think I'm okay. I'm not even sure if it would have been fatal. Normally you'd need to remove my pretty head to kill me, but I really felt like I was dying. It was strange. Whether you nearly killed me or not, you definitely drank almost my entire blood volume. But it seems like the bags refilled me again."

Her brow scrunched down.

"Wait a minute. You drank my blood. A *lot* of my blood. And it didn't taste like shit? Or make you sick?"

With bulging eyes, I shook my head. "No. Not at all. In fact, it's like it's what my body needed. It cured the blood lust, and once I started drinking, I felt even more powerful than I already did. A *lot* more powerful."

"More powerful?" Her eyes widened.

"Yeah. I can't quite explain it. But I felt something change inside me, and I really do feel better now. More like myself and less like someone who wants to go on a killing spree."

"Well, I'll be damned," she whispered. "You must need to feed on vampire blood. That's why the human stuff wasn't fixing your blood lust. It's not what you needed. And regular vampires can't drink vampire blood. It tastes horrible and comes right back up… just like food. But not for you."

"Are you saying I need to feed on vampires?" My eyebrows shot to my hairline.

"I don't know." She pushed off the ground and paced back and forth. "I guess maybe? Human blood didn't make you sick, and it secured your transformation, so that means you can drink it, but maybe your body prefers vampire blood. I mean, it would be *crazy*, but so is the fact you can go in the sun, your eyes glow, you get claws, and you're stronger than the original vamps… and apparently even *stronger* now."

She blew out a puff of air. "Stay here for a second. There's something I want to try."

Before I could answer, she flashed out of the bunker. A few moments later, she flashed back.

As she walked up to me, she opened her hand to show me several red berries. "Here. Try to eat these."

"What happens if I can't?"

"If vamps try to eat food or drink, it just comes back up

*Exorcist* style. Something happened with our digestive systems when the Picts cursed us, and we can't keep anything down. Only blood. But I'm wondering if maybe you can."

"It won't kill me if I can't keep it down?"

"No. You'll throw it back up."

"Okay." I shrugged and took the berries from her hand. After sucking the air through my teeth and giving her a look, I popped them into my mouth and swallowed.

Annella stepped aside and stared at me, blinking.

After several long moments, she said, "Anything? Do you feel sick?"

I shook my head. "No. Not at all."

She scoffed and started laughing. "Holy shit. You can eat human food too. This is unreal."

"Wait. Are you saying I don't have to live off blood?"

She lifted her hands and shrugged. "I have no idea, Owen, but you certainly can eat human food. If a vampire took a handful of berries, they would be doubled over and spewing them on the floor already."

I'd been desperate for death just hours ago, feeling like my whole life had ended.

And it had. Leeya had killed me.

But Annella had been right when she'd begged me not to give up. There was still a chance I could control this monster inside me and maybe, just maybe, find a way to live a normal life.

"We have a lot to figure out," Annella said. "We're going to spend as much time up here as we have to until we understand everything about you, and we are sure you're safe to be around people again... and vampires." She arched an eyebrow.

"I promise I won't feed on you."

"You may have to." She shrugged. "You may need vampire blood to survive. We don't know anything yet, but we're going to figure it all out together."

It felt like she'd lifted the crushing weight off my shoulders, and I knew that no matter what, we'd work through this together.

Now, if I could just figure out how to stop wanting to kiss her.

# Chapter Eight

## OWEN

I searched my surroundings for Annella, and even though it was nighttime, I could still see everything as clearly as if it had been noon. When there was no sign of her, I turned my senses toward my hearing.

Without focusing it, things sounded like they had before I turned. Nothing amplified until I used the skills she'd taught me and honed in on a sound or an area. It was one of my favorite tricks she'd taught me in the week we'd been out here.

A week filled with frustration, fear, and despair as I struggled to adapt to the changes in my body. But finally, a week later, I'd started to wield control over the monster inside me.

Thanks to Annella.

I closed my eyes and remembered how to activate my hearing, then started searching through the sounds of the forest.

The soft, rushing water of the creek behind me.

A bird flapping its wings.

A squirrel chewing on nuts.

Everything I heard was so crisp and clear. It was incredible the sounds I'd never noticed in the world before, and now I could pick them out individually, focusing on one sound at a time before moving on to the next.

Pain seared through my side from the power of an unexpected blow. It sent me tumbling to the ground, dirt and leaves scraping my skin as I slid to a stop. In a flash, I leaped to my feet. I saw her immediately, leaning against a tree, grinning as she waggled a finger at me.

"Tsk, tsk, tsk. You let your guard down."

I wiped the dirt off my ass and chuckled.

"Nice moves."

After casually strolling a few steps, I flashed to her side, picked her up, and tossed her on the ground. She grunted when she hit the dirt.

"Tsk, tsk, tsk. You let your guard down," I teased.

Annella glared up at me before bursting into laughter. "And so the student becomes the teacher."

I held out my hand, and she took it in hers. Just like every time our skin touched, we both froze before quickly hurrying away.

The training all week had been hard… but resisting the desire to annihilate her with a kiss every second of it had been harder.

She pushed me to test my abilities every day—hearing, sight, speed, strength. We honed every one of my skills.

Then she trained me to resist the urge for blood that at one time seemed impossible. Taught me how to feed on blood bags enough to survive and be strong, but not overindulge and re-trigger the bloodlust.

Annella had succeeded in making me safe to be near humans again.

We hoped. We hadn't gotten a chance to test it out yet.

She'd helped me overcome all the obstacles that had seemed impossible to hurdle, but she hadn't done a damn thing about those feelings for her that refused to go away.

"How are you feeling strength wise?" she asked as she picked up a fighting stick.

"Pretty good," I answered as I grabbed the other one from where it leaned against a tree.

Annella stepped into the clearing as she spun her stick around, baiting me in to fight her. "Are you as strong as you were yesterday?"

I shook my head. "No. Weaker still."

The corner of her lip lifted in a smirk. With a flash, she came at me with her stick, swiping my legs out from under me before darting away.

"Fuck," I grumbled as I jumped back up to my feet.

The first two days here, I'd been considerably stronger and faster than her, but since then, each day, I seemed to weaken back to the strength of a normal vampire. Now she could wallop me when we sparred, and I tried not to be upset about it.

"You feel weaker, but not ill, right?"

"Right. I feel fine, but just not as all-powerful as I did when I first transitioned. And especially when I drank a bunch of your blood."

With a flash of movement, Annella crossed the clearing, jumped on my back, wrapped her legs around my neck, and flipped me to the ground. By the time I hit my feet, she was leaning against a tree again with that oh-so-familiar smirk.

"You gotta keep your guard up, Owen."

"You're too fast!" I argued but started laughing. "Damn, girl! Take it easy on me!"

"Did you take it easy on me when you could kick my arse a few days ago?"

I opened my mouth to argue but just chuckled. "No. I whooped it."

"Exactly. You were all confident and cocky and 'look at me all stronger than an original vamp.' Now? Not so much."

Another flash of movement and I flew across the clearing and landed in the stream. When I came up, I spit out the water that I'd inhaled with my gasp.

"Now my clothes are wet! Rude!" I teased as I strode out of the water. Annella just grinned as she spun her stick.

Water poured off my clothes as I emerged from the stream. I grabbed the bottom of my wet t-shirt and pulled it up over my head, pausing to wring it out. When I looked up, I saw Annella staring at my abs while she gnawed on her lower lip.

I smirked.

Nope. It wasn't just me who had to fight the chemistry still crackling between us.

With her distracted, I sped across the clearing and caught her around the waist, tossed her over my shoulder, and flashed back to the stream. Annella screamed as I dropped her in the water.

She came up spitting and swearing, cursing me as she sent a spray of water into my face.

"Did something distract you to make you drop your guard?" I asked as I stood in the rushing stream and tightened my pecs. Once again, her eyes drifted to them, and I saw the desire igniting in her eyes.

"Lucky break," she taunted as she rose from the water.

Now it was my turn to stare as I looked down at the wet

clothes clinging to her body. Her white t-shirt revealed the black bra underneath it, and my cock pressed against my jeans. Before I had another second to appreciate the incredible view, the water enveloped my head as Annella shoved it into the stream. When I shook free and stood up, she had already left the stream and leaned back against her favorite tree.

"Yep. I'm definitely stronger than you," she teased as she wrung the water out of her shirt.

"Am I going to keep losing my powers? Why are they dwindling?" I asked as I left the stream and pushed my wet hair from my eyes.

Annella's eyes drifted over my shirtless torso again.

She slid her gaze back up my body to meet my eyes. "I have a theory."

"Yeah? What's your theory?"

"Well, when you died and turned, you had my blood inside you. You were stronger than me even immediately after your transformation. Then you drank my blood, and you were even stronger still, right?"

"Right."

The first day after I drank her blood at the cabin, I was almost twice as strong and fast as I'd been before—which was already stronger than an original.

"You've been fine all week on human blood, so we know you can live on that, and eat food, but I think vampire blood, or maybe it's original vampire blood, increases your powers."

"Interesting." I shook the last of the water from my ears. "So, you think if I drink your blood again, I'll go back to full powers."

"Maybe." She shrugged. "It's worth a try, though. And if that works, then we can try feeding you regular vamp blood and see if it makes you as powerful or if it's just original vamp blood that does it."

My gaze swept her body. "Look at you, Sherlock Holmes."

"I'm as much brains as I am beauty." She waggled her eyebrows.

"So, what's your plan? You want to feed me a little of your blood to test the theory?"

"I can't think of another way to try it out."

As excited as I was to taste her decadent blood again, I also couldn't quell the panic churning inside me that I may go too far and kill her.

"Maybe you should just put a little in a glass for me."

"Scared you're going to kill me?"

I walked toward her, towering over her small frame leaned up against the tree. "Yeah. I am. I haven't tried a live feed since I almost killed you last week."

"But you *didn't* kill me. So, I think we need to try a live feed again, and I'm the perfect one to try it on."

She tipped her head and pushed her wet hair off her neck. "Go ahead."

"Annella," I whispered as I fought the fangs trying to spring forth once I saw her pulsating vein. "This isn't a good idea."

"You've got this, Owen." She peered up into my eyes, and though I saw the slight concern in them, she let out a breath and said, "I trust you."

Hearing her say the words drove deep the need to protect her and make sure no harm came to this woman I cared so much about.

Especially harm from me.

"Go ahead, Owen. Drink."

My fangs clicked as I slid my hand behind her head. I

heard her heart speed up as I leaned down over her neck. With one last reminder to myself not to lose control, I slid my fangs inside her.

Annella moaned and pressed her body into mine while I pulled her against me. It wasn't just the blood making every nerve in my body fire; it was feeling her in my arms… feeling her soul connecting with mine in a way I couldn't comprehend.

I pushed her backward, driving her body into the tree as I clamped down ever harder.

Annella's arms wrapped around my neck as she leaned back and offered me more of hers.

Pure passion coursed through me as I drank her in.

The last time I'd fed on her, I'd been in a frenzied state, incapable of wanting anything but blood. And almost killing her in the process.

But this time, I felt in control.

This time I felt like I connected with her instead of wanted to drain her dry.

As my powers surged along with the passion, I knew it was time to let go. I slid my fangs out of her neck and leaned back, worried maybe I'd gone too far again.

"Are you okay?" I whispered.

Annella looked up at me with eyes hooded with desire. "That was amazing," she murmured. "That was… incredible. I felt… I don't even know. I just… I… I want to…"

Before I could say another word, she rose on her toes and pulled my mouth against hers. I didn't hesitate to return the kiss. Grabbing a handful of her hair, I yanked her head back as I drove my tongue inside her mouth.

Annella met my force and matched it. Her hands traveled up my body, spreading across my chest as she raked her fingernails into my skin.

As we kissed, we connected differently than we had when I'd drank her blood. It deepened the emotions already coursing through me.

"I want you," I growled into her neck as she slid her leg around my thigh. "I want you so bad."

"We shouldn't," she whispered, but her hand drifted down my abs toward my jeans button.

"Fuck," I ground out as her fingers worked it open.

My desire for this woman overwhelmed my every sense. I grabbed her face and held it between my hands as I kissed her harder.

My heart pounded in my chest as her hand started into my pants. Then her phone rang.

*Fuck!*

It shattered our passion like a shotgun shell had hit it, and Annella froze in my arms.

"It's Lothaire," she panted. "I haven't checked in yet tonight. If I don't answer, they'll come here. I need to get that."

"Yeah. You should," I said between panting breaths as I pressed my forehead into hers.

After one last pained look, she flashed over to her phone at the cabin.

"Hello," she answered.

I paced in circles as I tried to get my testosterone to simmer down and my dick to simmer down with it.

Which was impossible when I glanced over at Annella pacing on the porch of the cabin in her soaking wet clothes. All I wanted to do was help her get out of them.

"Yes. He's ready. No, really. He can handle it. We'll check it out, and if we see them, I'll call, and we'll wait for you," Annella said before hanging up.

From the sounds of it, we weren't about to pick up where we'd left off.

*Son of a…*

"Lothaire says they have a potential hit on Clan Lennox. It's in the city close to us, so he's asked us to go check it out."

"You really think I'm ready to go into the city? To be near people?"

She looked at me with confidence. "Yes. I know you are. And I'll be right there at your side."

"Okay," I said. "I trust you. If you say I'm ready, then I'm ready."

"You are." She smiled. "And if they are there, we will call my family in and put a hurting on those bastards who kidnapped me and killed you."

"Yeah. We are." I matched her grin. "You know why I can say that with confidence?"

She furrowed her brow.

I grabbed her by the waist and threw her across the clearing, then darted across it and caught her before she hit the ground.

As she stared up at me with wide eyes, I grinned wider. "Your theory is correct, Sherlock. I'm back to full power, and I'm ready to smoke some fucking vampires."

Her lips curled up as her eyes narrowed. "Then let's go smoke some vamps."

# Chapter Nine

## ANNELLA

Now I understood what humans meant when they explained the euphoria of a vampire feeding on them. What I'd felt when Owen fed on me tonight was hotter than any sex I'd ever had. It had been transcendent… and I wanted to feel it again, and again, and again.

And *again*.

My mind kept replaying the images as we sat on the side of the building, surveying the city block below. My attention should have been laser-focused on spotting anyone that resembled a member of Clan Lennox, but instead, it kept drifting over to the man I wanted to pounce on like a wild animal.

And that was what my feelings for him were.

Wild.

I lacked control over them, try as I may. I'd spent the better part of every second of every minute this past week trying *not* to kiss him. Reminding myself that not only was he a descendent of disgusting werewolves, but he was also an unpredictable hybrid hard-wired to hate me and my family.

And kill our kind.

But when I was overstimulated from the oxytocin, or whatever the hell released in me when he'd fed, I'd tossed all my good sense out the window and thrown myself at him.

And the kiss had been as good as the feed.

What was it about this man that made me feel things I didn't even know I was capable of feeling?

He awakened something inside me. I didn't know if I'd ever be able to put it back to sleep.

But I had to try.

At least for now, so I could focus on the mission. And the mission wasn't in those green eyes staring back into mine.

The ones I could gaze into all night long.

*Damn it!*

"You okay?" Owen asked.

I swung my legs back and forth over the edge of the building. "Yeah. Fine. Just sick of waiting. I wish someone would show up already so we could get confirmation they're here. The sun comes up in less than an hour and nada."

"Maybe it was bad intel."

"Maybe." I shrugged. "But we have to check out every lead."

"Yeah, I get that. It's just uh, too bad about, uh, the timing." He rubbed a hand across the back of his neck as he started to swing his legs as well.

I pinched my brow. "The timing?"

"Yeah. The call to come here right in the middle of the, uh, the kiss."

The man twice as powerful as me looked sheepish while he peeked over.

And it was hot.

"Yeah. The kiss." I clucked my tongue as I looked past my feet at the hundred-and-fifty-foot drop. "We probably shouldn't have done that."

But I wanted to do it more.

"Yeah." He cleared his throat. "Yeah. You're right. The whole mortal enemies thing kinda makes it complicated and shit."

"Yeah. Exactly."

I peered over at him and licked my lower lip.

Impossible.

It was impossible to resist kissing him. Even though I shouldn't, I leaned in. Then, movement in front of the building across the street caught my eye.

"Wait," I said as I stopped my lean.

"No. You're right, we shouldn't." He shook his head.

"No. Not that. Well, yeah, that too. But look," I whispered as I pointed at the redheaded woman and the redheaded man walking into the building. "I think that's Leeya and her brother Leith!"

"Are you sure?" He squinted to see them better, but they disappeared inside.

"No. Not sure."

"Should we go check?"

I shook my head. "We should probably call Lothaire."

"Don't you want to make sure it's them before we call?"

"I guess maybe we can sneak over there and take a look? Just to be sure before we get everyone flying up here."

Owen nodded, and we hopped off the building together, dropping the fifteen floors and landing side by side. We flashed to the corner of the building and flattened against the wall.

"Follow my lead," I whispered.

He nodded his acknowledgment, and we crept inside the eight-story building.

I focused my hearing as we tip-toed down the dimly lit hall. From the looks of it, this was some kind of commercial building. Each door on the first floor had a different business name, and Owen and I popped the locks on each one and carefully peered inside. When we got to the last door, he broke the handle and stuck his head in.

"Cool," he whispered. "A recording studio. I've always wanted to record an album."

"Seriously? You're thinking about making an album right now?" I whispered back. "Focus!"

"Sorry." He pulled a face, and we slipped back into the hallway.

Floor by floor we searched, listening and looking for any signs of Clan Lennox. When we got to the fourth floor, I held up my hand and paused. Tipping my ear toward the sound, I listened up the stairs until I fixated on the voices talking.

"Leith, you'd better hurry the fuck up," Leeya said. "There's no doubt some rat has told Lothaire we're here, and it's only a matter of time before he and his fucking family show up. Just finish up and let's get the hell out of here."

From the sounds of it, they were on the top floor.

"They're here," I whispered. "We need to call Lothaire."

"Think he can make it in time? It sounds like they're about to take off."

Shit. He was right. It would take my family at least twenty minutes to run here, and by then, Lothaire and Leeya could be gone.

"How strong do you feel?" I asked him.

His eyebrows rose. "Like I could knock this entire building down if I wanted to."

I listened again and heard just a few other voices up there.

"It sounds like it's just a handful of people. Let's take them out."

"Kill vampires? Oh, hell yeah. I was born and bred for this." He grinned.

I pulled out my phone and shot Lothaire a text.

*Me: Found them. They are getting ready to leave. Owen and I are going in.*

*Lothaire: Are you sure you can't wait?*

*Me: No time. Don't want to risk them getting away and will be light soon.*

*Lothaire: Be careful. I'll send Aiden, Thorne, and Emilia. They'll be there soon.*

I slid my phone back into my pocket. "Aiden, Thorne, and Emilia are coming since they don't have to worry about the sunlight. They'll be here to clean up whatever mess we've left behind."

"Should we wait for them?"

I lifted my lip and smirked. "I've been waiting months to drench my hands in Clan Lennox blood. I'm not waiting another minute. And I've got you with me… and you're filled to the brim with my blood. We can take them. Let's go."

Owen and I crept up the stairs to the top floor. When we got outside the door, I gave him a sharp nod.

With a powerful kick, I sent the door flying into the expansive room.

"Hello, old friends!" I said as I flashed into the room. "Miss me?"

It only took a split second for me to realize the major error of my decision. There weren't a few vampires up here in this loft.

There were dozens.

Dozens of vampires standing quietly along the walls.

Dozens of vampires who'd intentionally stayed quiet while we entered the building.

Dozens of vampires all with knowing eyes boring into me.

*Fuck. A trap.*

"So predictable," Leeya said on a sigh. The red dress plunging between her cleavage dusted the ground as she sauntered toward us. "But where are the rest of your wretched family? I don't see them. We were expecting the whole lot of you."

She pointed to the television screen with video footage of the stairwell and camera angles around the entire block. They'd known we were coming this whole time.

Owen stood at my side, and I heard his deepening breaths.

"They missed the Evite. Junk mail or something." I shrugged.

"That's too bad," Leith said as he stepped forward in front of a wall of vampires and stopped at Leeya's side. "I was looking forward to seeing Lothaire."

His red hair matched his sister's, but he dwarfed her in size. If they went nose to nose, Leith and Lothaire would probably be evenly matched in the height department.

"Oh, he's looking really forward to seeing you too." I grinned like a Cheshire cat. "*Really* looking forward to it."

"We can take them," Owen whispered.

"There's too many. We need to run for it," I whispered back.

"The great Annella is running?" Leeya laughed. "I'm a little disappointed. Though, from the looks of it, and being so obviously outnumbered even for an original, I don't blame you one bit. And your friend here isn't an original, so he's not as powerful as you… wait a minute."

She stepped forward and tipped her head, then her bright red lips parted in a laugh. "I know you! You're supposed to be dead. I killed you, so I should know."

"Didn't take." Owen's shoulders broadened as he straightened up even taller.

"Well, I'll be." She shook her head as she gave him a coy smile. "I don't know how you did it, but vampirism looks good on you. If you want to switch sides and join me, I'd still be happy to have you."

Owen's laugh echoed through the empty space, causing Leeya's smile to falter.

"Pass. Hard pass. I think I'll take certain death over being stuck with a psycho like you."

Her eyes narrowed as she stepped forward, but Leith caught her by the shoulder.

"Enough, Leeya. That's not why we're here."

"Why *are* you here?" I asked, hopefully stalling long enough for Aiden, Thorne, and Emilia to arrive. It would still be a hard fight, but the odds would tip a little more in our favor.

"You didn't really think we were stupid enough not to realize the minute we showed ourselves that you would come running, did you?" Leith said.

I sucked the air through my teeth. "Actually, I kinda did."

Leith just chuckled and shook his head. "Figures. You originals think you're so much better than that rest of us. Think you *know* better than the rest of us. But it's time to step aside and let new blood guide us into the future."

"And I suppose you think it should be you." I snorted.

"Yes. I do." He lifted his chin, accentuating his long, braided red beard. "For six hundred years, Lothaire has ruled with an iron fist, but it's past time to end his reign… and every one of Clan Mackay." He stepped forward and grinned. "Since he didn't bother to show up, I guess we'll start with you."

I stood up taller, my muscles twitching as they prepared for the fight. We would try to run, but the vampires blocking every exit would make it difficult to get away.

"You may take us, but not before we take out a bunch of you." I passed a glance over the vampires still standing like robots. "This is your one warning to stand with me, stand with your *King* Lothaire. If any of you lift a hand against me, you will be sentenced to death."

Leeya laughed, and Leith joined her.

"It won't work," Leith said. "They've been influenced to fight to the death for us."

*Influenced?* Impossible. Vampires couldn't influence other vampires unless…

"Did you influence them as humans and then turn them?"

"To fight a war, you need an army."

I narrowed my eyes. "You know that is against vampire law."

Leith rolled his eyes. "An outdated one. Don't kill the humans. Don't turn the humans. Humans, humans, fucking humans. Humans are a means to an end for a vampire. Food. And it's time we started putting vampires first."

There it was—the reason Clan Lennox wanted to take control. There had been rumblings of Leith's desire to harvest and breed humans, treating them like livestock for vampire feeding. Lothaire had banished the idea, but Leith still couldn't be deterred.

"We live in harmony with humans. Why would you want to change it?"

"Harmony?" He scoffed. "We lurk in the shadows, and we can't even *feed* the way nature designed, from the vein, because of security cameras, cell phones, and fucking satellite cameras. It's time to come out of the shadows, show the world we exist, and then show them who's actually at the top of the food chain."

"Lothaire will stop you."

"Lothaire can try. But my army will stop him." He crossed his arms and nodded to one of the vamps in the corner. "And we'll start with you."

The vampire in the corner flipped a switch on the wall. I screamed as my skin nearly ignited into flames, searing from the intense UV lights assaulting me from overhead.

"Kill them!" Leith commanded.

His vamps stood on the outside of the lights and threw chains that wrapped around my waist, securing me from several sides at once and preventing me from running.

"Annella!" Owen shouted.

His arm snaked around my waist as he folded me underneath the shade of his immense body. With one yank, he pulled all the vampires holding the chains into the UV lights. My skin was ready to burst into flames any second, but they weren't an original like me. They shrieked as their skin erupted into a blazing inferno. Another pull and Owen broke the chains around me, then he flashed across the room and slammed me into the dark corner, out of reach of the rays.

"What the hell? Kill the lights and go get them!" Leith commanded.

The lights flicked off as I stayed pressed into the corner, trying to recover from the searing pain. My speed healing kicked in, but not before I heard thundering footsteps coming toward us.

I glanced up at Owen and saw the green ignite in his eyes. With a loud roar that shook the air around us and rattled my bones, he popped out his claws and spun over the top of me.

I watched in amazement as he sent body after body flying, each one absent the head. His teeth and claws sliced through their flesh with ease as he tore through them.

"What the fuck is he?" Leeya shouted, and I glanced in her direction.

She stood stunned at her brother's side, wide eyes staring at Owen, who continued decimating every vampire who came at him.

The pain in my body dissipated, and I glanced down at my already healed skin. When I looked up, I narrowed my eyes at Leeya.

She saw the intent in them and grabbed Leith by the hand. "Run, Leith! We have to run!"

He gave one last stunned look toward Owen and then took off at her side. I wanted to go after them, but when I shot up from the ground and landed at Owen's side, more vampires stood between me and my prey. I started tearing through the bodies along with him. Blood soaked the concrete floor as we battled our way through the last of the vampires. The final one fell with a thump at my feet, and I stood panting as I surveyed the room for any signs of Leith or Leeya. They were nowhere to be found.

Endless carnage.

Dozens of vampires dead.

And Owen had done almost all of it single-handedly. His powers were even greater than I'd realized.

Then I glanced at where I'd last seen Leeya and Leith. They may have escaped, but lying on the floor, I saw the purse Leeya had carried into the building when we'd spotted them. With that purse, Catrain could run a tracking spell, and that bitch couldn't hide ever again.

"Annella, are you okay?" Owen spun around and grabbed me by the shoulders.

The green glow in his eyes softened as he looked me over closely.

"Yes. I'm okay."

He exhaled a deep sigh of relief and pulled me into his arms. "Fuck. I thought you would burn to death."

"For a second, I thought I would too."

The power of the UV lights was stronger than any I'd ever known. These were special lights, and that meant Leith and Leeya had been planning this for some time.

What they hadn't planned on was Owen.

"I'm okay because of you," I said as I looked up into his now soft eyes. "Thank you, Owen. You saved me."

He slid a hand along my face and stroked my cheek with the pad of his thumb. "I'll always fight for you, Annella. Always."

As he leaned down to kiss me, I threw all my reservations out the window.

Fuck that he was born a werewolf.

Fuck that he was now a hybrid.

Fuck all the messiness that could come with this kiss.

I didn't care about any of it as his lips closed in on mine.

"Annella! Are you okay?" Aiden called from the stairwell.

"Son of a bitch!" I whispered against Owen's lips as they paused just before touching mine. "You have got to be kidding me."

# Chapter Ten

ANNELLA

"Annella?" Thorne called.

Owen pressed his forehead against mine and heaved a heavy sigh.

"Over here," I called back as I shook my head against his.

Owen and I broke apart just before Aiden, Emilia, and Thorne flew around the corner to where we stood. When they slammed to a stop, their mouths dropped open as they surveyed the bodies piled up around us.

"What in the actual fuck?" Thorne covered his mouth. "How?"

"Owen," I answered. "I have a lot to tell you guys about his abilities, but the fact is, when he feeds on vampire blood, he is at least twice as strong as us, if not more. He saved me."

Aiden blew out a breath as he kicked a head with his foot. "Damn, man. This is… impressive work."

"Thanks, I guess?" Owen shrugged. "I haven't ever killed vampires before, so I'll take your word I did good."

"You did good. You saved my sister. Thank you." Aiden reached out and shook Owen's hand.

"This is disgusting." Emilia wrinkled her nose. "I'm sorry. I'm new to this whole scene." She waved a hand over the bodies. "Blech."

"Why don't you go wait over there, baby," Aiden said before kissing her cheek.

"Good idea. I just need a minute."

Emilia stepped over the bodies and hurried to the corner of the room.

"Want to tell us what happened?" Thorne asked.

"Well, for starters, it was a freaking set up. They had those ready." I pointed to the ceiling and the rows of UV lights. "They are super-powered UV. I almost started on fire the minute they turned on."

"Whoa," Aiden recoiled. "Usually, only direct sunlight can do that. UV lights weaken vampires and hurt, but they can't kill them."

"Exactly," I said. "These felt like direct sun. If it weren't for Owen, I'd have been dead in a few more seconds."

"Again. Thanks, man." Thorne held out his fist, and Owen bumped it.

"Happy to help."

"But the UV lights were just part of it. The rest of it was the dozens of *influenced* vampires waiting to kill us."

"Influenced vampires?" Aiden furrowed his brow.

"Yep. Leith has been influencing humans to fight for him, then turning them into vampires."

Thorne and Owen's eyes widened in unison.

"Whoa," Thorne breathed. "That's not good."

"No." I scoffed. "Not fucking good at all. Who knows how many he has? But these guys were willing to walk straight into death for him. Like robots."

"Stepford vampires," Owen said. "That's what I was thinking while they just kept coming at me."

"And you killed them all by yourselves?" Aiden looked around at all the bodies again.

"Owen took out most of them while I recovered from the UV lights. I helped at the end."

Thorne and Aiden's stared at Owen and shook their heads in unison.

"I'm really glad you're on our side." Aiden ran a hand behind his neck. "Damn."

"Leeya and Leith got away." I scowled. "But, Leeya left her purse. If we take it to Catrain, she should be able to run a locator spell."

"Catrain is on the island, getting her sister ready for her ascension ceremony. I'm going there later today, and I can bring it to her. As soon as we get back, we'll run the spell."

"Oh, shit. That's this week, isn't it?"

Thorne nodded. "Yeah. Alpia takes over as leader of their tribe tomorrow."

When Thorne met Catrain, she'd been the one to inherit the throne of her tribe… and the considerable power that came with it. But her love for Thorne had made her step down from her birthright and give it to her sister, Alpia, instead. And once Alpia rose to power, she'd agreed to remove the sunlight curse from all of us.

Which reminded me…

"The sun will be up any minute, and not until Alpia lifts this curse, unlike you lucky bastards, I'll cook in it."

"Oh yeah." Thorne shook his head. "I forgot we have to watch that with you still. But not for long."

"I need to get somewhere safe." I glanced out the window and saw the sky starting to lighten. "Now."

"The recording studio," Owen blurted. "It's light and

soundproof. We can hide there until the sun sets. It's Sunday, so no one should be scheduled to record."

"We'll clean up here," Aiden said. "You just get safe. Meet us back at the castle tonight, you can fill us in on the rest and we'll make a plan."

"I'll see you tonight," I said quickly before flashing out of the room.

Owen kept pace with me as we rushed down the stairs. The rays of light started coming through the windows on the way down and scalded my skin as I passed through them. When we reached the first floor, he blocked the sunlight with his body and pushed me inside.

"Ouch!" I said as I looked at the burns on my arm. "That freaking hurt."

Owen closed the door and sealed us inside the room.

I rubbed a burn and watched it start to heal. "Thank you. That was close. Too close."

When I turned around and looked at Owen, I saw the fire burning in his eyes.

In one swift movement, he crossed the room and slammed me up against the glass wall dividing the room.

"No more talking. No more interruptions. No more excuses." He lowered his mouth to mine, and I inhaled his breath. "Fucking kiss me."

The look of pure desire in his eyes obliterated any other thoughts in my mind other than wanting him inside my body.

I tossed my arms around his neck and pulled him down for a kiss so intense it nearly exploded my mind. His powerful arms yanked me against him as he drove his tongue deeper inside my mouth. Raw, uninhibited need controlled my body as I clawed at his shirt, breaking our kiss only long enough to push it over his head while he yanked mine off as well.

The feeling of his skin on mine ignited every nerve in my body as I fumbled with the buttons on his jeans.

I wanted him.

*Needed* him.

Now.

He held me captive with his kiss, his hands on my body were the cell holding me tight. I was a prisoner to our desire and wouldn't try to escape even if I could.

But I couldn't. The connection between us was too strong to break.

And I didn't want to.

He moaned into my mouth as I reached into his pants and took his rock-hard cock in my hand. He bit my lip as I pumped my hand up and down the impressive shaft.

"Fuck, Annella," he growled against my lips.

His hands slid down my body, cupping my breasts before moving to my back and releasing my bra with a quick snap. When his fingers squeezed my nipples, I cried out in his mouth.

"Take me. Now," I whispered.

With lighting fast movement, Owen yanked my pants and underwear off my body. His powerful arms wrapped around my ass as he picked me up and pressed me into the glass. I wrapped my legs around him, and his hard cock pressed against the place that needed him most.

"Do you want it?" he ground out.

"Yes," I breathed as I cupped his bare ass.

"Condom?" he asked, and I shook my head.

"Immortals. We can't get pregnant. Take me now."

Without another word, he drove himself so deep inside me that I struggled to exhale the gasp trapped in my lungs. I writhed on him, pushing him even deeper inside me as I captured his kiss.

Our desire magnified as we used each other to try to extinguish the passion that had burned between us since the first time we locked eyes.

A passion that still didn't dissipate.

Owen slid me off his shaft, spun me around, and pressed me into the glass as he kicked my legs open. He lifted my hands over my head, pressing them into the cool glass as he covered them with his own. He lowered his body to allow him to connect with mine, and I gasped as he entered me again.

The weight of his body driving into mine pressed me tight to the window, and my panting breaths fogged it up as I struggled to stay on my feet.

"You're mine. Always mine," he rumbled before he pulled my hair and tipped my head back so he could claim me with his kiss.

"And you're mine," I said, before spinning around and pushing him across the room. He landed on the mixing board, and I flew on top of him, straddling his lap as I slid down the length of him.

Owen groaned as I rode him, our bodies connecting in a way that I'd never imagined they could before.

"Drink from me," I whispered as I felt my body closing in on the release I knew would be explosive even without his fangs inside my neck.

Owen grabbed my hair and tipped back my head, sinking his teeth into my neck as I wrapped my legs around his waist. I screamed out my pleasure as it hit heights I didn't think I could stand another second. I exploded on him with cries as he moaned while his body trembled against mine.

Boneless and satiated, I collapsed against him. His arms closed around me and held me against his chest while we struggled to catch our breaths.

"Damn, baby," he whispered into my ear. "You're amazing."

"You're not so bad yourself." I leaned back and grinned.

Owen matched it and leaned up, pressing a soft, gentle kiss on my lips.

It was such a stark contrast to the powerful, explosive connection we'd just experienced.

A stark contrast to the powerful man who'd just slaughtered dozens of vampires and held me so gently now in his arms.

"That was definitely worth the wait," he said on a sigh.

"Was it ever," I agreed as I pressed my head into his tattooed chest.

"As much as I want to sit here and hold you, the sliders for the soundboard are digging into my ass."

"Oh, shit," I laughed as I slid off him. "Sorry about that."

"Don't be sorry," he said as he stood. "I was so into it I didn't even notice until just now."

My gaze raked his incredible body.

Tattoos spread across his chiseled and defined pecs. The abs I'd felt with my fingers were chiseled and hard, like a sculptor had taken great care to create a perfect masterpiece. When he walked past me toward his discarded clothes, I couldn't help but stare at the perfect, round ass flexing with every step.

Pure physical perfection.

"Here," he said as he tossed me my t-shirt and jeans. "Not that I want to see you cover up that incredible body, but on the off chance someone comes into the studio on a

Sunday, I don't want to share the view with anyone else." His eyes slid over my curves, and it caused my skin to prickle. "Mine."

*Mine.*

I shouldn't be letting a werewolf, or now a hybrid, lay claim to me, but one look in those eyes of his, and I couldn't even come up with a witty comeback. I wanted nothing more than to be his, and for him to be mine.

Even though deep down, I knew we still shouldn't.

# Chapter Eleven

## OWEN

I watched Annella's sexy body disappear beneath the jeans and off-the-shoulder t-shirt I wanted to rip back off her again. Even though I'd just had the greatest orgasm of my life, I already felt the urge for another round.

After all that waiting—all that wanting—it'd been even better than I'd imagined. And it wasn't just the sex, though that had been mind-blowing.

It was connecting with her. Feeling her moving with me. Feeding from her and feeling her essence coursing through my veins while her body linked with mine.

Transcendent.

Being with Annella had been transcendent.

"So, that just happened." She chewed on her lower lip as she slid down the wall and sat beside me on the floor.

"Yep. That just happened." I sucked my cheek.

"Yep."

The awkward silence settled over us like a heavy blanket.

"We probably shouldn't do that again," Annella said

quickly. "We'll just call it a momentary lapse of concentration. Like we just needed to get that out of our systems so we can move on."

*Move on?* That was the last thing I wanted, but I nodded anyway.

"Yeah. Just got it out of our systems."

It was anything but out of my system. If anything, it had driven my need for her right into the damn core of my system. My need for her now controlled every thought in my mind.

Annella pressed her head back into the wall, and it exposed the long, creamy lines of her neck. A neck I wanted to feed on. A neck I wanted to kiss while I felt her body writhing on top of mine again.

*Fuck.* After that mind-blowing experience, no way could I shove down the feelings for her that grew with each second in her presence.

"Well, I'm stuck here all day, but you can go in the sun. If you want to go do something, maybe go grab a burger or something since you can eat food. I'll just meet you back here at sunset."

I scoffed. "As much as I would kill to taste some real food that isn't blood or forest berries, I only passed a couple humans on the street when we came into town last night. While I didn't have any desire to kill them anymore, I still don't trust myself out there. Not yet. We need to do some more work to make sure I'm safe."

"Oh, shit. That's right. Yeah. We don't need you going on a rampage through the city. Hopefully, tonight we can test you around some humans and see how you do."

"I don't want to get my hopes up, but I have a good feeling I will be okay. Ever since I had your blood, I haven't craved human blood. I've only craved your blood. Or maybe it's vampire blood in general because killing those vampires with my teeth tonight was pleasurable when I got their blood in my mouth."

"Really?" She arched an eyebrow. "Vampire blood in my mouth makes me want to puke."

"Yeah, really. I would take vamp blood over human blood in a heartbeat."

"That must be the vampire-hating wolf in you." She rolled her eyes. "Better watch my back, or you may still slaughter me in my sleep."

"Hey." I bumped her with my shoulder. "I won't go crazy and kill you."

"You don't know that." She lifted a bare shoulder and dropped it. "None of us understand you or how you work. For all I know, your deep hatred for my kind, for *me,* will surface when I least expect it and…"

She sliced her finger across her neck.

"You really don't trust me?" I asked, surprised to hear it.

"Honestly?" She lifted her brows. "No. I don't."

"Wow." I blew out a breath. "I guess I didn't realize that."

"You're twice as powerful as me. You're a hybrid of sorts with a hatred of vampires that was built into your species. They created your entire species to hunt *my family.* I'm sorry if I'm not going to forget that and turn my back on it. I need to be careful."

"Maighread Mackay is scared of something," I teased.

"Hey," she warned. "I'm not *scared* of you. I'm cautious around you. You haven't proven yourself safe yet. Maighread Mackay isn't scared of anything, but she's also not an idiot."

"Why did you stop going by that name?"

She stood up and walked over to the drum set and slid her hands around the cymbals.

"No reason other than it's outdated. Annella is my middle name, and a few hundred years ago, I switched to that because it's more modern. Aiden and Thorne changed their names to be more modern as well. It helps us blend in a little better." She arched an eyebrow and gave me the side-eye. "And, *no,* it's not because I'm ashamed of Maighread Mackay if that's what you're thinking. I have no qualms about killing all those werewolves. Every last one of them deserved their fate. I'd do it again if I could."

The wolf in me snarled at her comment, but I fought the urge to let the snarl move up to my lips.

"You don't regret genocide? Well, attempted genocide?"

"When the entire species of werewolves were created to *kill us*, then no. Hell no. It was self-defense, plain and simple." She tapped the cymbal, and it rang through the room.

"When the werewolves appeared, my family and our clan that had survived the transition, were just living a fairly quiet life with our new powers. We lived a pretty peaceful existence for almost a year. We still fed on humans and killed the occasional one as we learned to control our urges..."

She turned and looked at me and speared me with a knowing stare.

"*Urges* you understand well now."

I pressed my lips into a thin line.

Yeah. I understood the urges.

"And unlike you, we didn't have anyone to teach us how to feed without killing, but we were getting better on our own. It became rare to kill a human during a feed. Then out of nowhere, in the middle of the night on a full moon, these *huge* wolves come flying into the town we'd created for ourselves. They killed over a dozen of our clan, and we finally had to run. Every full moon for months, they'd come for us, killing way more of us than we did of them. They even killed our Chiefton, and that's when Lothaire inherited the position and became the leader of all the vamps. But after the fourth raid, I managed to capture one. Imagine our surprise when I went to kill it, and the gigantic wolf turned into a human."

"And then you tortured him, I bet." I rolled my eyes.

"You bet your arse I did." She scoffed, flicking her wrist. "And it's a damn good thing I did. It was then we found out it was humans shifting into wolf form. Until then, we just thought they were some strange, giant wolves. We also found out that the Picts had created them, that they couldn't turn humans into werewolves and make more, and that they were strongest under the full moon. After finding out their entire existence was to eradicate us, Lothaire decided the only way to survive with our dwindling numbers was to turn an army of humans into vampires. So we did. And then we hunted your kind down."

"Very successfully," I added.

"Your damn straight we were successful. I loved every second of killing the wolves. They'd taken so much from us… and they took Edine."

Sadness filled her eyes as she looked at me.

"Edine?" I asked.

"My best friend. We'd been born just a day apart and had been raised like twins. The morning after the fourth attack, the wolves came to the caves we slept in to get the prisoner we had. They snuck in while we slept. A battle started in the cave, and we realized we were stronger than them without the full moon. Something they realized too, so they retreated, but one of them got ahold of Edine and dragged her out of the cave. I tried to stop them, fought to hold on to her, but they ripped her from my hands, and pulled her into the sunlight."

Her blue eyes glistened from the tears building up in her eyes.

"I stood helplessly in the cave and watched her burn. My best friend. My sister. I stared into her eyes as she left this world. And you're damn right. After that, I wanted every single one of those fucking dogs dead."

Annella looked away, and I saw the hard swallow as she choked back the tears.

"I'm so sorry, Annella. I had no idea."

"Why would you? Just like the Picts, your kind has turned *us* into the villains. We weren't the villains, though. We started out with almost a hundred members of our clan. When we were done with the war against the wolves, there were just nine original vampires left. Nine."

Compassion lingered on my lips. "So, that's why you waged war with us on that fated night."

"We had no intention of turning more humans into vampires, but after the wolves attacked us in the cave, and we dwindled down to less than fifteen originals, we knew we had no choice. We split up and spread out, turning six other tribes into vampires and creating an army of over a hundred immortal warriors. Then we tracked your kind down and eliminated the threat."

"I've heard the story countless times growing up. The night all the wolves slept in the valley and awakened to the sound of screams. After weeks of vampires taking out some of the smaller camps, all the wolves congregated into one large camp to protect themselves with their numbers. But as they slept, over a hundred vampires surrounded them, leaping off the top of the cliffs and slaughtering them before leaping back to safety. Since the moon wasn't full, the vampires were stronger, and in one night, you wiped out the entire pack. Except one."

"I still can't believe we missed one. We really thought we got them all. Imagine our surprise this year to find out that werewolves still exist."

"One lone wolf escaped, and she carried a pureblood wolf child in her belly. It was that woman that saved our entire line. Her name was Marsle. She vowed that day to protect her family from the vampires, and in order to do so, she created the rules that no werewolf could ever shift after their first transition. She married a human she met a few months later and had twelve other children, all with the werewolf gene. Each one continued her traditions of teaching their children the rules of changing and protecting the pack from the vampires she knew couldn't be defeated."

"So, all these years you've been living among us, reproducing and growing stronger. How do we know you aren't just waiting until you have enough werewolves to rise up and destroy us?"

I lifted a shoulder and let it drop. "There are rumors of some packs of wolves that want to get revenge on the vampires, but mostly, we just want to live our lives peacefully. Yeah, the desire to kill vampires is inside us. I won't lie and say it's not. But I'm sitting here in a room with you right now, and I don't have the urge to kill you at all."

"Not at all?" She arched an eyebrow.

"I want to do other things to you, but killing you isn't one of them." I smirked and stood up.

Annella's pupils dilated as I approached her. Her breath trapped in her lungs as I stepped in front of her, her lips slackening as I leaned down.

"What are you doing?" she whispered as I got closer. "We shouldn't."

Instead of giving her the kiss I knew she wanted, I continued my lean and reached past her, grabbing the guitar behind her by the neck.

"Just getting a guitar," I said into her ear as I stood.

Her long exhale blew through my hair as I stood back up.

"Don't worry. You've made yourself clear. I won't kiss you again until you ask for it."

"I won't," she said quickly as she looked up into my eyes.

I lifted my lips into a smirk. "You will."

Before she could argue back, I turned around and strode across the room to the stool. I sat down on it and lifted my knee, propping the guitar on it as I slid the strap over my head.

"What are you doing?" she asked.

"If I'm going to be in here all day, I'm going to take advantage of my first time in a recording studio. The acoustics in here are supposed to be amazing, and this guitar is more expensive than any guitar I've ever been able to afford. Do you mind?"

"No. Not at all," she answered.

I started strumming on the guitar as Annella walked back to the wall and slid down onto the floor.

She sat and listened to my private acoustic show, and I loved how when I sang, it made me forget everything that had happened to me.

That I'd died.

I'd turned into a hybrid.

I'd been disowned by my father.

I'd betrayed my bloodline by taking Maighread Mackay into my arms and my heart.

When I sang, I was just Owen Hunter again. A man who loved music. A man who dreamed of a day he could stand on stage and play for sold-out venues. A man who wasn't a bloodthirsty killer.

After my third song, Annella shook her head. "Wow. You're incredible. Your voice is amazing, and you can play the bass and the guitar. Impressive."

"Thanks." I set down the guitar. "I definitely sound better in here. They weren't kidding about perfect acoustics in a recording studio."

A genuine smile played on her lips. "It wasn't just the acoustics. You're really talented."

"I've always loved music. My mother used to sing to me as a child, and I loved singing with her. The rest of my family is in protection careers, like the military, police, and firefighters, but I've just always loved music. It's been my dream since before I can remember to record an album. But now? I have no idea what all this means for my music career."

Annella patted the ground next to her. I sat beside her and rested my elbows on my ripped jeans.

"We'll figure it out. You can walk in the sun and eat real food, so there's really no reason you can't go back out with your band once this is all over."

"As long as I don't want to kill my bandmates." I chuckled.

"Yes. As long as you don't want to kill them, you'll be fine."

My breath brushed the top of her head, and I had to fist my hands to keep from pulling her close. "You really think I'll be able to have a normal life?"

She shrugged. "I don't see why not. Most vampires don't interact with humans much because it's hard to explain the no eating and no sunlight thing. It means we have to influence them a lot."

"Did you influence me?" I tipped my head.

She sheepishly smiled. "Maybe."

"You did!" I laughed and pushed her with my shoulder. "What did you influence me about?"

"Well, when we first came to your bar, we influenced you to think the bottles of blood we gave you, and you served us, were special Bloody Marys."

"That was blood?" I laughed.

"Yep."

"I really thought it was Bloody Mary mix."

"Of course you did. That's what we influenced you to think."

"Anything else I don't remember?"

She chewed on her lip. "Um, maybe that I fed on you a couple times."

My eyes widened. "You fed on me?"

"The first night I saw you bartending, I took you in the stockroom for a snack."

"I remember going in there and kissing you. Our first kiss, actually." I smiled at the memory of the gorgeous woman pushing me against a wall and pulling me down for a kiss.

"After we kissed, I drank a little of your blood. It was some of the best blood I'd ever had. I influenced you to forget any time I fed from you."

"Holy shit." I chuckled. "Influencing really works because I have zero memory of any that."

"It's how we can safely feed on humans without killing them to protect our secret existence."

"And my blood was good, huh?" I don't know why I felt proud that my blood had tasted good, but I did.

"I can't believe I didn't put it together back then, but werewolves have decadent blood. I hadn't had it in centuries, so I didn't place the taste."

"Damn." I shook my head and laughed. "That's kind of horrifying."

"You asked." She laughed.

"And that's it? You didn't influence me any other times?"

"Nope. Just to ignore my feeding and blood drinking. And now that you're feeling better about humans, I'll teach you how to do the same."

"I still think I'd rather drink your blood," I said.

"And you can. As long as you don't drain me of every drop, it doesn't affect me at all."

"Oh, I think it affects you," I teased.

Her ivory cheeks flushed pink. "I *meant* it doesn't hurt me."

"Don't I know it."

She joined me in laughter and slapped my shoulder. "Don't get cocky. Now, we need to rest because we are going hunting for Leeya as soon as we can get out of this recording studio and get back to Catrain. Her tracking spell will locate Leeya anywhere she tries to go."

"Get some sleep," I said, gesturing to my shoulder.

Annella hesitated, then leaned her head against it. I lowered my head on top of hers and closed my eyes, listening to her breathing as she drifted to sleep.

# Chapter Twelve

## ANNELLA

I stood at the side of the man we'd just snagged outside the restaurant and pulled into the alley. I'd influenced him not to run or be frightened.

"Go ahead, Owen. Just look deep into his eyes and tell him what you want him to do."

Owen's impressive height forced him to lean down to get eye-to-eye with the man. "I want you to stand on one foot."

The man pushed his glasses up on his nose and furrowed his brow. "Why?"

"Really believe it, Owen. Mean it," I said.

He narrowed his eyes and tried again. "I want you to stand on one foot."

The man shrugged and lifted his leg.

"I did it!" Owen exclaimed, but I shook my head.

"No. He wouldn't have questioned it with a shrug."

"Son of a…," Owen breathed. "This is harder than it seems."

"Only the first time. Once you figure it out, it's easy

anytime you do it again. Just try to *really* believe that you have power over his thoughts and mean what you're telling him. Put your foot back down," I said without influencing the man.

He did.

"If he was influenced, he couldn't do that unless you told him, since you're the one that influenced him. Watch his pupils. They'll dilate then constrict if it works."

Owen exhaled a deep breath and looked deep into the man's eyes. "I want you to stand on one foot."

Like a spring had shot his leg off the ground, the man stood obediently on one foot.

"Did I do it?" Owen's excited eyes met mine. "I think I saw the pupil thing happen!"

"I think you did!" I looked at the man. "Why are you standing on one leg?"

"I don't know," he responded with a shrug.

"Put your leg down," I said without influencing him.

He started to lower his leg but lifted it quickly again. "I can't. I don't know why I can't, but I can't."

"Holy shit," Owen said, eyes widening. "I did it."

"You did it." I grinned. "Now, don't forget to undo your compulsions on things like this. If you don't, this poor guy will be stuck for eternity standing on one leg."

"That's not good." Owen shook his head, then leaned down. "You can put your leg back down now."

The man lowered his leg.

"Now, the next part is a little trickier. It's important to get your wording right when you're influencing someone to forget about your interactions with them. If you just say, 'leave and forget me,' they will still remember *what* happened, just not *who* was there. The best thing to say is,

'Forget what happened here and that we exist. Nothing out of the ordinary happened tonight.'"

Owen nodded and leaned down. "Forget what happened here and that we exist. Nothing out of the ordinary happened tonight."

The man nodded his head and walked off casually.

"Did it work?" Owen asked.

"Let's go be certain." I flashed in front of the man and looked deep into his eyes. "Answer honestly. Do you remember us, or what happened here tonight?"

He furrowed his brow. "No. Nothing out of the ordinary happened tonight."

"Good." I smiled. "Have a nice night and forget what happened here and that we exist. Nothing out of the ordinary happened tonight."

He started walking again, and I spun around and beamed at Owen. "You did it! You didn't want to feed on any of the humans we passed, and you successfully influenced someone. It's official. Your vampire training is complete."

"That's it?"

"That's it. The rest is more learn-as-you-go. And you can be in the sun and eat human food, so it's even easier for you than most new vamps."

"Speaking of. Mind if we grab a burger and a beer before we head back to the castle? I'm still dying for some real food."

"Of course." I pointed to the bar across the street. "After you."

Owen and I went inside and sat together at the bar. I checked my phone, but still no word from my family that Catrain was back to run the locator spell. Until she returned, we couldn't locate Leeya, so I'd used the time to practice with Owen in the city.

And it had been a big success. If it weren't for the fact I needed him to help me with Clan Lennox, we'd normally be parting ways.

The thought of parting with him caused a knot of agony to twist up inside my stomach, but that had been the deal I'd made with him. I'd teach him how to use his new powers without hurting anyone, and he'd help me defeat Clan Lennox. After that, he was free to go.

"This is *so fucking good*," Owen said around a mouthful of burger. "You are seriously missing out."

"I haven't had human food in six hundred years. I can't even imagine what that tastes like."

"Like heaven. It's literally like heaven in my mouth right now. I haven't had anything but blood in a week."

I chuckled. It was exciting enough that with Catrain's sister taking power, the sunlight curse would be lifted soon. But deep down, I hoped she'd be able to return us to our original powers. The ones Thorne, Aiden, and Emilia had. The ones it seemed Owen had. They could eat food, needed no blood to survive, and could enjoy the sun. Yet they remained immortal with all the strength, speed, and other perks that came with it.

The best of both worlds.

"So, now that Catrain's sister is the head witch, that means you'll get your sunlight curse lifted, right?" Owen asked before taking another huge bite of his burger.

I reined in a smile. "Yep. When Catrain returns, she'll locate Leeya, and then we'll go get our curses lifted."

"And you're not sure if you can be like Thorne and Aiden or just get to go in the sun?"

"Exactly. Catrain's mother, Liùsaidh, has been in power

for decades. And she *hates* us." I laughed. "She believes that vampires are an abomination, and we should all be dead."

"Ouch."

I arched a brow. "Don't lie. You felt the same way about us until you became one."

Owen laughed. "True story."

"Liùsaidh could definitely give us all our original powers back if she'd wanted to, like she did with Thorne, but she wouldn't."

"Then why did she do it for Thorne?" Owen took a swig of his beer.

"Because the thought of her precious daughter dating a bloodsucker was too much for her to bear. So, she fixed it, so he wasn't."

"Well, wasn't he lucky?"

Laughing, I shook my head. "So fucking lucky. And now that she's retired from her position of leader of the tribe, Catrain's sister has all her powers. And she's *hoping* she can figure out how to do for all of us what her mother did for Thorne."

"But no guarantees?"

"No guarantees. Removing the sunlight curse, yes, for sure. But the big one, reverting us to how we were, that's the tricky one."

"Well, I really hope she can, because if she does, the first place we're coming is here for one of these burgers. You've gotta have one."

He wrapped his lips around the double burger and bit down.

Did that mean he'd still be around after we killed Clan Lennox? I didn't want to overanalyze the simple phrase, but it made my heart jump in my chest.

And then it sunk.

Owen was powerful… too powerful. And even though I started to trust his werewolf instincts wouldn't force him to harm me, what if I was wrong? Or worse than harming me, what if he slaughtered my family?

Was it safe to be with a hybrid who could end every one of us with ease?

Deep in my gut, I felt that he wouldn't hurt me. I felt his desire to protect me and be with me.

But just as deep, the same gut told me he was hard-wired to kill us… and powerful enough to do it.

It left my head spinning while I stared at the man I wanted to kiss every second of every minute of every day.

The same man who deep down, though I refused to truly admit it, terrified me.

*Ding.*

I broke my spiraling train of thought to check my cell phone.

*Thorne: Back on the mainland and heading to the castle. Meet us there.*

*Me: On our way. Back in twenty.*

I stuck my phone in my purse and pointed at Owen's beer. "Finish that up. Catrain is back, so it's time to go."

Owen shoved the last bite of burger in his mouth, then chased it with the beer. The sound of the glass slamming on the bar echoed through the restaurant.

"Let's do this." He stood up and offered me his hand.

When our skin connected, flashes of our lovemaking whipped through my mind. I could almost feel him inside my body again. Hear his raspy breath in my ear. Feel his sweaty skin sliding against mine.

And it almost dropped me to my knees.

"You okay?" he asked as I stumbled.

I blew out a quick breath and plastered a smile on my face. "Yep. I'm good. Let's go."

Before he had a chance to press me anymore, I pulled him around the corner where no humans could see us and then took off in a flash. Vampires moved so fast that, unless a human saw us disappear, we could pass right by them without their eyes detecting us. Owen and I raced through the city side by side, then out into the countryside toward the castle where my family awaited.

---

"We're back!" I called as I pushed open the castle door.

Owen followed behind me, pausing to look at the floor where we'd first found him. "Wow. It feels like years since I woke up on the floor here. But really, it's just been a week."

"You've been through a lot in a week."

He scoffed as he shook his head. "Yeah. My whole life changed. Forever. And literally forever, because I'm freaking immortal now."

I chuckled and gestured for him to keep following me. We got into the family room, and my family wasn't sitting in their usual spots. Instead, they stood as a wall of wary vamps.

"Hey guys." I passed a glance over them.

"Welcome back, Annella," Lothaire said to me, but his eyes never left Owen. "How is… everything."

By *everything,* he meant Owen.

"We're good. He's good," I said with a confidence I didn't know if I should have. "I think."

*Is he good?* What if he was playing me and intended to

tear apart my family the minute we got here? Killing Clan Mackay was the entire reason werewolves existed, and now I'd brought an almost invincible one into my home.

"You sure?" Lothaire arched a bushy brow.

"Yes?" I answered as a question.

"That's not really reassuring," Grizella said. "We heard how strong he is and what he did to all those vampires."

Owen lifted his hands, and the movement caused everyone to stiffen.

"Listen, I know you guys don't have any reason to trust that I won't hurt you. I get that. Hell, I wouldn't trust me either. I was a complete wreck the first and last time you met me. But thanks to Annella here, I'm under control. I swear to you I won't hurt you."

"But you drink vampire blood." Mark pulled a face. "We're like lobsters to you, and with these powers we're hearing about, we're like lobsters sitting in one of those claw machine tanks just waiting for you to pluck us right out and serve us up for supper."

Owen laughed. "You're right, Mark. I do drink vampire blood, but I can control it just like you can control feeding on humans. Annella, do you mind if we show them a demonstration?"

I bit my lip and nodded, then lifted my wrist to his mouth. When his fangs sank into my wrist, I closed my eyes for a moment as I felt our bodies connecting. It pulled me to that place of ecstasy that I never wanted to end. But after a few seconds, he released my wrist, and I snapped back to my senses.

"See. Complete control. I'm not a bloodthirsty monster anymore."

"Do I have your word you won't hurt my family?" Lothaire lowered his head and locked eyes with Owen.

Owen stepped forward, causing my family to stiffen again. When he extended a hand, Lothaire appraised it with a cautious glance, then stepped forward and took it.

"You have my word, Lothaire. I promise I won't harm any of you. And I am a man of my word."

"As am I." Lothaire gripped his hand. "I am not accustomed to not being the most powerful man in the room, and it's unsettling knowing that you can harm my family. Although, I'm quite certain the lot of us together could still take you out."

He arched an eyebrow and gave Owen the silent warning.

A warning Owen heeded.

"I know you could. And I would never hurt you guys. Annella saved my life, and though I know that my bloodline is your enemy, it's in the past that we wanted to kill each other. This is a new day. A new time. And now I understand more of the history that I'd never heard before. You were just defending yourselves from us."

"We were," Lothaire said, continuing to grip his hand. "We never would have started a war with your kind if they hadn't started it first."

"Well, maybe going forward, we can find a way to make peace between the werewolves and the vampires. Maybe they can come out of hiding."

"I would be happy to discuss it. As the leader of the vampires, it is well within my power to do so."

They shook one last time, and I saw the armistice pass between them.

"We welcome you into our family, Owen. We're happy to have you on our side."

*Welcome into our family.*

Those weren't words Lothaire said lightly. By saying them, he meant it when he vowed his trust in Owen.

That meant maybe *I* should trust Owen. It was clear he'd convinced Lothaire of his intent. And Lothaire wasn't one to fall for a ploy. He had a knack for reading people with a glance, and he'd deemed Owen safe to join us.

Aiden and Thorne stepped forward and greeted him with a brief hug, followed by Emilia, Mark, Grizella, and Catrain.

It seemed they'd followed Lothaire's lead in trusting him. So why was I still struggling so hard to believe him?

Why was I so scared of trusting the man who had saved me? The man who'd resisted the urge to kill me even before he got his urges under control?

Maybe it wasn't fear for my safety that made me want to keep him at bay… maybe it was fear for my heart.

For the first time in my life, someone had the power to hurt me… and not just physically. I cared about Owen, and I had since before his transition.

And even more since.

It terrified me to think I wanted something more than just a quick tumble with a man.

I wanted all of him, and I wanted to give all of myself to him.

And that terrified me.

What if I opened my heart up to him and he rejected me?

What if he would always see me as Maighread Mackay, the slayer of his people instead of the woman he'd fallen for inside a crowded bar?

It was hard enough to admit to myself how much I cared for him, but it seemed impossible to admit it to him.

"Welcome back, Annella," Catrain said as she stepped away from Owen and pulled me in for a hug.

"Thanks, Catrain. How did everything go on your island? Did your sister ascend?"

Her face lit up. "Yes, she did. It was amazing to see my mother's magic pass to her."

"Are you sad it wasn't you?" I asked, tipping my head. "Maybe just a little?"

Catrain's gaze drifted to Thorne, and she shook her head. "Not at all. I have everything I could ever want right here."

Thorne grinned like a lovesick schoolboy and came over and bent her back in a kiss.

"Welcome back, Annella," he said after he stood her back up. "We missed you this week."

"Yeah, I missed you guys too. But it was a really productive week. We got Owen all sorted out and got him under control."

"Any issues?" Aiden asked.

"I hit a few rough patches," Owen answered, "but Annella was an excellent teacher."

I glanced over at Owen, remembering how he'd almost sucked me dry the first night we'd gotten there. "Yep. A few bumps in the road while we figured out all his unique powers, but we made it to the end without killing anyone."

"You were going to tell us more about his special abilities," Emilia said. "What are they?"

I blew out a deep breath and started going through everything we'd discovered. His ability to eat food, drink vampire blood, and the strength that came with it versus human blood. After I got done filling my family in on all of it, they just stared at him in awe.

"That's incredible," Grizella said. "I bet Leith and

Leeya are still trying to figure out what the hell happened. We really are lucky to have you on our side."

"I made Annella a promise to help stop Clan Lennox, and like I said, I'm a man of my word. I am happy to help."

"Speaking of special powers," Catrain said. "I spoke to my sister after the ceremony today, and now that she has my mother's powers, she inherited all the knowledge of the ancestors."

"Does that mean?" I struggled to say it out loud. "She can revert us back to our original powers?"

Catrain grinned widely. "Yes. She can. And," she paused and looked to Thorne, "she can make me immortal too. Then I can stay with Thorne for eternity."

"Holy shit," I breathed.

"Fuck yeah! Margaritas and pool parties, here we come, baby!" Mark cheered. "No man will ever be left behind again!"

"Thank you for talking to her, Catrain. It means the world to us." Grizella pulled her in for a hug. "I can't even begin to imagine what the original immortal powers feel like since I never experienced them, but I'm excited to live in the light again."

Lothaire had turned Grizella into a vampire after meeting her a few hundred years ago. She'd never gotten to feel the original powers that they had gifted us with when we first became immortal.

"It's incredible, Grizella," Aiden said. "After she performs the spell, you'll feel weaker than you do now at first, but in a few weeks, you'll be stronger than ever."

"We can go to the island any time you guys want, and she'll perform the spell," Catrain said.

"Let's go!" Mark started toward the door. "Seriously.

Scoot. Let's do this thing. We can hit happy hour tomorrow night!"

"Wait." I held up my hand. "We can't risk being weaker until we get rid of Clan Lennox. Aiden is right. At first, we'll be weaker and slower than even regular vamps. We can't give them any advantage."

"Son of a bitch," Mark grumbled. "You're right."

"Then we kill Clan Lennox and go through the transition right after," Lothaire said decidedly.

"Well, what the hell are we waiting for?" Mark placed his hands on his hips. "Do that locator spell, let's go kill some vamps, get the original powers, then get ourselves a proper cocktail to celebrate!"

"I'm ready to do the locator spell whenever you are," Catrain said.

As we glanced at each other, Lothaire nodded. "Let's do it."

We followed Catrain into the drawing room, where she laid a large map of Scotland out on the table. Thorne dumped out the contents of the purse we'd snagged and grabbed Leeya's ID.

"This will definitely work." Catrain placed the ID in the center of the map.

Owen stood at my side as Catrain closed her eyes and held her hands over the ID. Once she began chanting, it started moving to the north end of Scotland.

"This is crazy," Owen whispered in my ear, and his warm breath on my skin sent shivers snaking down my spine. "I can't believe magic exists."

Since meeting Catrain, it wasn't the first time I'd seen magic performed, but it still amazed me as well.

Not quite as much as the magical feelings Owen managed to keep awakened inside me.

"There. That's where she is." Catrain dropped her hands to her side as we all stared at the map.

"Well, I'll be damned," Lothaire said. "They went home."

"Home?" Mark asked.

"Yes. Clan Lennox used to have a castle up there. It's been abandoned for over a century, but I'd bet anything that's where they are."

"I remember it now. It's not far," Aiden said. "We still have plenty of time to get there tonight, wipe them out and get you guys safe before sunrise."

"Let's do this." I curled my fist up tight. "I'm sick of their shit and ready to end this fucking war."

"Sign me up," Thorne said, and a round of nods followed his statement.

"I'm with you." Owen looked at me, and the simple words startled me with their power.

I hoped he meant he wanted to be with me long after the battle tonight ended.

"Thank you, Owen."

His fingers brushed my hand and started my heart ricocheting around inside my chest.

"If Leith really is turning humans into influenced vampires, there may be a small army. Let's gear up."

As the strongest of the vampires, we didn't need weapons to fight, but Lothaire was right. With the number we'd seen in the city, we had no idea how many may be waiting for us at their castle.

"You come equipped with knives." I gestured to Owen's hands. "The rest of us need to grab weapons. We keep them in the armory. Follow me."

We all darted off to the armory, changing into our battle clothes and pulling our favorite weapons off the walls.

Lothaire picked up the ax he'd had for centuries, and Grizella opened the display case and grabbed her two favorite gold daggers. She'd taken them off a slave trader she'd slaughtered a few centuries ago.

Aiden and Thorne slid their swords into their back holsters, and it reminded me of how they looked going into battle before we'd become immortal.

"Do Emilia and I get something?" Mark asked.

"Take your pick. Whatever weapon you feel most comfortable with," Aiden answered.

"Most comfortable with? The only weapons I've ever wielded are my good looks and charm. But, oh! This one looks cool." He plucked a silver engraved sword with a fancy black handle from the wall. "I bet it would go great with my Gucci! Does it?" He held it up next to his black t-shirt.

"It goes perfectly." Emilia laughed.

"Here. Sling this over your shoulder and slide the sword in there," Thorne said as he tossed Mark a holster.

"Try these, baby," Aiden said to Emilia as he presented her with two daggers.

"These look more my size." Emilia fingered them, then twirled them around and almost dropped one. "I just have no idea how to use them."

Thorne grinned. "It's easy. Just stick the pointy end into the vampires and use them to cut off their heads."

Catrain crackled the lighting in her hands. "I don't need a weapon. I am one."

"Fucking hot, baby." Thorne blew out a whistle, then kissed her cheek.

I wore the black leather pants and top that always made me feel like a badass and had holsters for the daggers strapped to my thighs and two swords crossing my back.

I saw Owen's appreciate glance as he appraised my body in the skintight black outfit.

"Damn," he mouthed.

As much as I wanted to stand there and seduce him, I knew we had a job to do, and for me, Grizella, Lothaire, and Mark, we had to do it before the sun peeked over the horizon.

"Lead the way, Lothaire." I lifted my chin and jutted it toward the door.

Thorne grabbed Catrain around the waist since she lacked our speed but loved to go fast with him. When he had her tight in his arms, he nodded, and Lothaire bolted out the door. We followed behind him, racing through the countryside toward the clan that wouldn't be alive by sunrise.

## Chapter Thirteen

### OWEN

Nerves and excitement coursed through my body as we charged across the countryside. I'd be lying if I didn't admit the thought of killing vampires ignited something deep inside my core. The werewolf inside me salivated at the thought of tearing them apart.

It begged me to let it out of the cage… let it run free to rip apart every vampire in my path.

But one glance at the beautiful vampire running at my side, and I knew I had to keep it in check. Let it out of the cage, but keep it on a leash.

And thanks to her, now I could. I could wield it like a weapon and then recall it before it went wild and harmed her and her family. Like a trained guard dog, the wolf inside me had learned to yield to my commands instead of making them.

Lothaire led the pack, and after a twenty-minute sprint at full-speed, he raised his hand and slowed to a stop. We all lined up beside him at the edge of the forest.

"This is it," he whispered. "The castle is in a clearing

inside these woods. It has, or at least had, a curtain wall surrounding it."

"That shouldn't pose a problem for us," Aiden said. "We can scale walls."

"Exactly. I think we're best going in quietly. They have no idea we have Catrain who can do locator spells, and since they haven't here in over a century, they won't be expecting us to have thought of it. Let's use the element of surprise and try to quietly put down any vamps we find as we hunt for Leith and Leeya."

"Let's split up," Thorne said. "We'll go in pairs, each searching the castle for them."

"Good plan," Aiden agreed.

Annella and I nodded our agreement.

Lothaire looked into the woods toward the castle and pointed as he spoke. "Owen and Annella, take the north side. Aiden and Emilia go east and take Mark with you. Thorne and Catrain go west. Grizella and I will take the south. Move silently, kill anything in your sight, and we will find them."

"Are we sure she's still in there?" Emilia asked.

Everyone looked at Catrain. "I can run a spell again just to make sure she hasn't left since we ran the last one."

"Wait," I said as I closed my eyes. Inhaling a deep breath, I searched the smells surrounding us, sorting my way through the scents until I found Leeya's.

It was strong. Too strong for her not to still be here.

"She's here, I can smell her." I opened my eyes.

They all stared at me, stunned.

"You can smell her from here?" Annella asked.

I nodded. "Werewolves are expert trackers and have an incredibly heightened sense of smell. And we never forget a scent. I caught hers the night she killed me, and I'll never forget it."

"Damn," Annella breathed. "It's a good thing our smell isn't strong like yours, or we'd never be able to sneak up on Leeya."

I smirked. "Well, we've got the upper hand with mine."

"And Leith?" Lothaire asked.

I closed my eyes and searched the scents again, shaking my head when I finished. "No. No Leith. He's been here, but he's not here now."

"Shit," Aiden whispered. "Should we wait?"

"No," Lothaire said decidedly. "We take Leeya now, and we'll find Leith later. We aren't missing an opportunity."

"Then we go," Thorne said. "Everyone be safe. Remember, no mercy."

We all exchanged a nod of solidarity before Annella gestured for me to follow her. We moved quietly and quickly along the edge of the forest until we reached the north end. Together we crept to the edge and surveyed the field separating us from the castle wall. I started to move into the clearing, but she caught me by the shoulder.

"Wait," she said. "Before we go in, we should make sure you're at full power. Drink from me."

I salivated, but not just from thinking about the taste of her incredible blood, but from the anticipation of the connection crackling between us every time I fed from her. It was a connection I couldn't explain, but one that deepened every time I drank her essence.

Annella pushed her hair off her shoulder, exposing her long, creamy neck. My fangs popped at the sight of it. I stepped forward, wrapping my hand around her waist and pulling her against me. I slid my other hand behind her head, holding her steady as I leaned down and sank my fangs into her.

We both moaned as her warm blood coursed into my mouth. I dug my fingers into her hair, biting down harder as her life force merged with mine. Every cell in my body vibrated with the incredible power filling them to bursting.

Not wanting to take too much and weaken her for the battle, I forced my fangs back out of her skin. Pressing my forehead against hers, I closed my eyes while I let the emotions she stirred settle back down to a manageable level.

Emotions that felt a lot like love.

When I opened my eyes, and she looked up into mine, I knew right then those feelings didn't just feel a lot like love… they were love.

Undeniable, unquestionable, unending love.

It was all I could do not to let the words tumble out of my mouth, but I knew to Annella, I was just a means to an end. A weapon to wield in her war against Clan Lennox. She would never fall for a werewolf.

But the look in her eyes as she stared up at me made me question it.

*Does she feel the same?*

Was it possible my feelings weren't one-sided?

A crack in the bushes caused us both to spin toward it, but a deer hopped through the brush, and we both heaved a sigh of relief.

"Come on, we should go," she said.

As much as I wanted to stay there and stare at her, or kiss her, or tell her I loved her and always would, I nodded and followed her back to the edge of the clearing.

A vampire stood at the top of the wall, his gaze passing over the clearing we needed to cross. Dropping low to the ground, we slunk side-by-side through the tall grass until we reached it.

Annella went first, scaling up the stones. I followed her lead, realizing it was my first time scaling a wall and being surprised by how easy it was for me. When we reached the top, we crawled over the edge and stayed low as we used the stone ledge for cover.

Annella lifted a finger to her lips. I lowered myself to the ground and waited. I watched as she crept up behind the unaware vampire, sliding her sword from the sheath on her back as she approached. She rose behind him, and in one swift move, she spun around, slicing through his neck and catching his body before it thumped loudly on the stones.

Yep.

I loved this woman.

God, did I love this woman.

Then I felt it, and the feeling nearly dropped me to the ground. Being raised as a werewolf, I'd been told about it, but I'd never truly understood it until it happened to me.

Wolves mated for life. Once the wolf inside identified its other half, no other woman could ever take her place. Not in life. Not in death. Never. A wolf's love for its mate was pure and unending.

And my wolf had just claimed Annella.

And I agreed with that choice.

The wolf inside me, the one hard-wired to hate her—to kill her—howled its approval as she wiped the blood from her blade and slid it back into its sheath. It claimed her as its mate, and I felt the eternal connection to her solidify into something that could never be broken.

Ever.

"Come on," she whispered as she lowered herself to the ground again.

Even though I wanted to rush up to her, grab her in my arms, and kiss her until we couldn't breathe, I knew we had a job to do. There was a threat to the woman I loved, to my mate, and even the animal inside me wanted to seek out vengeance and eradicate the threat to her.

The threat to this woman we both loved.

With the quick tip of her head, she gestured toward a door, so I followed along behind her. A slow creak broke the silence surrounding us as she opened it, and we both cringed and paused, waiting for vampires to come running.

But none did.

Silently, we descended the stairs. I used my sense of smell to guide the way, and like an invisible tether, it pulled me toward Leeya.

"This floor," I whispered when we reached a landing. "She's here."

Annella gave a sharp nod and pressed her body alongside the doorway while I pushed it open. I peeked my head through and saw no movement along the long, stone corridor.

With a tip of my head, I gestured for her to follow me. We stepped into the corridor, and I used my sense of smell to guide me as we took slow, deliberate steps.

Leeya's scent strengthened with each step, and I knew we were close.

Very close.

As we closed in on the door I knew held her behind it, another door behind us opened. When I spun around, the startled eyes of a vampire met mine.

"Intruders!" he shouted a millisecond before I launched across the hallway and snapped his neck.

Annella and I froze for a moment, hoping that maybe no one had heard his warning.

Thundering footsteps echoing through the castle ended that hope in an instant.

The sound of the approaching vampires triggered my wolf to pound at the gate. I opened it up, snarling as my fangs and claws popped out. With Annella's blood coursing through me, I felt the power surging as every muscle in my body twitched at the ready.

A half dozen vampires flew down the corridor at us from both sides. Annella slid her daggers from her thighs, and we went back to back, preparing for impact. When they arrived, we fought our way through the bodies that threw themselves at us.

"Leeya's here! Up here!" Annella shouted to her family as we continued our battle against the newly turned vamps who lacked enough strength to seriously challenge us. But another thundering of footsteps brought not her family, but a couple dozen more vampires.

"Shit," Annella said as she wiped the bloody daggers across her thighs and slid them back into the holsters, drawing out her swords instead. "Get ready."

I was born ready for this, I thought as I lifted my lip. With a loud roar, I launched at the pack of vampires flying toward us. With each slice into their skin, and each bite into their bodies, I grew stronger and stronger, their blood and my inner desire to annihilate them driving me on. Fueling me. Igniting the power inside like gasoline on a flame.

As I tore blindly through the last of the bodies, I glanced behind me to check on Annella. Just seeing her in her tight black leather pants fighting vampires had me ready to drop to my knees. But I couldn't. I had to keep her safe. Keep fighting and kill all the vampires who would dare do her harm.

She caught my glance and flashed me an appreciative

smile as she slid her sword through the air, taking the head off a vampire without even looking.

So fucking hot.

And from the way her pupils dilated as she watched me, I knew the feeling was mutual.

A sound behind me caught my attention, so I spun back around, swinging my claws at the body in front of me. Just before I connected, I stopped, my eyes widening when I saw Lothaire's face staring back at me. The wolf inside me snarled at the vampire and wanted to finish the lethal blow, but I yanked on the leash and pulled it back, lowering my hand from his neck.

"Sorry." I retracted my fangs. "Thought you were one of them."

Lothaire held my eye contact and curled his lip in a half-smile. "Glad you're on our side."

As the bloodlust dissipated, I saw the bodies piled around me, and that Annella's family had joined the fight at some point. I'd been too laser-focused on the vampires to even notice when they'd arrived.

"Leeya?" Aiden asked.

"She was in there." Annella pointed at the doorway.

With a powerful kick, Aiden sent the door flying into the room. As expected from the commotion we'd caused, instead of finding Leeya, we saw the sheer curtains of the open window billowing in the breeze.

"Fuck!" Annella spit out. "She got away!"

I closed my eyes and inhaled the air, a sly smile lifting my lip as I finished. "No, she didn't. This way."

I launched forward and leaped out the third-story window, hitting the ground and springing off after the scent path she'd left like a trail of breadcrumbs behind her. I was faster than the Mackay family, and this time I didn't slow down for them. Surging forward, I let my hatred of vampires, and of the one who'd harmed Annella and killed me, drive me on.

It didn't take long for me to find her. I saw Leeya racing through the trees, her red hair trailing behind her. With a snarl, I pushed my body even faster, closing the distance between us in only seconds. Reaching out, I caught her by the hair and yanked, sending her sailing backward, tumbling through the dirt and leaves before she skidded to a stop.

Leeya leaped to her feet and snarled, but one look at me, and she widened her eyes as she prepared to bolt away. She only made it a few steps before Emilia appeared from behind a tree.

"Hello, Leeya." She smiled and placed a swift kick into Leeya's chest, sending her tumbling into the circle of original vampires surrounding her.

"Don't fucking move," Annella said as she stepped on her neck, digging a heel into her skin.

"Don't kill me," Leeya choked out.

"Oh, we're not gonna kill you just yet, Leeya." Annella smirked. "I've got plans for you. Plans like the ones you had when you kidnapped and tortured me. Those kinds of plans."

Leeya's eyes widened as the Mackay family all glared down at her.

Movement to the east caught all our eyes as a vampire bolted toward freedom.

"I got him!" Mark shouted as he sped off in that direction, tackling the vampire before he could get away. When he had the giant redheaded vampire pinned to the ground, I saw the shock on Mark's face.

"Gregor?" Mark said, stunned.

"Please don't kill me, Mark. They made me help them," Gregor said as he begged for his life.

"Shut up, Gregor!" Leeya spat, but Annella quieted her by digging her heel deeper into Leeya's throat.

Mark snarled and lowered his face into Gregor's. "You used me. Tricked me. Made me look like an idiot."

"I'm so sorry, Mark. I didn't want to. You have to believe me."

Gregor lay still in the grass as Mark bared his fangs.

"I could kill you right now." Mark snarled.

"And I deserve it," Gregor said as he submitted. "I'm so sorry, Mark. I never wanted to hurt you. You have to believe me."

"It's your decision, Mark," Lothaire interrupted the stare down. "Kill him or bring him with us as a prisoner. He wronged you, so the choice is yours."

Mark stared down at him, his shoulders heaving with his heavy breaths. After a long pause, Mark pushed off Gregor and stood.

"He may be important to Leith since we've seen them together twice now. Maybe he can help us find him, so I say he lives." He crossed his arms and looked back over his shoulder. "For *now.*"

Thorne and Aiden flashed to Gregor's side and hoisted him to his feet.

"Let's get them back to the castle. We can use them to figure out where Leith is hiding."

"I'll never tell you," Leeya spat as Annella yanked her to her feet.

"Well, I'm gonna have fun trying." Annella grinned.

"Wait," Catrain said. "We need to go back to the castle. Thorne and I found a whole dungeon filled with humans."

"Seriously?" I spun to look at her.

Thorne left Aiden with Gregor and went back to her side. "Yes. Close to a hundred. Catrain and I found them when we entered the castle through the dungeon. They said some were being used as food while the strongest were being turned into vampires."

"Jesus," I whispered. "That's horrific."

"Yes. It is." Grizella's eyes narrowed as they raked over Leeya. "Then we need to go free them. Now."

Annella had told me of Grizella's history as a slave before Lothaire saved her, and I saw the anger burning inside her emerald green eyes as she glared at Leeya. No doubt it conjured up memories from her time as a captive.

"Thorne and Aiden," Lothaire said. "Since you two can influence people and handle the sunlight, stay behind and clean up the mess we made and free the captives. Influence them to forget all this and get them to the city."

"We can grab a bus," Thorne said. "Just load them all up and bring them to the city with some story about a bus tour getting lost in the mountains."

"Let's do it," Aiden answered.

"The rest of you back to the castle. Gregor and Leeya are coming with us. We'll figure out where Leith is next."

"I've got Leeya," Emilia said with a smirk as she grabbed Leeya by the elbow. "Funny how the tables have turned, huh, Leeya? Should have thought things through before you kidnapped me and tried to force Aiden to drain me of my blood."

Leeya spat at Emilia's feet. "I should have finished you off when I had the chance."

Emilia shoved her forward toward Aiden with enough force Leeya almost fell. Leeya had no shortage of angry immortals all frothing at the mouth for her head.

I started to walk after them, but Annella caught me by the wrist.

"We'll see you at home," Annella said to them.

I arched an eyebrow, wondering why we weren't going to travel with them but didn't argue.

With a nod, her family took off. Thorne and Aiden raced back toward the castle with the hostages, while Lothaire took the rest of the family home. After they left, I turned to Annella.

"Why aren't we—"

She didn't let me finish the sentence. Annella launched into my arms, wrapping her legs around my waist as she consumed me with a kiss so powerful it almost dropped me to my knees.

I wrapped my hands around her leather-clad ass and flashed us back to the trees, pressing her up against one.

Her fingernails raked my skin as she yanked off my shirt.

"I can't wait another second," she whispered into my ear before nipping it. "I want you. Now."

It wasn't just me who'd been turned on to the point of exploding during the fight tonight. It seemed it ignited the flames of passion inside Annella as well.

Flames I was happy to help her douse.

We tore at each other's clothes while kissing each other so hard I worried I'd hurt her. But she didn't ease up on her enthusiasm, and the pain I must have caused her only seemed to encourage her on.

I spun her around, lowering her to the ground before yanking off her leather pants. Annella tore at my jeans, ripping off the button, yanking down the zipper, and tugging them over my ass. I kneeled between her legs, sliding myself against her.

But instead of impaling her with the passion that urged me to plunge inside her now, I hovered above her, then lowered myself down to her lips.

Gently, I pressed my lips against hers, closing my eyes while I inhaled her breath.

"I love you, Annella," I whispered against her lips. "I need you to know that."

Her breath trapped in her lungs, and her eyes fluttered open. They searched inside mine as her chest rose and fell with her quickened breaths.

"I know I'm a werewolf, and I know you're Maighread Mackay, and we're supposed to hate each other, but I love you. I have loved you since the second I laid eyes on you. And you may just want me to help you stop Clan Mackay and never see me again, but I need you to know that I don't ever want to leave your side. And ever for an immortal is a long fucking time."

After a lengthy pause, she whispered, "I'm scared."

*Scared? Annella?*

It seemed impossible this woman could be scared of anything, but fear crept into her passionate gaze.

"I will never hurt you, Annella. Ever. I have my wolf under control, and even he would go to war and die for you."

She gently shook her head. "I don't mean physically. I trust now that you won't hurt me. But I've never done this. I've never opened myself up to a man. And it… it terrifies me."

Her vulnerability made my heart swell inside my chest. I pushed a piece of hair from her face.

"I love you, Annella. And yeah, falling in love is scary as fuck, even for an immortal hybrid… and an original vampire. You have as much power to crush me into nothingness as I have over you. More. But that's what love is. It's trust. It's giving your heart to someone, even when there is no guarantee they won't crush it in their hands. But you do it anyway, because it's impossible not to. You already have my heart, and you always will. Do with it what you will. And I'm asking now for yours in return. I swear to you, Annella, I will never hurt you. I'd sooner crush my own heart than yours."

She chewed on her lip as she slid her hands alongside my face.

I brushed my finger across her lips. "Just tell me how you feel about me. Tell me what I *know* I can feel every time I look into your eyes."

Her worried gaze searched mine before it softened, and she whispered, "I love you." It sounded so meek and timid from the powerful woman I'd fallen for. "You have my heart. Always. And I don't ever want you to leave my side."

My heart detonated in my chest with the power of her words. I exhaled a sigh as I smiled, leaning down to kiss her again.

She slid her hands through my hair, pulling me down and deepening our kiss. I slid myself inside her, catching her gasp in my mouth as I moved inside her body. Our connection only strengthening with each movement.

Our sweaty bodies slid against each other as we rode the wave of ecstasy together, panting into each other's mouths as we came in unison.

When we finished, I rolled off her and collapsed at her side.

We lay on our backs staring at the sky. I reached over and slid her small hand into mine, closing it tight inside my fingers. When she looked over and smiled, it tipped my entire universe upside down.

We were a team. Partners. And I knew that this woman would be at my side for all times.

Right where she belonged.

# Chapter Fourteen

## ANNELLA

When I opened my eyes, the first thing I saw was Owen's green ones blinking back at me.

"Good morning, beautiful," he said, then kissed me on the nose. "Or, I guess I should say good evening."

It felt surreal waking up in his arms… but right.

I pressed my head into his chest, and he closed his arms tight around me.

"Hi," I whispered as I traced the ink on his smooth chest with my fingers.

"Hi," he whispered back. "Is it weird waking up with me?"

I peeked up from his chest and shook my head. "No. Actually, it feels…"

"Normal."

I grinned. "Yeah. Normal. Like we've kind of always been."

Just last night, I'd handed him my heart, and already it felt like we'd been together for years. Like he was a permanent part of my life and waking up in bed with him was the most natural thing in the world.

Usually, I'd have snuck out of bed long before he woke because sleeping with a man and *sleeping* with a man were two very different things for me. I never stuck around for snuggles.

But with Owen, I couldn't imagine anywhere else I'd rather be than in his arms.

"You're not regretting this, are you?" Owen asked.

I shook my head and rested it back down on his chest. The steady drum of his heart soothed me.

"No. Not at all. Are you?" I peeked back up and arched an eyebrow.

"Regretting this?" He chuckled and pulled the sheets off me then flipped me onto my back in one swift move. "Who in their right mind would regret having this all to themselves?"

I giggled while he pressed kisses all over my naked body.

"What would your pack think of you kissing all over *Maighread Mackay*?" I accentuated my name like the villain they'd made me out to be.

Owen rolled onto his back and pulled me against him. "They'd probably skin me alive if they knew."

I sucked the air through my teeth. "Then we probably shouldn't tell them, huh?"

After a long pause, Owen said, "Did your brother mean it about a truce with the werewolves?"

"Lothaire means everything he says."

"Maybe we really can find peace between our kinds. As a werewolf, I know how amazing it would be to have the freedom to be ourselves… the freedom to change. Even though we can control it and we don't *have* to change, the wolf inside us wants to come out. It wants to run. It's hard never letting it free. I think it would be incredible if the werewolves could shift sometimes and let their wolves out."

"As long as they understand they can't hunt vampires, I don't see why we couldn't work that out. Honestly, we had no idea your kind existed until a couple months ago, and even then, we thought there were just a few left on Catrain's island. If we'd have known about you on the mainland, we probably could have worked out a truce centuries ago."

Owen chuckled, and his abs tightened underneath my hand with the movement.

"To think we could have ended this feud centuries ago. Never in a million years would any werewolf have believed me if I'd have told them Clan Mackay didn't want us all dead. To werewolves, vampires are bloodthirsty murderers."

"And now you've seen we're not. Not in the slightest. In fact, we help more people than we hurt."

"Yeah? How is that?"

I dragged my fingertips along the defined lines on his stomach. "Well, for one, we helped wipe out slavery."

"What?"

"Yep. After Lothaire met Grizella and we really understood what slaves went through, we freed thousands and thousands and *thousands* of them. The trouble was, slavers just kept getting more. So, in every battle to end slavery, we showed up to fight with Grizella leading the way."

"Seriously?" Owen looked down at me, and I shrugged.

"Oh, yeah. We'd fight on the side wanting to end slavery and made a much bigger difference than just releasing individual slaves."

"Please tell me you fought in the Civil War in the United States."

I grinned up at him. "You bet your arse we did! That was a bitch, and honestly, we really helped the Union Army.

Half of those battles would have gone to the south without us intervening."

"Well, I'll be damned." He laughed. "My whole life, I've heard nothing but vampires slaughtering innocent humans, and it turns out you've done more for humans than most people on this planet."

"Yeah. We kinda kick arse."

"Yeah. You do." He pulled me up for a kiss. "My girl kicks the most arse ever."

*My girl.*

I'd never been anyone's girl before, and as I stared down at Owen, I knew I'd never be anyone's girl again.

For the rest of eternity, I'd be only his.

"The sun set thirty minutes ago, and we really should be down there figuring out what's up with Leeya," I said on a sigh. "I'm being irresponsible right now."

"I like being irresponsible with you." Owen yanked me back into his arms.

"You're tempting me to go for round six. Or is it seven now?" I pressed my finger to my cheek while I smirked.

"Seven, and I say we go for eight."

"Later. We're already late." I leaned up and kissed him quick then flashed over to my closet. "Let's go downstairs and find out what's up with Leeya and if they got any leads on Leith."

Owen stuck out his bottom lip as I dressed. "Boo to clothes and leaving this room. Being naked in here with you is way more fun."

I pulled on my boots over my jeans. "Just remember, once we've killed Leith, I can go get reverted to my immortal powers and go get a burger with you at that bar."

"Fuck." He bit his lip. "I really want to take you for a

burger there. Okay, point taken." He flashed to my side and pulled on his clothes. "Let's go."

I laughed as he took my hand and pulled me down the hall.

When we got downstairs, Mark stood at the bottom of the staircase wearing a smug smile.

"How are you even walking right now?" He shook his head as I approached. "Because all I've heard all freaking day is the two of you all bow-chicka-bow-wow." He swiveled his hips and ended with a thrust. "And I've seen the outline of that thing." He waggled a finger at Owen's crotch. "It ain't small. I'm just saying, you shouldn't be walking, Annella."

"Mark!" I slapped him on the shoulder as we passed by. "Don't be a pervy perv and be listening in on our bow-chicka-bow-bow. Vampire etiquette says no using vamp hearing to listen to other people's sexy time! Gross!"

"Vampire hearing?" He snorted. "Yeah, no vamp hearing needed. Every human in Scotland heard you two last night. Even if I leave the country and wear earplugs, I'm still not gonna be able to tune that shit out."

"Well, it's that good," I whispered as I kissed him on the cheek while I passed. "Don't be jelly."

Mark smacked me on the butt, then glanced at Owen's. "Well, I am jelly. You got any brothers?"

"Three," Owen said with a smile.

"You got any *gay* brothers?" He waggled his eyebrows.

"Not that I know of, but you can always give it a whirl. They're pretty open-minded."

Mark bit his fist. "Damn. If they have an ass even half as good as yours, don't mind if I do. Werewolves for everyone."

"How's it going with Leeya?" I asked as I moved to the

kitchen to get some blood. I offered it to Owen, but he just shook his head, and I remembered he'd just fed… on me.

Mark sat at the counter and rested his head on his hands. "She's not talking. Grizella gave her hell all day, but no luck. Aiden and Thorne got back a little bit ago from returning all the prisoners, and they are down there now."

After downing my blood, I tossed the empty bag in the garbage. "I'll get her to talk. Coming, Owen?"

"That bitch killed me. Of course, I'm coming."

I looked to Mark. "You coming?"

I saw the pained look on his face as he diverted his eyes. "No. I'm just gonna stay up here."

"You okay?" I reached out and touched his hand. He didn't need to say it for me to understand the conflict brewing inside his eyes.

"Yeah. I know he's a dick and a user and all that shit, but it's still hard seeing him down there all tied up… and not in a sexy way." He pushed out his lower lip. "And I still feel so stupid for falling for his lies."

"Hey." I walked behind him and closed my arms around his shoulders. "Don't you dare blame yourself for what happened to me. I'm just sorry someone hurt you. And I promise you I'll make him pay for it. No one messes with my Marky Mark."

He giggled while I plastered dozens of kisses on his cheek.

"And you girls are my Funky Bunch." He kissed me back.

"We'll always be your Funky Bunch. And right now, I'm gonna go Funky Bunch on Gregor's ass."

Mark and Owen furrowed their brows.

"Yeah. Now that I've heard what I said, it doesn't make sense to me either."

They both burst into laughter.

"Thanks, baby. I needed a laugh."

"Anytime, lovey. We'll find you when we're done."

After one last overly dramatic kiss on Mark's cheek ending with a *mwuah,* I took Owen by the hand and led him through the castle to the doorway into the dungeon.

When I pressed it open, he paused. "Is there seriously a dungeon? Like a *dungeon* dungeon?"

I nodded. "Yep. This castle is over six hundred years old, and back then, dungeons were all the rage. Now we use it for dickhead vamps who get out of line."

"This is so weird. Just a couple weeks ago, I was just a wannabe rockstar/bartender. Now I'm a hybrid vampire/werewolf heading into a dungeon to interrogate a vampire prisoner with my original vampire girlfriend. This is beyond strange."

*Girlfriend.* That was beyond strange to me.

But a good strange.

Owen followed me through the dark, stone hallway to the cells at the end.

"Any luck?"

Aiden and Thorne both shook their heads.

Thorne leaned against the bars. "Nothing yet. But we'll keep working on her."

"Fuck you," Leeya said, following it up with a well-aimed spit.

I flashed across the cell and slapped her across the face.

*Crack.*

"That's for spitting on Thorne."

*Crack.*

"That's for kidnapping and torturing me."

*Crack.*

"*That's* for killing my fucking boyfriend."

When I stood back up, Leeya spat blood onto the floor. The cut on her lip healed immediately.

"If I'd have known he had your blood in his system, I'd have cut off his head. Guess I'll just have to try again. Although, I'm dying now to know what he is." Her gaze raked Owen up and down. "At the warehouse when you fought, you were something else. Not just a vampire. Something Leith and I have never seen before. Tell me. What are you?"

Other than my family, no vampire knew werewolves existed. And certainly none knew a hybrid did. And I didn't intend to let Clan Lennox in on our little secret.

Secret weapon, that was.

"Don't you worry about him. I'm the one asking questions here."

She ignored me and kept appraising Owen. "Leith *really* wants to know more about you, and so do I, so why don't you stay here with me awhile and we can… chat." Her red eyebrow rose as she drew her tongue along her crimson lips. "I'll show you mine if you show me yours."

Owen snarled, and I leaned into her face, raising my hand to slap her again. "Where is Leith? Tell me. Now."

"It won't work," Aiden cut in. "We worked her over all day, but she didn't give up anything on Leith."

I arched an eyebrow and leaned down into Leeya's face. "They're a lot nicer than I am."

It was only a millisecond, but I saw the fear in her eyes. My reputation was well known in vampire circles.

A reputation that made most vampires run.

"I'll die before I tell you."

And though I saw the flash of fear in her eye, I also saw the strength return. Leith and Leeya would never turn on each other. She would die before she broke.

*Fuck.*

"Where's Gregor?" I asked as I pushed off the arms of her chair.

"Two cells down," Thorne answered.

I narrowed my eyes. "I'll get you to talk, Leeya. First, I need a date with Gregor. He made my Marky Mark pull a sad face."

I marched out of the cell and kicked open the door to Gregor's. His shaggy red hair covered his eyes as he hung his head low, and he didn't struggle against the chains tying his hands behind his back.

"Do it," he said defeatedly. "I deserve it."

"Yeah. You do deserve it." I cracked my knuckles. "Mark didn't deserve to be a pawn in your stupid fucking game."

"No, he didn't. And I'm so sorry I played any part in it. Do what you must to me. I won't fight."

I paused, tipping my head while I appraised him.

Was it possible he'd really regretted his part in my kidnapping? His part in betraying Mark?

*Nah. He's probably just a good actor.*

"I'd like it better if you fought, but I certainly won't hold back, regardless." I grinned.

"Don't hold back. My sister is probably already dead now that I got caught, and she was the last family I had. Add that to how shitty I feel about Mark, and if you could just put me out of my misery and toss me out in the sun, I'd appreciate it."

What was that? A twist of sympathy in my gut?

Me? Sympathetic? Never.

"What's that about your sister?" Owen asked, stopping me with a hand on my arm.

I clucked my tongue. "Owen. He's lying."

"No. Let him speak."

With a huff, I leaned back against the bars. "Okay. Let's hear it."

He lifted his head, and his beautiful blue eyes, heavy with sadness, met mine. "I already told them everything."

"Then tell me," Owen said. "I want to hear what happened."

Gregor sighed and shook his head. "It's just me and my sister. We grew up in the foster system, and about a year ago, she turned eighteen. She went out to celebrate her birthday with me, and we ran into Leith and Leeya at a bar. I didn't know it at the time, but Leith influenced us to come back to his place with him. When we got there, he turned me into a vampire. Told me he was making an army to take down Clan Mackay."

"And you just joined up with him?" I arched an eyebrow.

"Of course, I did. I didn't know anything about you guys, or that Lothaire was our true leader or any of that. I only knew what Leith and Leeya told us. And I had nowhere to go. I was a vampire, and he took a liking to my sister and kept her." Gregor shook his head, and I saw the hatred ignite in his eyes. "He keeps her to feed on. Something about enjoying the taste of her blood."

"Why didn't you free her?" I asked. "Surely, you had ample opportunity to get her out of there in the past year."

Gregor scoffed. "Oh, I had plenty. But he influenced her not to run. No matter how hard I tried, she'd run back to him. And the last time I tried to break her out, Leith told me he'd kill her if I tried again. And then he started forcing me to do stuff for him or he'd threaten to hurt or kill her. I had to do it." Gregor looked up, and his sad eyes searched mine. "You have to understand. I would do anything for her. She's my family. My only family."

That pang of guilt plucked inside my stomach again.

*Shit.*

I would do anything for my family too.

But what if he was lying? Or worse… influenced.

"How do I know you're not influenced to Leith, and if we believe you and let you go, you won't kill us or just run back to him?"

"You don't." Gregor shrugged. "But I'm not. It wasn't until about three months ago that Leith realized he was turning us all into a vampire army, but most of us didn't want to fight with him. For every ten vampires he'd turn, eight would sneak off in the night. And they didn't have sisters he could hold hostage to control them. That's when he realized he needed to influence humans before turning them. *Then* he started to build his army. And fast."

"How many?" I asked. "In his army?"

Gregor scoffed. "Hundreds. Maybe a thousand by now."

My eyes bulged at the number. "Holy shit."

"He's hell-bent on taking you all out."

"And we're hell-bent on destroying him." I snarled.

"And he's *really* interested in you." He jutted his chin at Owen. "After he saw you fight in the warehouse, he's determined on figuring out what you are so he can make an army of you."

"Great," I grumbled. "Just what we need."

"He can't make an army of me because we'll be killing him long before he has a chance," Owen said confidently.

"Let's hope so."

If Leith figured out what Owen was, and that werewolves still existed and could be turned into hybrids, this war would take a turn in a hurry… and not in our favor.

"What do you think?" Owen whispered in my ear. "I mean, I'm new to the whole torture and interrogate part of this, so maybe I'm an idiot, but I believe him. I don't think he wants to be with Leith."

Rolling my eyes, I turned and looked at him. "Every single person I've ever tortured makes you think they're the good one, and you've got it all wrong. Every one of them. It's not until you really turn the screws that they will admit the truth."

I turned back to Gregor.

"So, let's start turning those screws."

As I stepped toward him, he lowered his head and slumped forward. There was no fight in him, that was for sure.

"Wait," Mark's voice stopped me in my tracks. "Don't hurt him."

"Mark?" Gregor looked up, his blue eyes searching for the voice.

Mark stepped around the corner, crossed his arms, and leaned up against the wall. "Is it true? You really only did what you did to me because Leith has your sister?"

"It's true, Mark. I never would have betrayed you, and I *was* truly loving being with you the night we were together. If I had a choice, I would never have left your side. Ever. I swear it. I swear it on my sister's life." Sadness flooded his eyes again. "If she even has one now that I've been taken."

"How can I believe you?" Mark pushed off the wall and paced back and forth. "I mean, fool me once, shame on you. Fool me twice, shame on me. And I'm not about to wear shame. It doesn't go with my skin tone."

"I don't know how to prove it to you, but I just want you

to know, believe me or not, that I did really connect with you that night, Mark. I almost told you a hundred times what was happening and begged for your help and the help of Clan Mackay, but I was too scared it would backfire and he'd kill Meagan."

Mark arched a wary eyebrow and lifted his chin. "I *want* to believe you, but I still don't."

"What do you want me to do, Mark?" I turned and asked my friend. "I can torture him to the truth, or we can leave him to you. The choice is yours."

Mark chewed on his lip while he stared at Gregor. After a long pause, he shook his head. "We won't torture him… *yet.* Let me just take some time digesting this story."

"He's in your control. You tell me whatever you want, Mark."

"Thank you." He kissed my cheek, and I gestured to Owen to follow me out of the cell. When I glanced back, Mark stood cross-armed in front of Gregor, staring him down.

Aiden came out of Leeya's cell. "This could take a while. We're going to starve her of blood for a couple days and weaken her. Once she's weaker, I hope we'll be able to get her to tell us Leith's whereabouts."

"And Gregor doesn't know?"

"No. He told us all the places he's been with them, and several are ones we know about, but he doesn't know where Leith is right now. The last he saw him was in Glasgow. Apparently, Leith was supposed to meet them at the castle last night, but Leeya got a text out to him when we attacked. He won't go back there. He's in the wind."

"Shit."

"Yeah." Aiden clucked his cheek.

"I guess we'll hold out a few days and try again when she's weakened. If not, we kill her."

Mark poked his head out of Gregor's cell. "Now, the big question is, which one of us gets to kill her?" He pointed at himself. "I vote me."

We all raised our hands, then laughed as we looked around the room.

"She's the one that killed me," Owen said.

"She stalked me and tried to kill my fiancé," Aiden challenged.

I lifted my hand higher. "Um, she kidnapped me, and she *did* kill my boyfriend. *Did* kill trumps *almost* killed."

"I just really hate her." Mark shrugged. "She made fun of me for *years.*"

"I guess we'll flip for it when the time comes," I said with a laugh.

Everyone put their arms down and agreed.

Aiden stretched and blew out a breath. "We'll figure out Leeya later. In the meantime, we'll keep hunting for Leith through our contacts as well."

I patted Aiden on the shoulder and walked out of the dungeon. When Owen and I got upstairs, he looked distracted.

"You okay?"

"Yeah." He nodded his head, then slowly shook it. "No."

I pulled his hand in mine. "What's wrong?"

"All Gregor's talk about family and doing anything for them and watching you with your family… it's made me realize that because of this, I lost mine."

"I'm so sorry, Owen." I squeezed his hand. "Is there anything I can do?"

"No. I can't go home."

"Can't you? I mean, they're your family."

He blew out a puff of air. "They *were* my family. Now I'm the thing they hate the most."

"The last time you saw them, you were in a bloodlust frenzy and out of control. You're different now. You owe it to yourself to go home and try again. You owe them a chance to accept you as you are *now*. A powerful, under control hybrid."

He stared at his feet for a moment and then looked up. "You know what? Yeah. I do need to try again. And I want you to come with me to meet them."

My eyes saucered. "Your *werewolf* family?"

He nodded harder. "Yes. You're right. The last time I saw them, I was completely out of control. But now that I've got a handle on this whole hybrid thing, I should try again. Even if they don't accept me, at least their last memory of me won't be of some blood-thirsty lunatic. And I want them to meet you and see that you aren't the monster we'd all been led to believe. Will you come with me?"

"Of course." I slid my arms around his neck and pressed a kiss to his lips. "I will go anywhere with you, Owen. And if there is a chance we can get you your family back, then we have to take it."

Owen tucked a piece of hair behind my ear and kissed me again. "Thank you, Annella. I love you."

"I love you too," I said with a smile, then pressed my forehead against his.

And love him, I did—more than anything I'd ever imagined.

# Chapter Fifteen

## OWEN

I stepped onto the dock holding Annella's hand. Even though she'd offered the helicopter, I opted for the ferry. Riding it over to visit my family had been part of my life for the past decade since I'd moved to Scotland. Today especially, I needed to feel like me, not the monster who'd darkened their door last week.

I needed to show them I was still the same Owen they'd known all their lives.

What a different feeling it was this time around. Last time I was here, all I could think about was draining everyone around me of blood. I'd been terrified and frenzied, running around in hiding like a wild animal.

This time, I felt in control and settled with my new self. With my new life.

A life at Annella's side.

I'd thought about contacting my brothers over the past week to let them know I was still alive, but I couldn't bring myself to answer their messages pleading with me to tell them I was okay. Until now, I'd thought it better for them to think I was dead. Easier for my father at least to not envision his son running around draining humans of all their blood.

But now that I had my urges under control, I was ready to face my family again.

No. I couldn't just call and tell them I was okay. I had to *show* them I wasn't the monster who'd knocked on their door and nearly killed them the last time I was here.

At least I had to try. I wanted them to be part of my new life, and it pained me to think they might tell me I was no longer welcome in their world.

"Come on." I pulled her around a corner where no human could see. After making sure no one was around, we took off at a full sprint and raced down to my father's house. After we arrived, I stood holding her hand in the front yard for a minute before finding the courage to go inside.

It was Sunday night, which meant all three of my brothers and my father would be around the dinner table. A family tradition I already missed and hoped one day maybe I could be part of again.

Maybe.

With a stilling breath, I knocked on the door.

"If you're a Jehovah, take your bible and shove it up your arse," my father called, and I heard the deep laughter of my three brothers. "If you ain't sellin' something, then come on in."

"Why don't you wait out here for a minute," I said as I twisted the handle.

Annella nodded and kissed my cheek before I stepped inside. "Good luck. I love you."

I stared into the eyes of the woman I couldn't believe was mine. "I love you too."

Fear like I'd never known coursed through my body as I stepped into my childhood home. I walked toward the dining room and smelled the pizza and ribs, and I knew the three of them would be drinking beer.

A traditional Hunter family Sunday night feast.

We'd had the same thing every Sunday for years.

With one last deep breath, I stepped into the dining room.

"Hey, guys," I said as I pulled my lips into a tight, awkward smile.

"Jesus feck." Clutching his knife in his hand, my father leaped out of his chair. "What the hell are you doing here?"

Slowly, I raised my hands as I swept a gaze across my three stunned brothers and then focused it on my father. "I am so sorry about how I acted the last time I was here. I was in transition and didn't know how to control myself yet. I promise you, I'm safe now."

"Christ, Owen." Logan stood and rubbed a hand over the stubble that had grown on his face since I'd last seen him. "We thought you were dead."

"I tried," I said on a sigh, then chuckled. "God, did I try. Turns out, I'm really hard to kill."

Torin rose and appraised me with a wary eye. "You're okay now?"

"Yes. I swear. I'm completely in control of this thing. I won't hurt any of you."

Tears glistened in Colin's eyes as he took a cautious step toward me. "You're alive. I can't believe you're alive."

My little brother, who wasn't so little anymore, tossed his arms around my neck and squeezed me tight. I closed my eyes and returned the hug.

"I missed you guys. So much. And I'm so sorry for the

way I behaved the last time you saw me. I can't imagine what you must have thought."

Colin patted my back and pulled out of my embrace. "We didn't know what the hell to think, other than that you were dead. Fuck, Owen. We called your phone so many times, but it just went straight to voicemail. We spent all week mourning you." He pointed to the plate at my seat at the table. "We even set you out a beer and food tonight in memorial."

My heart hurt that they'd spent the week mourning me. I couldn't imagine what it would be like to lose one of my brothers. They meant everything to me.

"I'm so sorry I didn't answer. I wasn't ready to talk to you guys. Not until I got this under control. I didn't want to risk hurting you."

"So, you're good now?" Logan moved toward me. "No more crazed Owen?"

"Complete control." I lifted my hands and stepped forward to pull him into a hug.

He squeezed me tight, slapping me on the back before we broke apart.

Torin, the most cautious of my siblings, was the last to approach. "It's good to see you again, brother." He clapped me on the back and squeezed me tight. "We don't give a shit what the hell you are. Werewolf. Vampire. Faery. Unicorn. Doesn't fucking matter. You're our brother. Always will be."

As I hugged him, I looked over his shoulder into the eyes of my father.

They weren't the same welcoming ones I saw when my brothers looked back at me. Anguish still consumed his stare.

"Pops," I said as I broke out of my hug with Torin. "I'm

so sorry about how I behaved last time I was here. I can only imagine what you think of me. But it's me now. I'm still me. I'm still your son, Owen."

The agony in his eyes deepened. "No, you're not. My son died that night. You're a monster walking around in his skin." He shook his head, then looked away and whispered, "Just go. Get out of my house."

"Pops, please," I started, but he turned his back to me.

Lowering my eyes to the ground, I turned on my heel and started out of the dining room, but Logan caught me by my shoulder. He paused when he did, likely waiting for me to send him sailing across the room like the last time I'd been here, and he'd tried to stop me. But this time, I was in control.

"Pops," Logan said sharply. "Owen is our brother. He's your *son*. And we don't turn our back on family. Not for anything. Not fucking ever. Now get over yourself and turn around and look at him. Look at your *son*."

My father's shoulders lifted and rose with his deep breaths, but he just shook his head and continued staring at the wall.

"It's okay." I pressed my hand on Logan's that still rested on my shoulder. "I shouldn't have come back. He made that clear, and I should have respected his wishes."

"Fuck that," Torin said as he stepped to my side. "I can tell you're different from the last time you were here. I can see it in your eyes… the eyes of my brother. You belong here with your family. Pops, turn your stubborn arse around, and look at him. It's Owen."

My father ignored the plea.

"Dad." Colin stepped to my side as well. "Don't turn him away."

My father just shook his head again. "You're a vampire now. You kill people."

"No. I don't," I answered. "In fact, vampires don't kill people. It's the number one rule of their code."

"Bullshit." My father scoffed. "Vampires kill humans to survive. They always have and always will."

"Seriously," I said. "They really don't. Most vampires now drink blood from donated bags."

"Really? They aren't out slaughtering innocents?" Colin asked.

"Yes. Really. And I should know. I just spent over a week with them, and not one human suffered. They drilled it into my head that no vampire can harm a human. Ever."

My brothers passed a look between them.

"And even though they made sure I knew not to hurt humans as I fed, it turns out I really don't need to worry about it. I don't need human blood to survive."

My brothers mirrored a shocked expression.

"For real?" Torin said. "But I thought you were a vampire."

"I'm a hybrid it turns out. Part vampire, part wolf. And stronger than both. I can eat human food, go in the sun, and I prefer vampire blood to human."

"Holy fuck." Colin laughed. "You can drink vamps? Now that's something that should win your approval, Pops."

"Yep. I drink vampire blood. But I can also have that beer." I nudged my chin toward the place that had been set for me.

"Well then, sit the hell down and have one with us." Logan grinned.

I waited for my father's response, and slowly he turned around. Wary eyes met mine.

"You don't hurt humans?"

"No. Never."

"And what about werewolves? Will you hunt them now?"

I scoffed. "God, no. Fuck. The wolf inside me still wants to shred apart vampires, and in fact, he's taken out a few dozen already. But my wolf is alive and well, and he'll never hunt another wolf."

"You've killed vamps?" Colin's eyes widened.

"Oh, yeah. It's a seriously long story, but Annella, the woman who accidentally turned me, her family is at war with these bad vamps who want to harm humans. I've been helping them eradicate the rogue clan."

My father tipped his head, appraising me cautiously again.

Logan pulled out the chair that I usually sat in. The place at the table with a plate of food and a beer in my honor. "Have a seat, Owen. Tell us about it."

I looked at my father and waited for his response. With a low grumble, he nodded at the chair.

My brothers and father each took their seats. It felt strange to sit at this table and feel unwelcome, but my father's cautious gaze warned me not to get too comfortable here.

As I took a sip of my beer, he watched closely. "So, you aren't *really* a vampire? If you were, you couldn't drink that."

"Not completely. I'm something new. A blend of both species."

"And what of the vampires? Now that they know werewolves are alive, are they going to hunt us?"

All four sets of eyes stared at me, waiting.

"No. In fact, Lothaire Mackay, the original vampire, is still the leader. He's my friend now, and he said he is more than willing to talk to us about a truce so we can stop hiding and can start shifting again."

"Seriously?" Logan almost choked on the word.

"Seriously."

"Bullshit," my father said on a snort. "Vampires would never let us live if they knew we still existed."

"Actually, they would. And they don't hate us like we always thought. In fact, our history is a little skewed. We hunted them to near extinction. They only defended themselves to survive."

I grabbed a slice of pizza and my beer, then told my family the story of the vampires and the werewolves. They listened closely, all surprised by the facts our werewolf history had left out.

"So, you see? They weren't out to kill us, and they'd already been learning how to survive without harming humans. We drove them to defend themselves, and if the roles were reversed, we'd have slaughtered all of us too. It was survival, and they won. As long as we aren't going to hunt them, they don't care if we're out here in the world. Lothaire rules the vampires, and what he says goes. All we need to do is sit down with him and come up with a treaty."

"And you're seriously talking about Lothaire Mackay… as in *the* original clan of vampires? The ones we heard about all our lives?" Torin asked.

"Yes. That's who I've been with all week."

"What about *her*?" My father asked, his eyes narrowing. "What about Maighread Mackay? Please tell me you didn't make peace with that werewolf slaying psycho."

"Yeah! Did you meet *Maighread?*" Colin lifted his hands like claws and made the same monster face we'd made as kids when we told stories about her.

Oh, God. This was the second part of the night I'd

dreaded. Just as my father started to soften to my presence, I had to tell him that not only did I know Maighread Mackay, I'd fallen in love with her.

I cleared my throat and blew out a deep breath.

"Maighread Mackay is Annella. My girlfriend."

For a moment, I worried the table would be covered with eyeballs because everyone's popped open so wide, I thought they might fall out.

"Shut. The. Fuck. Up." Colin opened his mouth in an "o."

"You're shitting us," Logan said as he set down his beer. "No way."

I sucked on my cheek as I rocked back in my chair, balancing it on two legs. Something my father always yelled at me for. "Yep. Annella and Maighread are one and the same. But you need to understand she isn't the werewolf slaying psycho we heard about. She's actually kind and fiercely loyal. She's amazing, really. And I love her."

"Holy balls," Torin said before downing half his beer.

"And…" I gritted my teeth and grinned sheepishly. "She's outside waiting to meet you."

"Outside?" My father bellowed. "You brought an original vampire to *my* house? She'll kill us all!"

All three of my brothers looked ready to jump into battle in a moment's notice, but I lifted my hands and gestured for them to stay seated.

"Annella won't hurt you. I'm telling you. Everything we know about vampires is wrong. Dead wrong. If you just give her a chance, I know she will win you over like she did me. And my wolf. He claimed her as his mate."

"Your wolf did *what*?" Logan said.

As werewolves, they understood what it meant to have

your wolf claim a mate. It was never questioned who your wolf chose, and everyone in the pack respected the bond.

"Your wolf claimed her as a mate? Maighread Mackay. An original werewolf slaying vampire?" Torin asked, then slammed the rest of his beer.

"He did. And that should tell you right there that she's not the monster you think she is. My wolf recognizes she's not a danger to our kind. And so do I. And so will you if you'll allow me to invite her inside."

"No way," my father spit out. "I'm not having a *vampire* at my table. I'm still trying to get used to having *you* here."

"She's his mate, Pops," Logan said. "We don't question the bond. If his wolf chose her, then she's part of our pack, and we welcome her into our lives. That's the rule. Are you really going to go against that?"

His jaw ticked as he ground his teeth while I waited for his answer.

"Fine. Invite her in. But if she kills your brothers, don't say I didn't warn you."

I chuckled and shook my head. "She won't. Annella," I called, knowing she could hear me and had heard everything we'd said. "Please come in."

The front door creaked, and I got up and hurried to meet her and walk her in. She gave me a wary glance, but I encouraged her with a smile and an arm around her shoulder as I walked her into the dining room.

When we got there, my family stared blinking at the woman our kind had been created to kill.

She lifted her hand in an awkward wave. "Hey. I'm Annella."

It was so surreal seeing her standing in my childhood dining room.

And surreal to see the most powerful woman on the planet looking nervous.

"Come sit by me." I guided her around the table, then pulled her chair right next to me.

We both sat down, then she placed her hands in her lap as she looked across the stunned faces staring back at her.

"So, this is Maighread Mackay." Torin broke the ice.

"That's me." She shrugged and picked up the knife from beside my plate, twisting it between her fingers. "The were-wolf slaying psycho."

For a moment, everyone froze, but then her smile stretched across her face, and she laughed and handed me the knife. After a collective sigh of relief, my brothers joined her.

"Jesus, Mary, and Joseph," Logan said on a chuckle, "I thought for a second we were gonna be vampire fodder."

"Nah." She laughed. "Killing unicorns is where it's at these days."

They laughed along with her, and I saw the tension easing from everyone's shoulders as they started to joke back and forth with her.

Almost everyone's shoulders.

My father still watched her with cautious eyes for the better part of an hour, sizing her up as she and my brothers took turns razzing each other like old friends.

"Mr. Hunter," Annella said, turning her attention to my father. "You raised a good man." She slid her hand over mine and squeezed. "A really good man. A better man than I've met in over six hundred years. You don't need to worry about him turning into a monster. It's impossible. Owen is a good soul, and he loves you. He loves his whole family."

My brothers smiled as she passed a glance at all of them.

"Owen's heart broke when he felt like he disappointed you. I saw the wreckage. I was the one who helped piece him back together. And I hope that now you can see the boy you raised is still the man sitting at your table. The best man. And I hope you'll embrace him again like you once did. You don't have to accept me. I understand if you can't, and I'm okay with that. But you need to accept him. Accept him for who he is now and love him like you always have. Love him like I do."

Silence settled over the table. My father swallowed as he stared at her, and I saw the shimmer of tears glistening in his eyes.

"I do love you, Owen," he finally said, his words barely a whisper. "I love you, son. And I'm sorry I let my bias toward vampires force me to turn my back on you. Can you forgive me?"

I swallowed over the lump in my throat as I nodded and pushed back my chair. My father and I rose, each stepping forward until we met in the middle, folding together in a hug.

"I'm so sorry, father. I didn't ask for this, but I hope you can continue accepting me the way I am now. And accepting her... the woman I love. My mate."

He patted my back before breaking apart our hug. His attention turned to Annella, and we all held our breaths as he stepped to her side and reached out his hand.

Annella eyed it up before taking it and letting him pull her to her feet.

He looked into her eyes and smiled. "I may be a stubborn arse, but I'll admit when I'm wrong. And I was wrong about you and your kind. It may take me a while to truly accept all this, but I will in time."

"I promise you we aren't the monsters you think us. And

I will keep working on showing you that as we get to know each other."

"I don't doubt it." He smiled slightly. "Thank you for saving my boy. I owe you a debt of gratitude. And I'm honored that he, and his wolf, have chosen you for their mate. Welcome to the pack, Annella."

She let out the trapped breath as she smiled. My father wrapped his arms around her, and she returned the embrace, squeezing him tight.

"Ay!" Logan cheered, and my brothers joined him.

They clinked their beer bottles together as they rose to their feet, then each took a turn welcoming her to the pack with a hug. She looked so petite as each one of my brothers towered over her and wrapped her in their muscular arms.

After they'd all welcomed her to the family, we sat back down. Annella and I spent hours talking with them, laughing as we told them about how we'd met, how I'd awoken on her floor, about Clan Lennox, and all the adventures we'd already been on. My brothers told her about their jobs and their lives but were most curious about her centuries on this earth. They wanted to know all about what life used to be like.

After we'd exhausted ourselves late into the night with the conversation I'd missed so much, I slapped my hands on my thighs and pushed up.

"I hate to cut this short, but we have to catch the ferry back before sunrise. Annella can't go in the sun."

"Yet." She lifted a finger. "Next time I see you guys, we're hitting the beach. I'll kick your arses at volleyball."

"Deal!" Colin laughed, and my brothers joined him.

"It was really nice meeting you all," Annella said. "Thank you for welcoming me into your family. My brother will be really excited to speak to you guys about spreading the word about a treaty. We don't want to harm you, and we don't want you to have to hide from us anymore."

"We appreciate that, Annella," my father said as he rose. "I look forward to meeting your family someday."

"You will, Mr. Hunter."

"Please. Call me Jack," he said. "Mr. Hunter is too formal for family."

She smiled and pulled him in for a hug.

My heart swelled as I watched the woman I loved hugging the most important people in my life.

"Well, we've got some vampires to kill, so we'd better get going." Annella broke from her hug with Torin.

"If you need any help killing those vampires, give us a call. Killing vampires is kinda why we exist." He grinned.

"We may take you up on that." Annella tipped her head.

"Just say the word and let us off our leashes. I'd be honored to fight at your side," Logan said.

"Thanks, guys." I made my way through, hugging each one. "I really appreciate your help. And I appreciate you letting me back into your lives. I missed you guys. A lot."

"We missed you too, brother." Logan patted my back. "And don't be a stranger with that girl of yours. We need some feminine energy around here. This entire house reeks like testosterone."

"Maybe you guys should find a mate of your own and fix that problem?" I arched an eyebrow, but they all shook their heads and laughed.

"Women? Fuck that." Torin laughed. "I don't need some woman telling me what to do."

"Hear, hear," Colin agreed while Logan nodded.

"You'll find your mates, and when you do, I look

forward to seeing all three of you carrying their purses," Annella teased as she nodded toward hers.

They howled with laughter when I slid it over my shoulder.

"Laugh now," I said as I adjusted the red purse. "Your time is coming, boys."

"Get your arse out of here!" Logan kicked me in the butt as we headed toward the door.

"I'll be back soon."

"Sunday night dinner. You'd both better be here." My father pointed a finger at each of us.

The simple invitation felt like the biggest one in the world.

"Wouldn't miss it for the world, Pops."

He shook my hand and clapped my back. "See you soon, son. And it was nice to meet you, Annella. I look forward to you whipping the rest of my boys into shape too."

"Challenge accepted." She waggled her eyebrows before kissing him on the cheek.

Annella and I walked out of my house, and I grabbed her by the hand and pulled her into my arms.

"I fucking love you," I said before I bent her backward with my kiss.

"I fucking love you too," she answered between kisses.

"Thank you for doing this with me."

"It was great to meet your family. I love them."

"And they love you. Just like me."

She smiled and squeezed around my neck, rising on her toes to give me one last kiss before we raced back to catch the next ferry home.

# Chapter Sixteen

## ANNELLA

"Your dad reminds me so much of Lothaire." I swung my hand, moving Owen's with me as we walked hand-in-hand down the ferry dock. "Like a big, terrifying Grizzly bear on the outside, but a teddy bear on the inside."

"That's my Pops," he said with the same smile that hadn't left his face since we'd left his family home.

When I'd been training Owen all week in the cabin, the agony he'd felt over his father's rejection had been enough to make him want to end his existence. Knowing how much it mattered to him to have his father's love and approval, I knew how much tonight meant to him.

And to me.

I'd felt like a knobby-kneed high school girl meeting her boyfriend's parents for the first time, and it had terrified me. Not only were they his family, but they were werewolves—my sworn enemy. But by the end of the night, they felt like my family too. A family I couldn't wait to belong to.

I tugged on his hand. "Let's buy a boat. Since you don't

want to helicopter over there, we can take it over and visit your family more often without having to wait for this stupid ferry. It's a pain in the arse having to follow the schedule when I need to worry about getting somewhere safe before daylight again."

"Soon, you won't have to." Owen smiled.

"You're right." The thought of the freedom that would come without the curse made me smile from the inside out. "But we should still get a boat. I want to visit your family a lot."

"They really loved you."

"And I loved them."

"But no one loves anyone more than I love you." Owen slipped his arm around my waist and yanked me against him, claiming me again with his kiss.

"And your wolf?" I asked between kisses. "Tell me about that."

A bashful look passed over his face. "You heard that, huh?"

"Sorry. I didn't mean to eavesdrop, but I had to know how it was going in there. Now tell me, what did you mean by your 'wolf claimed me as its mate?'"

"I didn't want to freak you out because it's pretty much like popping the question to a girl on the first date."

I widened my eyes. "That serious, huh?"

"*More* serious. And I know you're a little hesitant about relationships, and me, so I didn't want to tell you and freak you out."

"What does it mean?"

"For werewolves, there is only one mate for us. And when our wolf claims its mate, there can never be another. That's it. Forever."

"Forever?" I arched a brow. "What if your mate dies?"

Owen lifted his shoulders and dropped them. "Then we live the rest of our lives alone, like my dad."

"What if your mate doesn't return the affection?"

"It's rare. Even though they don't claim a mate at first glance, and our wolves take their time to be sure, they instantly recognize their mate. But on the rare chance our mate rejects us, then we spend the rest of our lives alone."

"Seriously?" I choked. "If I was to break up with you, you'd never date again?"

I shook my head. "No. Never. There can only be one for us, and once we find our mate, we'll never love another. We live and will die for the one we love. Why? You planning on breaking up with me?" He challenged me with a playful look.

"No. Hell no." I rose on my tiptoes and kissed him. "But knowing you will literally never be with another woman but me, is pretty intense."

"Exactly." He shook his head. "That's why I didn't want to tell you. I thought it might scare you off."

"If you were any other man on the planet, it would. I'd be hauling arse for the hills."

"But with me?" He stroked my cheek, and I pressed it into his hand.

"But with you, it just confirms the way I feel about you. For me, this is it. You're it. Always and forever, Owen."

His smile lit up the dark around us.

"I love you, Maighread Annella Mackay. And I always will."

We kissed again, then I glanced at the sky. "We should probably hurry if we're going to try to get back to the castle before sunrise. Or we can just go to the apartment a few blocks up."

"Whatever you want," Owen said as he took my hand.

Even though I knew it would be easiest to go to the apartment, Leeya was back at the castle, and I was itching to have another go at her. If we made it back to the castle before sunrise, I could start my fun sooner.

"It will be close, but if we go fast, we can make it back to the castle. If we cut it too close, we've got a couple hideaways along the way I can duck into for the day."

"Whatever you say, baby. Just lead the way."

I pulled Owen around the corner into the alley, and after a quick glance over my shoulder to make sure no one could see us, I prepared to sprint away. But before I could take a step, a bright light blinded me, and pain seared through every inch of my skin.

"A UV light!" I screamed as I tried to bolt to safety, but another light stopped me in my tracks.

I saw the shadows of the vampires holding the lights, and from the looks of it, there were dozens appearing all around us. Too many for even Owen and I to fight. And I didn't stand a chance in the lights.

"Annella!" Owen shouted, reaching for me. Before his hand took mine, a giant chain flew past me and wrapped around his upper body, clamping his arms to his sides.

Owen roared, shifting into his hybrid form and snapping the chain from his body. Another chain wrapped around him. Then another. And another.

One by one, the vampires surrounding us tossed chains around him, binding his arms and his feet.

"Owen!" I screamed as I struggled to get to my feet and fight for him.

"Run, Annella!" he shouted as he raged against his restraints. "Run!"

The UV light weakened me to the point running wasn't

possible. I clawed at the pavement as I struggled to get to Owen.

"I'm not leaving you," I said as the pain in my skin reached unbearable heights.

"I can't break them, Annella! Don't worry about me. Just go. Go!" he screamed.

I knew I only had seconds left before the multiple lights would cause me to burst into flames. And then there was nothing I could do to save him.

I'd be dead.

Knowing he needed me to survive so I could get help, I dug deep into my resolve and found the last remnants of my strength. "I'll be back for you!"

With a powerful push, I launched myself out of the UV light and sprinted to the ocean, plunging beneath the waves to cool my burning skin and hide from the vampires I could hear diving in behind me. They grabbed at me, but I fought them off then darted through the water at speeds no regular vampire could sustain, staying under for several minutes. When I knew I'd lost them, I shot onto the shore and pressed my hands into my thighs while I regained my senses.

Owen. They had him.

And by *they*, I meant Leith and his influenced army. I didn't know how they'd found us, but that didn't matter right now. What mattered was finding him. I reached for my phone to text my family to race down and start hunting for him, but only saw a black, dead screen.

"Fuck!" I shouted as I tossed it back into the ocean that had fried it.

A quick glance to the sky, and I knew I might not make it home in time. But my impromptu swim stole my opportunity to call my family and tell them to start hunting for

Owen. If I didn't get home now, no one would know he was missing for another fourteen hours.

Fourteen hours before we could even start the hunt.

No. I had to get home. Tell my family.

Torture Leeya for the answer to my question…

*Where the fuck did they take him?*

Gritting my teeth, I pushed off into my fastest sprint ever. My love for Owen and my need to get him back safe fired through my muscles as I raced the sunrise. As the minutes ticked on, the sky lightened by the second. If I miscalculated my abilities, no one would ever know they had taken Owen.

I'd be dead.

I couldn't let that happen. I had to find him.

The final stretch home, the golden rays of the sun peeked above the horizon. I ran harder, pushing myself to impossible limits. As I raced up the long sloping hill to our castle, the sun's rays nipped at my heels while they spread across the countryside. I could feel the heat threatening to ignite my skin.

Owen's face flashed into my mind, and my need to see it again reignited the strength I needed to outrun the sun. With one last push, I launched at the castle door, smashing through it and rolling across the floor and into the corridor to the dungeon.

I didn't even take a second to catch my breath or appreciate the impossible feat I'd just performed. Instead, I flashed to the cell at the end of the dungeon and pushed Aiden and Throne out of the way.

"Where is he?" I screamed as I grabbed Leeya by the neck.

"Annella? What's going on?" Aiden said as he stepped back to my side.

"You'd better fucking tell me where Leith would take Owen, and you'd better tell me right fucking now, Leeya."

I popped out my fangs and snarled, tightening my grip on her neck.

"Who has Owen?" Thorne asked as he flashed to my side.

"Leith," I growled. "They took him. They ambushed us outside the ferry dock."

"What?" Thorne and Aiden echoed.

"Tell me right fucking now, Leeya." I tightened my grip on her throat. "I know he must have been planning this since he saw Owen fight. You know where he'd take him. Now tell me right fucking now!"

Instead of fear flickering in her eyes, I saw the resolution to resist me deepen.

"Good for Leith. I knew my brother would figure out how to catch him. There are hundreds of places he could have taken him. You'll never find them."

"Fuck!" I screamed as I slapped the back of my hand across her face. The force of my blow knocked her unconscious, and she slumped forward in the chair.

"Tell us what happened," Aiden said as he grabbed my hand.

"They jumped us on the dock when we got back to Scotland. They must have followed us to the ferry and waited for our return because they were ready. They had those fucking UV lights again, and I couldn't fight back."

"Do you have anything of his that Catrain could track?" Thorne asked. "She was up all night trying to find a way to track Leith, and she just went to bed, but I can call up there and wake her."

I shook my head. "I don't have anything of his. How stupid is that?"

"From now on, we all leave a belonging in a safe. Then Catrain can always track us."

"Good idea," Aiden said. "But that doesn't help us now."

*Track him.*

"Hand me your phone." I opened my hand, and Aiden dropped his phone in.

After a quick Google search, I found Owen's father's number and dialed it.

"Hello?" he answered.

"Jack? It's me. Annella."

"Annella? Is everything okay, hon?"

My lip quivered, and tears threatened to spring from my eyes. I swallowed over the lump in my throat. "They took him. They took Owen."

His already deep voice dropped several octaves. "Who took my son?"

"The vampires we told you about jumped us at the Scottish ferry dock. They want to find out what he is and use him to their end. We can't let that happen. We can't let them hurt him. I love him, Jack. Please help me. I need you and your sons to track him."

A long pause stretched out between us that felt like an eternity.

"I'll call the boys. We'll hop on the next boat and track him. We'll find him, Annella."

I breathed a sigh of relief. "Thank you. Bring a belonging of his. In case you can't find him, Catrain can run a tracking spell. But if you find him first, just call me on this number. It's my brother Aiden's phone. Tell us where you are, and as long as the sun is set, we'll be there. Just don't engage until we're there."

"I'll call you as soon as we locate him. Don't worry, hon. No one takes my son and gets away with it. We'll find him."

He hung up without another word.

"Who was that?" Aiden asked as I handed him back his phone.

"Owen's father. They can use their wolf senses to track him."

"Great idea," Thorne said. "If they are even half as good as he is, they should have no trouble locating him. In the meantime, I'll alert the others and see if they have any other ideas to find him."

"Thank you, Thorne," I said on a sigh. "We have to find him."

Aiden squeezed my shoulder. "We will. And there's a very good chance Leith took him to trade for Leeya, so he won't kill him."

I lifted my eyebrows and nodded. Not only did Leith want to find out what Owen was, but he could use Owen as leverage to release his sister.

I hated to admit it, but Leith was smart. Two birds with one stone.

At least that meant Owen was probably alive.

For now.

---

After spending the day tossing and turning in my cell trying to get some rest so I'd be ready for the fight I intended to bring to Leith, I felt the sun set. I stretched and climbed off the cot I'd used as a bed to nap in and walked toward Thorne and Aiden.

"Any word from the Hunters?"

Aiden nodded. "They called a couple hours ago. They

picked up his trail, and they were gonna follow it and call us when they found him."

Lothaire, Mark, and Grizella appeared beside us after coming down from their light-tight rooms.

"Have they found Owen?" Lothaire asked before taking a long swig of blood from a cup.

"No. But they're looking," I said as I wrapped my arms around my big brother's neck and hugged him tight, fighting the tears that wanted to pour out again.

He squeezed me back. "Owen is strong, and we won't stop hunting until we find him. He'll be okay."

"He has to. I love him." I sniffled.

"Why would they take him?" Mark asked.

"Probably to trade for Leeya, but also because of what he is," I answered with certainty. "There's no doubt Leith wants to know so he can use him to his own ends."

Lothaire's face darkened. "That can't happen."

"We know," Aiden said.

"And you're sure I can't track him?" Catrain asked as she walked in with Emilia at her side.

"No. I don't have anything that belongs to him, but his family is bringing something that does in case they can't find him by…" I paused and glanced at Leeya, who listened intently. "*Looking* for him."

Lothaire nodded his understanding.

"They won't find him." Leeya snorted.

"Shut up, Leeya-ch," Mark said, then flicked her on the forehead.

The phone rang, and I grabbed it from Aiden.

"Hello?"

"Annella. We found him," Jack said.

My heart lifted at the words. I flashed away with the phone far enough that Leeya couldn't eavesdrop.

"Thank God. Where are you?"

"I don't understand the newfangled technology, but Colin said he'd ping you the location as soon as I hang up."

"Good idea. Once you send that, we'll be on our way. Just don't try to save him until we get there. Leith has been building an army, and there could be a lot of vamps."

He blew out a long breath. "Oh, there are a *lot* of vamps. We're watching them now. At least a hundred, maybe two."

"A couple hundred?" My eyes widened. "We're original vampires, so we're significantly stronger than them, but we can't take that many without help. I can't ask you and your—"

"I'll stop you right there. We're fighting for Owen. And it's a full moon tonight, so we'll be stronger than every last one of you."

"Thank you, Jack. I appreciate knowing you're on our side."

"I'll have Colin pong or ping you or whatever the hell he's doing, and we'll see you soon."

"We'll be there."

I hung up the phone and flashed back to my family, handing it back to Aiden. "They found him. They're sending the location, but there are hundreds of them."

Leeya smirked, and I wanted to smack her.

"Hundreds?" Lothaire arched an eyebrow.

"Yes. But Owen's family will fight, and it's…" I stopped when I glanced at Leeya and then looked up toward the ceiling.

Lothaire got my meaning and nodded. "Well, that will certainly help."

"Should we call in some of our allies?" Aiden asked.

Lothaire shook his head. "I don't trust anyone that isn't

in this room at the moment. We can't risk someone giving Leith a heads up. With all of us and Owen's family, we stand a chance."

"I can help," Gregor called from the other cell.

We all exchanged a look and then went in by him. When we entered the cell, he looked up from his restraints.

"I can help. I swear to you, I don't want to help Leith. I want him dead, so I can get my sister back. I'll swear loyalty to you and fight at your side as long as you promise to help me save my sister."

"Traitor!" Leeya shouted, but Grizella popped her head back out and silenced her with a glare.

"How could we ever trust you?" Thorne asked.

"I know it's asking a lot, but I swear to you I want to help."

We all looked to Mark, who twisted his lips up as he stared at Gregor.

"Mark? What do you think?" Aiden asked. "You spent all night down here talking to him."

Mark placed his hands on his head and blew out a deep breath. "I…" He paused and looked at Lothaire for a long moment, then dropped his arms and shook his head. "I believe him. I think we should trust him." He paused again. "Or maybe I just *want* to believe him."

"Trust your gut, Mark," Emilia said. "What does it say?"

Mark looked at Gregor and slumped his shoulders. "I trust him. I do. I don't want to be 'that guy' and just forgive everything that happened when he bats his eyes at me, but deep down, I really do trust that he'll help us."

"I will, Mark. I'll fight for you. I'll always fight for you."

They exchanged a soft smile, and Mark turned to

Lothaire. "Do it. Free him. I'll take responsibility if he betrays us."

Lothaire nodded for Mark to release Gregor, and he quickly unlocked the chains. When he finished, Gregor stood up and wrapped his arms around Mark, hugging him tightly.

"You won't regret this, Mark. I'm going to spend the rest of my life making it up to you."

"I'm holding you to that," Mark said. "Just please don't fool me twice and make me wear the shame suit, okay?"

Gregor leaned back and took Mark's face in his hands. He pressed a long, soft kiss against Mark's lips. Mark nearly melted into a puddle of contentment as he sighed.

"I will never betray you again," Gregor said between kisses. "Never."

"I believe you." Mark wrapped his arms around Gregor's neck and kissed him again.

"Come now and swear fealty to me." Lothaire interrupted their embrace.

Gregor kissed Mark one last time and then kneeled in front of Lothaire.

"I swear to you, Lothaire Mackay, that I will fight at your side and give my life to protect you and your family." His gaze drifted to Mark, who clutched a hand to his chest. "All I ask in return is that you help me rescue my sister."

"You have my word," Lothaire said, pressing a hand onto Gregor's massive shoulder. "When we kill Leith, her compulsion will be broken, and she'll be free."

"Thank you," Gregor said, then stood and returned to Mark's side. They held hands and turned to face us.

"Owen needs us." I passed a gaze over all of them. "I love him, and I know that each one of you knows what that feels like."

They all looked at their partners, the loves of their lives, and nodded.

"We need to save him and bring him home. So, everyone go suit up, and we head out. We're not coming back without him."

They all nodded, and then Thorne jutted a head toward Leeya. "What should we do with her?"

I stepped over into her cell and smirked. "Well, Leeya. Looks like we found Leith without you. Your potential usefulness is officially defunct."

Even though I knew we needed her as a hostage, I still enjoyed the way her eyes widened as I stepped toward her.

"Wait," Aiden said. "We can't kill her."

Leeya's eyes lit up when she looked at him… the man she'd always love.

"Yet. Don't forget we may need her alive if we fail and we need to negotiate a hostage exchange."

Her brow furrowed as she realized it wasn't some connection to her that made him want to save her life. It was a temporary reprieve until her usefulness ran out.

"But the minute we don't need you anymore…" I lifted my lip as I dragged my finger across the base of my neck. Leeya narrowed her eyes in return.

Lothaire crossed his arms. "We should have her nearby for a trade if things go south. Aiden, secure her and bring her with us."

"Yeah. We can leash her up and make her follow like a *dog*," Mark taunted as he panted at her.

"I'll fucking kill you," she snapped and struggled against her chains.

"Zip it, Leeya. You run with us and keep your mouth shut, or I'll put you down on the spot," Aiden said as he undid the chains securing her to the chair and the floor, but leaving the chains keeping her wrists bound behind her back.

Leeya grumbled but moved along with him as he tugged her forward.

"Don't you dare lose her, Aiden," I warned. "We can't have her escaping and warning Leith. Owen's life depends on it."

"I won't, Nella. I've got her."

"Good." I nodded. "Now, everyone weapon up. We need every advantage we can get. Meet out front, and then we go to save my Owen."

They all nodded their understanding and took off to suit up. I did the same, slipping into my black leather outfit and sliding my swords and daggers into their holsters. When I got done, I raced downstairs and met my family out front.

"You have the location?" I said to Aiden.

He showed me the map on his phone, and I nodded. "Then let's do this."

I took off at a sprint with my family charging beside me and Leeya reluctantly running with us.

*I'm coming, baby.*

## Chapter Seventeen

ANNELLA

"There." I pointed to the four men leaning against the building down the street. "That's Owen's family."

"Lead the way," Lothaire said.

We crept through the shadows in the warehouse district until we got to them.

Not wanting to startle them, I whispered, "It's me, Annella."

"Shit, you scared me." Jack spun around as he grabbed his chest.

"Sorry." I wrapped my arms around him and hugged him tightly. "Thank you so much for coming."

Logan, Torin, and Colin all embraced me as well. After greeting them, I turned around and pointed at my family.

"Hunter family meet the Mackay family. This is Lothaire, Grizella, Aiden, Emilia, Thorne, Catrain, Mark, and Gregor. This is Leeya. Ignore her. She's more like filth than family."

She glared at me and scoffed.

Ignoring her, I turned back and pointed to Owen's family. "And this is Jack, Logan, Torin, and Colin."

An awkward silence passed between the two families sworn to be enemies. I held my breath while I waited for someone to make the first move.

"It's a pleasure to meet you, Mr. Hunter." Lothaire stepped forward and extended a hand.

They matched each other in height and strong, masculine appearance. If they weren't enemies from opposing species, you could have mistaken them for brothers.

Jack's bearded jaw tightened as he stared at the hand of his rival.

Everyone watched in silence, waiting for the two enormous men to seal their alliance.

"Call me Jack," he said as he slowly took Lothaire's hand in his.

"Nice to meet you, Jack."

Lothaire and Jack shook hands, each giving each other a gentle nod of understanding.

"Thank you for coming to help bust out my boy," Jack said.

"We've grown quite fond of Owen. We want to help set him free. And please understand, we hold no ill will toward the werewolves. Please know you can shift freely in front of us."

"We appreciate the sentiment." Jack nodded. "We've gotten a good look at what's going on in there, and it ain't pretty. You're gonna need all four of us in wolf form to have a chance."

"Werewolves?" Leeya gasped. "Is that what Owen is? A werewolf? They still exist? I *knew* there was something—"

I covered her mouth and leaned into her face. "The deal

was to keep your mouth shut. Now shut it, or I'll let them have some werewolf fun with you."

She glanced at the Hunter boys, then stopped struggling against my hand.

"How bad is it?" Aiden asked them.

Logan stepped forward. "I've got experience in recon, so I snuck up and looked. They are all in that warehouse in the center there." He pointed into the distance at the largest building in the area. "Two stories with an outdoor balcony around the second one that gives a good entry point and the advantage of height. If we enter from the outside, we can slip through the second-floor windows. We've got an unobstructed view of the entire interior of the warehouse from up there. Seems all the vampires are on the first floor."

"And Owen?" I asked, my heart palpating at the thought of him held prisoner.

"He's there. They've got him strung up tight in the center of the warehouse. Chains stretch from posts and poles all over the building. It's like an unbreakable spiderweb he's caught up in, and there's no way we can sneak in and free him. There's no cover on the ground floor. Just a big empty warehouse."

"You've gotten a good look," Thorne said. "What do you think is the best plan?"

Logan nodded to Torin, who crossed his arms and stared at the building. "I work with the ERU, a tactical unit in Ireland. In my opinion, surprise is our best bet, and some kind of big entrance to stun them that can take out a bunch at once would be ideal, but I don't have any grenades or explosives."

"I do," Catrain said.

They furrowed their brow as they looked at her. "I'm a witch, and I can control the elements. I can produce a massive fireball that can take out a whole bunch of them at once. It takes a minute for me to generate the power needed, but once I do, I can whip it down into the most concentrated cluster of vamps."

"Will it kill them?" Colin asked. "I'm a firefighter, so I know a giant fire explosion could kill most people, but I thought nothing could kill vampires but beheading?"

I nodded my head. "Original vampires can't, but these aren't originals. With every subsequent generation of vampires, they are weaker and easier to kill. Leith Lennox is only a couple generations away so he'll likely withstand it, but the generation below him, these vamps he turned, shouldn't be able to."

"Then I say we bust in throwing fire," Logan said.

"I can throw one big explosion, and then it will take me another minute to restore enough power to do another spell."

"Hopefully, one is all we need to get the upper hand," Torin said. "We'll sneak around the perimeter, scale the walls, and get into position. We'll shift into wolf form on the ground so we're ready when we hit the top floor. Catrain, on my mark, you'll rain down fire, and the rest of us will use the confusion to attack and take out as many as we can while we break Owen's chains. If you see a chain. Break it. Once we've broken enough, he should be able to do the rest himself."

"It's a good plan," Lothaire agreed. "Does anyone have any concerns before we go in?"

"Do they have UV lights?" Mark asked.

Logan shook his head. "I didn't notice any, but that doesn't mean they aren't there. I wasn't exactly looking for them."

I looked at the Hunter boys and Emilia, Aiden, Thorne,

and Catrain. "You guys can handle the lights. If you see any bright lights go on, focus your energy on breaking them, so the rest of us don't burn."

They all nodded their understanding.

"That's my boy in there," Jack said as he looked us all over. "Now, I know our kinds haven't gotten along in the past, but I need to know you're gonna fight for my son."

Lothaire pressed a hand on Jack's shoulder. "Annella loves him, which means he's our family now too. We'll die before we give up trying to save him. You have my word. And I have your word you won't turn on us when this is all over?"

Jack gave him a sharp nod. "You have our word."

They exchanged a look of mutual understanding.

"Then let's move out," Logan commanded, and his vast experience as a military man shone through.

"What do we do with her?" Aiden gestured to Leeya.

Lothaire blew out a breath. "If it's as bad as Logan says, we need everyone in there fighting, so no one can stay behind with Leeya. We're far enough away Leith can't hear her even if she screams for help, but let's shove something in her mouth just in case. We'll tie her up tight and use her as a hostage if we fail."

"We won't fail," I said decidedly. "We will save Owen and put an end to Leith Lennox once and for all. Then you're next."

I turned my glare to Leeya. Her eyes narrowed as they met mine, then her gaze darted toward the warehouse, and I saw the intent in her eyes.

Before I could open my mouth to tell Aiden she was going to run for it, she used her vamp speed to slam her shoulder into him, dislodging him just enough she could yank the chain from his hands.

"Leith!" she screamed as she bolted toward the warehouse. "Leith! They're coming for you!"

"Fuck!" Aiden shouted as he lunged for the chain dangling behind her, but he missed it by only an inch.

Panic surged inside me. If she kept up that yelling and got much closer to the warehouse, there's no doubt Leith's vamp hearing would pick up on her cries.

And if she alerted him and got away, they'd kill Owen instantly.

"Stop her!" I shouted as I sprinted forward, and my family raced along with me. Leeya dodged my attempt to snatch her hair and darted the other way, narrowly escaping a grab from Lothaire. As I dug down into my original vampire speed to overtake her, she zigged the other way, just slipping past Thorne as he launched toward her.

"Leith!" she screamed again. "He's a werewolf! Leith!"

"Don't let her get away!" I shouted as she veered back toward the warehouse.

I pushed myself forward to top speed, and just when I reached out to snag her and put a stop to her flee for freedom, Mark darted out in front of her. With one long slice of his sword, he parted her head from her neck.

We all gasped and slid to a stop as Leeya's head rolled past our feet and disappeared behind the dumpsters.

Mark looked shocked as he glanced at his bloodied sword and then at the lifeless corpse at his feet. "Oops." He grimaced as he sucked the air through his teeth and bit down on his forefinger. "I probably shouldn't have killed our hostage."

With a slow sigh, I shook my head.

His grimace intensified. "Sorry, guys. My bad. It was an accident. She was getting away, and I totally panicked. And, honestly, I really hated that bitch."

We still stared dumbstruck at the quick turn of events.

Jack looked down at her body. "Well, I don't know who she was or what she did, but that was certainly one way to keep her restrained."

"It was Leith's sister. Among *many* other reasons we hated her, she's the one who killed Owen," I said.

Jack glared at her body, then spit on the ground. "Good riddance then. We don't need her. We're gonna go get my boy without her."

"Damn straight we are," I agreed. "And now we have no choice but to win this war, so let's go."

We all took one last look at Leeya's body as we passed it while we crouched low and moved with stealth along the buildings surrounding the warehouse. When we arrived at the one holding Owen, Torin paired us off two at a time and pointed to different sides of the building. I went with Colin, moving quietly until we reached the edge.

"I'm gonna shift now, so don't freak out and kill me," he whispered as we pressed against the wall.

"I'm not gonna kill you, you arse. You just don't go all werewolf and kill me." I pointed at the full moon illuminating the sky.

"You're my sister now, and Owen's mate. I'd sooner kill myself than harm a hair on your head."

I smiled and kissed his cheek. "I'm glad to be part of your family. Now let's go save your brother."

Before Colin shifted, I diverted my eyes.

"What are you doing? Scared to see me shift or something?"

"Um, I don't exactly want to see you naked. No offense."

He chuckled and shook his head. "Neither did the Picts

who created us. Part of our magic involves our clothes shifting with us. I don't need to get naked."

"Oh." I smiled as I turned back around. "I've only seen wolves in wolf form. I've never witnessed one shift."

"It's quick and painless… and I won't be naked. But I can't communicate with you after I shift."

"Can you communicate with each other?"

"Yeah. It's like ESP between members of a pack, but since you aren't a wolf, I can understand you, but I can't talk with you. But just know I'm watching your back. We all are."

"Thanks, Colin. I'm watching yours too."

With one last smile, he lowered his head and lifted his lips. It mesmerized me as I watched his body morph into the giant black wolf that stood almost as tall as me. His glowing green eyes locked with mine, and I couldn't help but have flashbacks to the last time I'd seen a wolf up close.

I'd killed it a few seconds later.

I reminded myself that it was Colin inside the terrifying creature capable of ending me in seconds.

Colin lowered his head, and even though I couldn't hear the words, I knew he was reassuring me. I nodded my understanding and pointed to the exterior balcony above us.

Colin launched off the ground, pushing off the brick wall and landing on the balcony with ease. I scaled up behind him, crouching beside him as we both peeked in the windows separating us from the vampires filling the expansive room below.

And in the center of them… Owen.

Even with his incredible strength, there wasn't any way he could break free without our help. Chains encased his waist, legs, and wrists, and they stretched across the room to every metal and concrete post in the building. I saw now what Logan meant by no cover. There was no way to get Owen out without a war.

A war I intended to win.

"What are you?" Leith shouted as he cracked a whip across Owen's face.

Rage reverberated inside me as my fangs popped out. I wanted to burst through this window and tear off Leith's head. Colin twitched beside me as his giant white fangs glistened in the moonlight while he snarled.

I placed a hand on him, steadying him as I gently shook my head.

"We wait until Catrain's first attack. Don't worry. We'll get them."

Colin narrowed his eyes and fixated them back through the window.

Catrain had said it would take a minute for her powers to charge up enough to throw an explosive fireball, so we waited until it was time to do our part and launch through this window to save Owen.

"What. Are. You?" Leith shouted, punctuating every word with a crack of his whip. "Tell me now! Just say the words, and I'll let you go."

Owen snarled at him, baring his fangs as he struggled against his chains. "Let me go? Yeah right. You'll kill me anyway. I'm not fucking telling you anything, Leith. You may as well just kill me now," he spat back.

"I don't want to kill you," Leith said a sigh. "I want to *control* you. Or if I can't control you, figure out what the hell you are so I can make more of you I *can* control."

Owen lifted his chin. "You'll never control me. And I'll never tell you what I am."

Leith stalked around him, dragging the tip of his whip along the muscles of Owen's shirtless back. "We'll see. At the very least, by catching you, I've assured the safety of my sister. Did you really think I'd just forget about her and leave her to her fate?"

Owen snorted. "I met her. I would. Although I'm sorry to report, she's likely already dead."

Leith chuckled as he continued his slow, deliberate steps.

"I saw the way Annella looked at you. She wouldn't dare harm a hair on my sister's head if it means getting you back. The Mackays may be a pain in my arse, but they aren't stupid. They'll know I'll be willing to trade. I may not have the strength of an army big enough to rescue my sister." He paused as he leaned up into Owen's ear. "*Yet*. But now that I have you, I'll offer a trade. You for Leeya. I'll use you to save my sister *and* find out exactly how you got your extra powers."

He came back around and leaned into Owen's face.

"And then I'll kill you all." His deep laugh echoed through the open space, bouncing off the concrete floor. When it petered off, he stood square in front of Owen. "But before I offer a trade, I want to know exactly how you got those powers I've never seen before. You have claws and more strength than even an original. You're not just a vampire. You're something else. How do you do it? Tell me, and the pain can end. You can go back to your beloved Annella."

He stepped back and let the whip crack across Owen's chest. His skin split open, and blood dripped down his torso before the wound started to heal. The stream of blood trickled into the pool forming at Owen's feet.

"Go fuck yourself," Owen spat back and got the back of Leith's hand across his face for his response.

My stomach twisted into knots as I imagined his agony.

Even with speed healing and his special powers, the crack of the barbed metal whip must be brutal.

*Come on, Catrain.*

I closed my eyes and shut out the sight of Owen being whipped, but I couldn't shut out the sounds of it tearing across his skin.

My eyes snapped open at the smash of a window. Catrain stood across the way, the giant fireball swirling in her hands before she chucked it through the window into a concentration of over fifty vampires gathered together.

"Now!" Logan shouted as the fireball exploded, sending bodies of vampires flying across the warehouse.

"What the fuck?" Leith screamed as he scrambled to his feet after being knocked back from the power of the blast.

Colin launched through the window, sending shards of glass spraying through the air. I leaped after him, landing at his side. His growl shook the surrounding air, and I snarled as I slid my daggers from my thighs.

Owen turned to look at me, his eyes wide with shock. "Annella."

The rest of my family landed on the floor of the warehouse, and the Hunter wolves echoed Colin's growl.

"Holy shit! Wolves!" Leith shouted as he leaped to his feet. "Kill them! Kill them all!"

Vampires flew at Colin and me, but his powerful jaws and claws sent them sailing away without their heads. I sliced my daggers through body after body, glancing over to see my family doing the same.

Three vampires jumped on Mark, and he snarled as he tried to fight them off.

"Mark!" Gregor shouted, quickly dispatching the vampire he fought and leaping to Mark's side. With a swift swing of his massive arm, Gregor sent them flying in the other direction.

I saw the look they exchanged before they turned back to back and started fighting again.

"The chains! Break the chains!" Thorne called, and I turned my attention to the chain nearest me. I drew the sword from my back and sliced through it. It recoiled from the release of pressure and flew toward the center of the room. I flashed to the next one, slicing through it as well.

One by one, we broke the chains as we fought our way through the dwindling vampires. At least a hundred still remained, but the Hunter brothers made quick work of them with the power of the full moon charging them up.

Emilia ripped a chain off the wall before racing toward another one. Two vampires got ahold of her, and she fought them off, sending them flying into the wall. Aiden appeared and took off their heads before they could get up and go after her again.

Owen struggled against the remaining chains. I ran toward him, but a bright UV light flicked on when I neared the center. Fiery pain seared through my body as it dropped me to my knees.

"UV light!" Mark shouted, and Thorne flashed across the warehouse and smashed it into pieces.

Another turned on, and I screamed in pain. A moment later, another crash of broken glass ended the agony. I looked up to see a wolf standing in front of the light.

"Thank you," I mouthed as I leaped back to my feet.

"Owen!" I shouted as I reached him and started snapping off the rest of his chains.

"You came for me," he said as he tried to wiggle free.

"Of course, I came for you. I'm your mate. It's you and me forever."

He smiled as I released the last chain. They fell on the ground with a clatter, and Owen wrapped me up in his arms.

I squeezed him back, exhaling a sigh of relief to have him back in my arms again. "As much as I want to stand here and hug you, we've still got some vamps to kill. Quick, take a sip of my blood and repower yourself."

"I love you, woman," he said quickly before sinking his fangs into the wrist I offered. After a few seconds of drinking my blood, he kissed me on the head before snarling and unleashing his claws.

Like a whirlwind of fury, Owen tore through the remaining vampires, sending bodies flying in his path. My family struggled to keep fighting as they stared at him in awe.

Leith cowered behind the last remaining vampires, but when Owen reached them and started making quick work of Leith's vampire shield, he took off toward the exit.

"Leith is running!" Gregor called. "Stop him!"

We all spun to see Leith making a sprint for freedom.

*Not this time, Leith.*

# Chapter Eighteen

## OWEN

I launched toward Leith, but Lothaire got there first. With one powerful blow, Lothaire sent Leith sailing onto his arse. Leith skidded across the floor and slammed into a concrete post.

"He's mine," Lothaire ground out as he strode across the warehouse.

"Lothaire," Leith begged, raising his hands. "I submit. I'm sorry. I submit to your rule."

Ignoring his pleas, he grabbed Leith by the shirt, throwing him so hard he broke through a concrete pillar on the opposite side of the floor. Lothaire was on him in a millisecond, grabbing him and throwing him again.

When Leith crawled on his hands and knees toward Lothaire's feet, Lothaire lifted a boot and pressed Leith down onto the concrete floor.

"Where is Gregor's sister, Meagan," he growled.

"Please, Lothaire. Don't hu—"

With a quick snatch, he caught Leith by the throat and lifted him into the air, pressing his nose into Leith's.

"Where is she?" he shouted so loud it rumbled through my bones.

"My apartment in Glasgow. She's safe there."

Lothaire nodded toward Gregor, who mouthed, "thank you."

As Lothaire lifted Leith higher in the air, my brother Colin took down the last standing vampire beside Leith.

It was incredible to see my brothers in wolf form and hear the thoughts in their mind, even though I hadn't shifted myself. It seemed my new hybrid abilities also retained the telecommunication a pack of wolves possessed.

*Me: You're here. I can't believe you came.*

*Colin: Of course we came for you, you dumb arse. You're our brother.*

*Logan: You hurt?*

*Me: No. I'm okay. You guys all okay?*

*Torin: Oh, yeah. Not a scratch. Christ, that was fun. Did anyone else think that was fun?*

*Pops: I've been waiting my whole fecking life to tear apart some vampires.*

*Me: I can't believe you guys are in wolf form. It's incredible.*

I smiled as I looked at my family in their true form for the first time, their wolves now freed as they stood beside the vampires we'd hid from our whole lives.

"Now for you, Leith." Lothaire tightened his grip on Leith's neck. "We warned you not to go against us, but you didn't listen, did you?" He lowered Leith's face close to his. "And now look what happened." He gestured to the carnage surrounding us as we all closed in around him. "You influenced humans to fight to their death and then turned them into vampires. Do you know how many vampire laws you broke? All those people are *dead* because of you."

"I'm sorry, Lothaire. I swear my fealty to you again. I swear it."

Lothaire laughed and shook his head. "It's too late for that, Leith. We're done with you and your sister. You've been given too many chances, and each time, you make the wrong choice."

"Lothaire. Please, just let us live. We'll be good this time. I swear it."

Lothaire shook his head as he smiled and revealed his blood-covered fangs. "It's already too late for Leeya. And it's too late for you, Leith."

"Leeya? Is she?" he whispered.

"Dead. Just like you're about to be."

His shoulders slumped as his eyes filled with agony. "Oh, God. Leeya. No. Not Leeya."

"She had it coming, and so do you. We gifted you both countless chances that you blew. And I know you have more influenced vampires somewhere. If I don't kill you now, you'll just come at us again and bring more."

"I won't. I swear it. I'll uninfluence them all."

Lothaire snorted. "I have a faster way to get them all uninfluenced. Do you know what it is?"

Leith's eyes widened.

"Kill the one who influenced them." With one swift move, Lothaire tore his head from his body. He held Leith's carcass for a few seconds before tossing him into the corner like discarded trash.

"It's done." Lothaire wiped his hands on his pants.

We all moved toward the center of the room, the wolves and vampires uniting. After my entire life being told of the blood war between vamps and werewolves, it warmed my heart to see them standing side by side as allies. My family of wolves and my new family of vampires all working together as one.

"Thank you for coming to save me," I said to everyone as I slipped my arm around Annella's shoulder then pressed a kiss against her head. "All of you."

My family shifted back into human form, and one by one, they came up and pulled me in for a hug.

"I can't believe werewolves and vampires just fought side by side. For me." I grinned.

"We all love you, brother." Logan clapped me on my back. "You know we'll always fight for you."

"And I'll always fight for you. All of you." I swept a gaze around the room. "You're *all* my family now. And it makes me so happy to see we can have peace between us."

Lothaire and my father exchanged a glance and a smile as Lothaire stepped up to him and extended a hand. "Jack, you have my word that no vampire will harm a wolf so long as this truce remains unbroken."

My father nodded and took his hand. "And you have my word, no wolf will hunt a vampire. We can coexist together."

They shook hands, then folded into a quick embrace.

I pulled Annella tighter against me and wrapped her up in my arms.

"You sure you're okay?" she asked as she pressed her head against my chest.

"Thanks to you, I am. I'll always be okay as long as I have you."

"Then you'll always be okay because I'm never leaving you. Ever."

She pulled back from my embrace and tossed her arms around my neck, pulling me down for a kiss so filled with love and passion, I thought my heart might explode.

"Aw! Get a room you two!" Mark called.

I turned to see him standing with his head on Gregor's shoulder.

I furrowed my brow. "I thought Gregor was our enemy?"

Mark scoffed. "That was *so* yesterday. He's my boyfriend today."

"And I'll be your boyfriend for always. I love you, Mark." Gregor lifted Mark's chin up and pressed a soft kiss against his lips.

Mark's smile stretched from ear to ear as he smiled up at Gregor. "Right back at you, baby." He sighed, then widened his eyes and looked to Lothaire. "Wait! Since I'm family, and Gregor is my lobster…"

Aiden and Emilia looked at each other and smiled as Lothaire furrowed his brow. "Lobster?"

"My lobster… the love of my life. Keep up. Can he come with us to get the original powers as well? If I'm going to be sipping margaritas in the sun for eternity, I need my big strapping hot Scot at my side."

Lothaire chuckled. "Anyone who can keep Mark busy and out of our hair is most welcome in this family. As long as it's okay with Alpia, it's okay with me."

Mark squealed and tossed his arms around Gregor's neck. "You and me forever, baby. You and me forever."

Gregor returned the embrace and kissed him again. "I

can't wait to spend my life with you. But first, I have to go make sure my sister is okay."

"Of course," Mark said and released his grip. "She's always welcome at our place if she needs somewhere to go."

"Absolutely," Lothaire said. "Whatever you two need."

"Thank you," Gregor said as he stepped toward the door. "I can't tell you how sorry I am that I was on the wrong side of the battle at first, and how grateful I am for your forgiveness."

"Welcome to the family, Gregor," Annella said. "As long as you take good care of our Marky Mark, you're always welcome with us."

Gregor's gaze slid to Mark, and he smiled. "I'll take care of him for eternity."

Mark sighed as Gregor blew him a kiss and ran out of the warehouse.

I laughed and shrugged. "Man. I missed a lot while I was gone. Anything else I missed?"

"You also missed me panicking and accidentally slicing Leeya's head off." Mark sucked the air through his teeth. "Now *that* you'd have wanted to see."

"You're right." I chuckled. "That is something I wanted to see. So much for us drawing straws on who got to kill her. Cheater."

"My bad." He smiled and shrugged.

"Well, Owen," my father said as he stepped forward. "Looks like you're safe and in good hands. Your brothers and I are gonna hit the road and catch the ferry home."

"Thanks, Pops. For everything." I pulled him in for a hug and squeezed him tight.

Logan, Torin, and Colin all came over and hugged me too.

"We'll see you for Sunday dinner?" Torin asked.

With a smile, I nodded. "Wouldn't miss it. Have the beer and pizza ready."

"I've got an idea." Logan lifted his finger. "Now that we have permission to shift, what do you say we move Sunday night dinner to my place next week. We can meet at my cabin in the woods, and all let our wolves out for a much-needed run through the forest."

Torin and Colin nodded hard.

"Yes. Fuck yes," Colin said.

We looked at my father. "I'm not gonna lie. My old bones are already aching from the fight tonight, but I sure as hell would love a good run with my boys."

"I'm in. I mean, I don't shift into a wolf anymore, but I'll still run with you guys."

My father crossed his arms. "Sunday night dinner and a run it is."

"I can't wait."

I shook my brothers' hands one last time, and they stopped to shake each one of the Mackay family's hands on their way out. With one last wave, I bid them each goodbye.

Thorne kicked a corpse at his feet. "Well, I guess we should get rid of all these bodies."

"Seriously. Clean up on aisle six." Mark pulled a face as he waved a hand over the carnage.

Annella chuckled. "After that, we need to figure out the plan to get to the island and get our curses removed."

"I am *dying* for a margarita," Mark said. "So, let's get these bodies buried or burned or whatever the hell we're gonna do with them and get our asses home. We can go to the island tomorrow night."

Everyone agreed, and we hurried off to dispose of the bodies and burn the warehouse down to hide all the blood we would never be able to scrub away.

---

After we returned to the castle, we all split up and went to our bedrooms. The sun would rise soon, and we needed our rest after a long night of killing and cleaning up the mess.

"How does it feel?" I asked Annella as she stripped off her clothes.

"What? Getting out of these blood-soaked clothes? Pretty damn good. I need a shower. That was some messy business tonight."

"No. Knowing this is the last time you will ever have to hide in your room all day out of the sun."

She paused as she pulled off her pants. Those bright blue eyes lit up even more. "Holy shit. You're right. This is the last day locked in a light-tight room."

"Pretty exciting, huh?"

"Very exciting." She smiled as she dropped the last of her clothes in the hamper.

I slowly pulled off my t-shirt and watched her hungry eyes roving over every inch of my inked skin. I arched an eyebrow. "How do you want to spend it?"

Annella pulled her lip between her teeth, and the passion lit up inside her eyes.

She turned on her heel, giving me a come hither look over her shoulder as she walked into the bathroom, her naked body begging me to follow it.

I moved into the bathroom with her and watched as she opened the glass shower door, holding my eye contact as she stepped inside and turned on the water. When it hit her naked body, I almost dropped to my knees. Instead, I dropped my pants and flashed inside with her.

Pressing her up against the tile wall of the shower, I held her face in my hand as I annihilated her with the kiss that

I'd kept envisioning to keep me sane while Leith tortured me. Her gorgeous face had kept me going. The need to taste her lips again helped me hold steady and endure.

Sliding my hand down her throat, I tightened my grip as I broke our kiss and peppered smaller ones down her neck.

"You must be famished," she whispered as she dragged her fingertips along my shoulders. "Drink."

Just the thought of sliding my fangs inside her coaxed them to pop out.

"I'm famished for more than just your blood," I whispered as I slid a hand under her ass and lifted her up. She wrapped her legs around my waist, and as I sunk my fangs into her neck, I sunk myself inside her.

The water poured down on us as we connected over and over again while I pushed inside her as I drank her blood.

She moaned as she got close, and I felt my passion surging to the point of exploding. I growled as I pushed her harder against the wall, pinning her with my body while I released my fangs and annihilated her with a kiss so deep it was bottomless.

Just like my love for her. It was endless, and I enjoyed the freefall as I dropped deeper and deeper, enjoying every second of the plummet.

One I knew would never end. Not for all of eternity, which was how long I knew I would love her.

She shuddered and moaned as she came, and I groaned into her mouth as I followed her over the edge.

After I held her against me panting for a minute, Annella slid down my body and blew out a breath. "God, I'm glad you're back."

"Thank you for bringing me back. I knew you would come for me."

"I'll always come for you." She paused and chuckled at the words. "Well, that too."

Laughing, I pulled her into the stream of the shower and kissed her again.

And again.

And again.

I never wanted to stop enjoying the lips of the woman I loved. My mate. And neither did my wolf.

"Can you believe that tomorrow I'll be able to sit in the sun with you?" she said as our kiss broke apart. "I still can't believe it."

"I'm most excited to take you out for a burger and a beer."

She grinned widely and nodded. "I can't wait. A lifetime of burgers and beers sitting in the sun with the man I love. Heaven."

*The man I love.*

Hearing the words still stunned me. How had I found a woman as amazing as Annella? To think I was created to be her enemy… to kill her.

But deep in my soul, I knew I was put on this earth to love her.

"Or…" she said as she drifted off. "Or now that you've fulfilled your pact to me and helped me with Clan Lennox, you're free to leave and go live your life."

She looked up at me, and uncertainty swirled around in her blue eyes.

I scoffed and grabbed her face in my hands. "What part of 'you're my mate' are you not understanding? I love you, Annella. Today, tomorrow, a thousand years from now. I will always love you, and I will always be at your side. You're stuck with my hybrid ass for all of eternity."

Her smile lifted those full red lips, and I claimed them again with my kiss, and my wolf inside howled his approval.

# Chapter Nineteen

## ANNELLA

"Everyone in?" Thorne asked he stood on the bow of the small wooden boat we all sat in.

"Present!" Mark raised his hand. "My buddy system buddy is present too." He lifted Gregor's hand, and Gregor just chuckled.

Thorne laughed as well, then took his seat beside Catrain and grabbed the oars. "Here we go."

My heart raced as we paddled through the dark toward the island where Catrain's sister, Alpia, would transition us back to our original powers from over six hundred years ago. Soon we could walk in the sun again and live a life not fueled by blood. It was incredible to imagine and remember what it had been like in the short time we'd lived that way.

The closer we got to the island, the thicker the surrounding fog grew. It was a magical barrier that prevented anyone from discovering the island. The thick mist had kept the last of a tribe of Picts hidden from society for centuries, and the rest of the world thought them extinct.

"We're here!" Catrain called into the fog.

It took only a moment for the fog to start swirling as it parted and disappeared, revealing the island we'd traveled to once to save Aiden's life.

Alpia stood on the beach at the side of a gigantic man I assumed was her new husband, a werewolf named Uradech. The tribe gathered behind them. It was amazing to see them in their native form. Leather loincloths and dresses left most of their tattooed skin exposed, and they clutched spears and bows far more primitive than we'd seen since many centuries past.

But the Picts were a proud people, and they clung to their traditions and heritage, refusing to move forward with the rest of the world.

The boat skidded onto the sand, and Catrain hopped out first.

"Alpia!" She raced to her sister and pulled her in for a hug.

Alpia's dark hair opposite Catrain's light made their likeness as sisters not obvious at first glance. But once I looked at them more closely, there was a clear resemblance between the two beautiful women.

"Hello, Uradech," Catrain said as she moved over to the massive man with more tattoos than even Owen.

"Welcome back, Catrain." He enveloped her in a hug as Thorne hugged Alpia.

I'd never met Uradech, but Catrain and Thorne had told us he and several of the men on the island were werewolves. I glanced over at Owen and caught him staring at Uradech, no doubt excited to see another of his kind.

Liùsaidh, Catrain's mother and the former leader of the tribe, stepped up to Alpia's side.

"Hello, mother," Catrain said as she hugged the frail-looking woman tight. "It's so good to see you."

"Hey, ma!" Thorne teased as he pulled her reluctant body against him. She grumbled but finally gave in and patted him on the back.

Liùsaidh hated our kind, and even though Thorne had slowly worn her down, she'd as soon slaughter us as save us. We hoped that once we were back to our original powers and didn't need to feed on blood, perhaps she'd trust us a little more.

Maybe.

"Come on, guys." Thorne waved us forward, and we all took tentative steps onto the sand.

"Welcome." Alpia stepped forward. "It is an honor to have you all here."

"Thank you so much for doing this for us, Alpia. I can't tell you how much we appreciate it," Lothaire said as he took her hand.

"It's my pleasure. Once I heard the *real* story of the vampire's betrayal, that wasn't a betrayal at all, I knew I wanted to help you get back to the powers and life we'd promised you. It's my honor to be the one to right the wrong of our people."

"We are so excited about this," I said as I squeezed Owen's hand tight. "I can't wait to stand in the sun again."

"And eat burgers." Owen smiled as he squeezed it.

"And eat burgers."

"Then I'm happy to do that for you." Alpia smiled.

"How does it work?" Mark asked.

"It will be over quickly. All you need to do is stand there, and I'll perform the spell that reverts you to your origins. It *will* be painful."

"Holy shit is it ever." Thorne blew out a breath as Aiden nodded in agreement. "But worth it."

"So, we just stand here?" I asked, still struggling to comprehend what was about to happen.

"Whenever you're ready, just line up, and I'll perform the spell on you all at once."

We all glanced back and forth, then Lothaire nodded his approval.

"Is it really okay I do this with you all?" Gregor asked as he hesitated, stepping forward.

"Ugh." Mark scoffed. "Of course it's okay. I love you, Gregor, and if you think I'm going to spend eternity sipping margaritas without you, you've got another think coming."

Gregor's smile grew as he squeezed Mark's hand. "I love you too, Mark. And I always will." Gregor leaned down and gave him a gentle kiss before standing up and looking at Alpia. "It's okay with them if it's okay with you."

Alpia shrugged. "I am happy to grant the original powers to any of you. Just step forward if you want it."

I glanced up at Owen, but he shook his head. "I'm good, baby. I've got all the immortality and powers I could ever want. I don't want to risk losing my werewolf powers and my connection with my brothers. But you go."

Uradech gave him a brief nod of brotherhood.

"Yeah. You don't need this spell done. You can already go in the sun and eat real food."

He leaned down and whispered in my ear, "And if I keep my hybrid powers, I can still feed on you while we do it."

My stomach flipped at the thought of an eternity of the pure, unadulterated bliss that I got when he fed on me.

"Deal," I whispered back, then kissed him and stepped forward with my family.

"Catrain," Alpia said. "Since you weren't immortal to begin with, and we've never tried this with a witch, we don't know if your magic will be available to you after the change. Are you sure you want to do this?"

Catrain looked at Thorne and nodded. "I want to be at his side for eternity. I want to do it."

Thorne grinned so wide I thought his face would tear.

"Very well, then," Alpia said.

I looked over at the faces who'd been part of my family for centuries, and the new ones who would be part of my family for all the centuries to come. Mark took ahold of my hand on one side, and Lothaire gripped it on the other. One by one, we linked hands as we stood in front of Alpia and waited.

She lifted her hands and started chanting. Searing pain shot through my body, coursing through my veins and my muscles, seeping into every cell in my body and making me feel like I'd explode from the pain any second. We dropped to our knees, screaming as the pain radiated through us. When I didn't think I could endure another second, as quickly as it started, it stopped.

I fell forward, pressing my hands into the sand as I panted and tried to catch my breath. The pain lapsed and left me feeling strange. An old familiar sensation started in my stomach and finished in my mouth.

"I… I think I'm hungry," I said quietly as I looked over at Lothaire. "For food."

He stared back at me, stunned. "I think I'm hungry too."

"I'm thirsty for a marg." Mark sat back on his heels. "Like I actually want to drink one. It worked. It fucking worked!" He tossed his arms around Gregor's neck and tumbled into the sand while he kissed him over and over again.

Catrain looked down at her hands, and we all held our breath as we watched. As much as we knew she'd choose Thorne and immortality over her gift of magic, we knew how devastated she would be to lose it. When I saw the sparks crackling along her fingertips, I pressed my hands to my mouth and smiled.

"They still work!" Catrain said, then turned to Thorne and threw her arms around his neck.

He spun her around in circles, kissing her repeatedly.

Grizella stood up and stared at her hands, then slid them over her body. "I… I've never felt like this before. I feel so…"

"Powerful." Gregor stood. "I feel more powerful than I ever could have imagined. And I don't crave blood anymore."

"You have the powers of the originals now," I said as I stood up with him, noting that while they felt more powerful than they had as vampires, I felt weaker, which we'd expected. "We all do. And they will only get stronger over the next few weeks."

"This is incredible." Lothaire pulled Grizella in for a hug. "Thank you, Alpia," he said over Grizella's shoulder. "Thank you for doing this for us. We're forever in your debt."

"It was my pleasure." She took Uradech's hand in hers. "I have my happiness, and now you all deserve yours. Now go out there and enjoy it."

We took turns hugging her goodbye, then climbed back into the boats. As we drifted away from the shore, the fog enveloped the island once again. Once back on the mainland, we all stayed quiet as we processed the overwhelming emotions coursing through us.

We were immortal, but with none of the downsides. I craved food, and no longer desired blood. Soon I could stand in the sunshine and no longer live as its slave. The world opened up to us now in ways we'd never imagined we could experience again.

"I've got an idea," Thorne said as he pulled the boat onshore.

"Yeah? What's that?" I asked.

He grinned widely with the mischievous smile he wore so often. "Just follow me."

Thorne grabbed Catrain by the hand. "You still got a need for speed, Maverick? Want to try out your vamp speed?"

Her eyes lit up with excitement as she nodded. Together they took off in a flash and disappeared over the hill. The rest of us shared a smile and took off after them.

I raced across the Scottish countryside, the wind whipping through my hair as I ran at Owen's side. He glanced over and grabbed my hand, grinning widely as we picked up speed. As Thorne and Catrain skidded to a stop, I looked around and smiled, recognizing the place immediately.

"Oh my God." I slid my arm around Owen's waist and let my gaze stretch out from the cliffs and across the ocean. "We used to come here all the time growing up. Remember sitting up here and watching the sunrise?"

"Of course, I remember," Aiden said, then chuckled. "I also remember jumping off them when we became immortal and realized the drop wouldn't kill us."

The memories on these cliffs flooded back to me.

Memories as humans. Memories as immortals. Memories with the family I loved so much… the ones still at my side.

Thorne stood on the edge of the cliff and turned toward us. "When Catrain temporarily blocked my sun curse, I watched the sunrise here. It was incredible to see it after so many centuries in the dark. I had a dream of sitting here one day with all of you and watching it rise. The sun will be up in fifteen minutes, and I would love to watch it with all of you."

"That sounds incredible, Thorne." Lothaire smiled.

"Grab a patch of grass," Thorne said, gesturing to the lush carpet of grass stretching right to the edge of the cliff.

"Hey, how's your sister?" Thorne asked Gregor, who held Mark between his legs.

"She's okay." Gregor smiled. "She's settling back into her apartment, and I'm going to stay with her for a few days this week and make sure she's okay. I influenced her to forget all the horrible things Leith did to her so she can get back to her life."

"That was kind of you," Grizella said. "She's better off not remembering all the bad stuff. It will help her heal and live a normal life."

"I hope so," Gregor said. "She already seems so much better and is talking about going to university. Thank you all for helping me save her."

Lothaire rested his chin on the top of Grizella's head as he pulled her against his chest. "You're family now, Gregor, and the Mackay family sticks together. Always."

The sentiment made me smile as I glanced down the row of my family, all lined up along the edge with their feet dangling over. The minutes ticked by, and with each second closer to sunrise, my heart raced faster.

As the first streaks of color streaked the horizon, Owen

pulled me close against him. Inch by inch, the sun appeared, and when I saw the top of the orange orb, I sucked my lip between my teeth as I swallowed over the lump in my throat.

"Oh, my God," I whispered as it climbed higher and higher, absorbing the darkness surrounding us.

"It's incredible," Lothaire whispered, then pressed a kiss to Grizella's head. "I can't believe I'm seeing the sun again."

We all sat in silence and stared at the beautiful colors awakening in the world around us. I hadn't seen the world bathed in the light in over six hundred years, and I'd forgotten how beautiful it was.

"Happy?" Owen asked.

"No," I answered. "There is no word in the language that can encompass my feelings right now. Happy doesn't even begin to cover it. I have you, the love of my life, my incredible family, and an eternity in the light again." A tear slid down my cheek.

He slid a hand across my face, brushing away the tear with the pad of his thumb as he lifted my lips to his.

"I love you, Annella. For now and for eternity. For every single sunrise." He kissed me, and it multiplied the warmth inside me that my skin felt in the sun.

"And I love you. Always."

"Are we doing this?" Thorne interrupted as he stood up.

I tipped my head, then realized his intention and smiled. "Oh, hell yeah!"

I leaped up and pulled Owen up with me. My family rose, and we held hands as we laughed and lined up on the edge.

Six hundred years ago, it had been just me, Thorne, Lothaire, and Aiden getting ready to plummet off this cliff and celebrate our immortality. Today it was all of us plus our new family… the friends and loves we'd found for ourselves over the centuries. As warm rays of the sun beat down on us, I looked down the row at the smiling faces of my family and the ones they loved.

They were all the lights of my life… the eternal lights I knew that would illuminate every moment of the rest of my countless days.

"On three," Thorne said with a huge grin.

Together we counted, "One, two, three… JUMP!"

Hand-in-hand, we jumped off the cliff together as a family… a family who would stick together for eternity.

# Epilogue

## ANNELLA

Mark shrieked, and I opened my eyes to see Gregor toss him through the air into the pool on the deck of our yacht. The huge splash sprayed up onto the chaise lounge chairs. I closed my eyes against the assault of water.

"Mark!" Emilia, Grizella, Catrain, and I all scolded in unison.

He popped back up over the edge of the pool, dripping water everywhere from his hot pink and blue crab-patterned shorts.

"My bad!" He sucked the air through his teeth as he playfully shoved Gregor. "Baby, look what you did. You pissed off the bathing beauties. You've upset my Funky Bunch."

"Your Funky Bunch is wet now." Emilia wiped the water off her large black sunglasses.

"Sorry, babies." Mark blew air kisses at each of us.

"Yeah, sorry, ladies," Gregor apologized.

I exhaled a long sigh. "I was getting a little hot in the

sun, so I suppose I shouldn't complain. You saved me a trip to the pool."

Mark flopped into the chaise lounge beside me and pulled Gregor down with him. "It's fucking hot out. Seriously. We should move to the shade."

I shook my head and relaxed back into my chair. In the three months since Alpia's spell, I hadn't missed a minute in the sun. After six hundred years without it, I felt like I needed to make up for all the lost time. The rest of my family felt the same, so we'd bought the mega yacht, enjoying an around the world trip. From one tropical shore to another, we soaked up every drop of sunshine we could.

"I'm good right here. And I'll be better when Owen gets back from the boys' fishing excursion."

Thorne, Aiden, Lothaire, and Owen had taken the jet skis to free dive and spear fish, though we weren't confident they would do anything other than drive around and race each other.

"Think they caught us dinner, or did they just screw around on the jet skis all day?" Grizella arched an eyebrow.

"The latter," Catrain said after swallowing the cherry from her pina colada. "If Thorne is involved, definitely the latter."

"I hope they bring dinner because I'm starving." I reached over, grabbed my mojito, and took a long sip. "Maybe we should have the chef whip us up some pizzas."

"Pepperoni." Grizella's eyes widened. "I cannot get enough of pepperoni pizza."

Like me, Grizella had been savoring every bite of food for months.

"Pizza tonight and maybe tacos tomorrow?" Mark said.

"I'll be gone tomorrow. Remember? Owen is recording an album with his band before the tour."

Despite the tricky situation, Owen managed to keep his true identity secret from his band. He and I took the helicopter to shore every couple of weeks and a jet back to Scotland, so he could perform in shows and visit his family. After hearing their last show, a record producer agreed to record a few tracks for them and potentially sign them to a label. I loved that his dreams were coming true, and that I got to sit in the front row and cheer him on while he did the thing he loved and continued chasing his childhood dream.

"Oh, shit. That's right. Well, more tacos for me. And now I can eat as many as I want, and I don't gain a single freaking pound. #winning!"

The buzzing of jet skis broke the silence, and I smiled as I sat up in my chair. "The boys are back."

Emilia, Catrain, and Grizella joined me in standing up and heading over to the edge of the yacht. We watched the jet skis barreling toward us, each jockeying for first position.

"Go, baby!" I shouted to Owen as he overtook Lothaire.

"Don't let him beat you, Lothaire! GO!" Grizella screamed.

Catrain snorted. "Thorne's got this. He's the king of speed."

"I don't know." Emilia smirked. "Aiden's looking pretty fast out there."

As they got closer, I could see smiles stretched wide across all their faces as they raced across the water, jumping the waves that broke their path, never letting up on the gas.

"Go, baby, go!" I screamed again as they closed in on the yacht.

Each one still fought for first place as they barreled toward the back of the boat.

"Open the garage!" I called to the crew down below.

They pressed a button and lowered the ramp into the

water that would let the boys drive the jet skis right into the boat.

"Here we go!" Emilia squealed as Aiden slid into first place.

Mark and Gregor joined us in cheering at the side, and we held our breath as the four guys, neck and neck, disappeared beneath the boat and into the garage.

"Who won?" Catrain asked as she tried to peer harder over the edge.

"Owen. Definitely Owen," I said with certainty.

Grizella shook her head. "Hundred bucks says it was Lothaire."

"My money is on Aiden," Emilia backed her man.

"I'll take that bet and put everything on Thorne." Catrain smiled.

We all shook hands and went back to our lounge chairs and awaited the victor.

"Bullshit!" Thorne said as he came up the stairs. "I had you by a mile!"

Aiden snorted. "Bullshit right back at you. I kicked your ass, and you know it."

Lothaire strode up behind them with Owen at his side, and the two giant men just shook their heads in unison.

"You two can argue all you want," Owen said, "because you're arguing over second place. I came in first."

"Whoa?" Lothaire said, lifting a hand. "I think you mean *I* came in first."

I lowered my sunglasses and looked at the girls. "I think none of us are winning a hundred bucks because they'll never agree on the winner."

They all nodded.

Emilia pulled her oversized hat onto her head. "I say we

each take our hundred bucks and go buy some new shoes when we hit the next port."

I lifted my mojito in the air. "I'm down with that!"

"Samesies!" Mark said. "I want in on the shoe shopping."

"Shoe shopping it is," Grizella said.

The four men approached us at the pool, each climbing onto the chaise with their woman.

"You guys saw me win, right?" Thorne gave Catrain a kiss.

"We saw no winner," I said as Owen pulled me into his arms. "All we see are new shoes."

Aiden furrowed his brow, but Emilia just waved off the look and kissed him.

"Whatever. I won, and you all know it," Owen said confidently, then laid back in the lounge and pulled me back with him. "But no matter who won the race, we're all winning tonight."

"Yeah? Why is that?" I asked.

"Because the boys and I went free-diving off the coast and pulled up over a dozen *huge* spiny lobsters. We gave them to the crew, and the chef will cook them up for us tonight."

"You guys actually did more than just race the jet skis?" My eyes widened. "I *love* lobster!"

I'd eaten one shortly after I could consume human food, the burger with Owen being the first meal I'd savored… but damn, lobster was yummy too. Aiden and Thorne weren't kidding when they'd said the new flavors of food in the world were worth giving up our immortality. I'd been on a non-stop eating smorgasbord and inhaled everything from lobster to burgers to sushi to cake and everything in between. All of us enjoyed every last morsel of food we could find.

"I love lobster too!" Catrain said.

"I know you do, baby," Thorne said back. "That's why I caught you the biggest one."

He waggled his eyebrows, and she tossed her arms around his neck.

"I got you two, Emilia," Aiden said as a look passed between them. I furrowed my brow as I wondered about their silent conversation.

"Who's up for cocktails?" Mark asked as he shook his empty margarita glass.

We raised our hands, but once again, Aiden and Emilia shared a look.

"What's happening over there?" I pointed a finger at Emilia and spun it around. "You two are hiding something."

They looked shocked that I'd called them out, and Emilia opened her mouth to say something, then snapped it shut.

"Well?" she said to Aiden, whose face tightened as he fought a smile.

"Well, what?" Thorne furrowed his brow.

Emilia took a deep breath as she pulled Aiden's hand into hers. He nodded at her as she grinned.

"We're pregnant." Emilia's face broke into a smile so bright it outshone the sun. Aiden's grew immediately to match it.

"Shut the fuck up!" Mark shouted before screaming so loud it rang my ears.

"You're kidding!" I joined him in the clapping, as did the rest of our family.

"I can't believe it," I said. "I didn't know we could get pregnant now! Can we seriously get pregnant?"

Emilia blew out a breath. "We didn't know it was possible either, but I started noticing symptoms a week ago. Not sure if it was possible, we scheduled ourselves for an ultrasound at the port we hit yesterday. It confirmed our suspicions. We're definitely pregnant. Listen."

Emilia placed her hand on her belly, and I focused my hearing. All the sounds around me faded away as I zoned it in. Then I heard it…

*A heartbeat.*

The tiny thumping of a new life pounded inside her stomach. My heart swelled in my chest at the thought of a baby coming into our lives.

Then I furrowed my brow as I heard another small, quick heartbeat.

"Two babies? Are you having twins?" I asked as I listened to the competing symphony of life.

Emilia shook her head and furrowed her brow. "No. Just the one. What?" She perked an ear and listened. The same shock started on her face that had started on mine, but then her gaze drifted from her belly over to Grizella's.

I saw the smile on Grizella's face and the proud one on Lothaire's.

"No!" Emilia squealed as she sat up. "Are you two pregnant too?"

Grizella's smile spread across her face as she took Lothaire's hand. "We were going to tell you all tonight. Yes. We're pregnant too."

"Oh my *God!*" Mark screamed so loud again I worried he'd hurt the babies' hearing.

I pressed a hand to my mouth as tears started in my

eyes. "I'm gonna be an aunty! I'm gonna be *two* aunties! I can't believe it!"

"Neither could we," Lothaire said. "It never occurred to us that with our original powers back, we could get pregnant."

"Well, shit," Thorne said as he blew out a breath. "We're falling behind, baby. Looks like you and I have some work to do because I'm putting a baby in that belly stat."

Catrain's eyes glistened with tears as she nodded her head. "Yes. So much yes!"

I was still too stunned to process that not only did we have one baby on board, we had *two.* And from the way Catrain bounced in Thorne's arms, it looked like three would arrive soon.

Owen nudged me. "Are we doing this too?"

"Do you *want* a baby?" I asked, shocked it was even an option.

Owen's eyes softened as he smiled. "I want one if you want one."

Since becoming a vampire, it never even occurred to me to dream of having a baby of my own. I'd given up on that girlhood dream long ago.

A dream that could now be a reality.

"Well, it's not like we've been using protection. Who knows? Maybe we already are." I bit my lip as I considered the possibility.

"And would you be okay with that?" Owen stroked my face.

After taking a deep breath, I smiled. "Yeah. I would be okay with that."

"So, we're not going to start using protection?"

I shook my head. "Not unless you want to."

"I don't," he answered quickly. "Let's try to do this."

I threw my arms around his neck and squeezed him tight. Not only did I have the man that I loved and the life that I wanted, but there was a chance we could start a family of our own. My engagement ring caught the sunlight and flickered in my eyes, a constant reminder of the love for each other I knew would never end.

"Well, that's just great." Mark huffed. "Everyone is having babies over there, but *hello,* some couples lack ovaries. One of you breeding bastards is giving a kid to Gregor and me to raise as our own. It's only fair."

He crossed his arms, and Gregor gave him a nod of solidarity and joined him. "Yeah. Mark and I want a baby too."

"We're not giving you our babies, guys. Sorry." Emilia flicked a wrist at him, then covered her belly with her hand.

Mark pouted for a second, then his face lit up. "Oh! We can adopt one! Let's find some little orphan vampire baby—wait. There are no vampire babies." His smile dropped.

Owen arched an eyebrow. "Sometimes werewolves are born without a family. What would you two say about raising a werewolf? I could teach you everything you need to know."

Mark's eyes lit up as he looked at Gregor. "Yes! Oh, please say yes. We will be the best daddies on the planet to some poor forlorn werewolf. We'll teach it everything we know. How to dress, how to dance, how to crush it at karaoke. Please, Gregor?"

Mark pressed his hands together and closed his eyes, mouthing *please, please, please* over and over until Gregor stopped his lips with a kiss.

"I would love to raise a baby with you, Mark. And a werewolf baby sounds perfect."

Mark squealed and threw his arms around Gregor's

neck, peppering him with dozens of kisses as he bounced up and down.

I leaned back against Owen and felt his muscular arms close around me in a tight embrace.

"I love you, Annella. Always and forever," he whispered in my ear.

"I love you too."

I sunk into his embrace and let his love envelop me like a cocoon while I watched the joy on my family's faces and imagined the bliss that would be coming when we all welcomed our little ones into the world someday. The next generation of immortal progenies to carry on our legacies and light up the world.

It was a world too wonderful to process, but a world that would soon be ours.

## More by Katherine Hastings

vinci-books.com/MillieAndMabel

**Dying was easy—staying out of trouble is the real challenge.**

Bored in Heaven, Mabel and Millie sneak back to Earth for mischief—only to land in a serial killer case. Teaming up with an FBI agent who can see them, the ghostly duo must catch a killer before the body count rises.

Turn the page for a free preview…

## Millie and Mabel's Afterlife Adventures: Chapter One

MABEL

I grabbed a flat, smooth stone from the edge of the dock and wound my arm back.

"What are you doing?" my best friend, Millie, asked from her spot beside me.

"Nothing." A mischievous grin spread across my face. "Just seeing if I can still nail a good skip."

But that wasn't true. I wasn't aiming for skips—I wanted a huge splash to drench my best friend. I hurled the stone with all my strength, targeting the spot right in front of her perfectly pedicured toes.

Instead of a satisfying splat, the stone hit the surface and took off, a small whirring blur that skipped perfectly seven times before sinking without a sound.

"Wow!" Millie exclaimed. "Seven perfect skips! Nice work!"

I groaned, planting my hands on my hips. "I wasn't trying to skip it. I was trying to splash you."

Millie let out a soft laugh. "I know, Mabel. We've been friends for ninety years. I can always tell when you're lying."

Unwilling to give up, I tried again, but as I tried to spike it into the water right in front of her, the stone just skipped a perfect, flawless series of hops across the pond's surface. I tried again. And again. My frustration grew with each failed attempt.

Her soft, grey curls moved in the gentle breeze. She looked over, her plump cheeks swelling with the smile that deepened the wrinkles around her eyes. "Are you done yet? I don't think Heaven will let you soak me since I don't want to be soaked right now. You know, Heaven. It always gives you exactly what you want."

I did know Heaven. Perfectly perfect Heaven we'd been living in for months of endless bliss... the kind of flawless paradise that was slowly driving me insane.

"Except I *want* to soak you! And this damn rock just keeps skipping off perfectly like I'm a freaking rock skipping champion!"

I tossed the last stone in my hand, watching it once again take off perfectly. Exhausted from my attempts, I flopped down on the dock beside her. "What's wrong with me, Millie? We have everything we could ever want with just a thought. We can paint masterpieces, learn any instrument, go anywhere we want with just a blink. Why can't I seem to be excited about it? What's wrong with me for not loving this endless perfection all the time?"

"There's nothing wrong with you," Millie said, her silver eyebrows furrowing slightly. "You're Mabel. You were never one for perfection. I know you're restless here, and Heaven can be a little… predictable," she said, then she opened her hand and with one big blink, a piece of chocolate cake appeared it. "But for all its constant happiness I know can irritate you, at least there's endless cake… and *no* calories." She grinned widely, her eyes lighting up as she looked at the plate. She took a bite, moaning with pleasure as she savored the taste. "Here. Have some cake. It will make you feel better."

I leaned forward and took a bite, the perfect flavors of the best cake I'd ever had filling my mouth. But in Heaven, everything I put in my mouth was the best thing I'd ever had, and instead of being excited for the perfect blend of chocolate and sweetness, I just felt more irritated.

I slung an arm around her shoulder. "Maybe Heaven is sometimes frustrating for me because I still feel like I don't belong here. Honestly, I'm still not sure why they let us into the good place. You know, back on Earth, we got into a heck of a lot of trouble."

"Oh yes we did. Kinda worried we'd end up down there." She pointed a chocolate-covered finger at our feet, and I burst into laughter.

I grinned at the memories. "I gotta admit, when I was fading away, I started to panic that Heaven had a list of all the things we'd done, and we were gonna get a big fat door slammed in our faces."

Her blue eyes widened. "Oh, that list would have been very, very long."

She pulled a face, and the two of us burst into laughter as memories of our legendary mischief invaded my mind.

"Like that time in third grade when Jenny called you an ugly troll, so I put gum in her hair?"

Millie started laughing. "Or that time sophomore year that Jimmy and his friends were tormenting you about your botched haircut, so I copied his handwriting and wrote a sappy love letter to the most popular senior girl, oh man, what was her name? Lacy? Lucy? I forgot. But then I slipped it in her locker, and she read it aloud to all her friends? Oh my word, everyone teased him the whole year even though he was constantly screaming he didn't write it." She leaned in, whispering as a sly smile lifted her lips, "And only you and I know he wasn't lying. He didn't."

"It served him right!" I frowned, remembering the hell that little brat had put me through. "I wanted to drop out of school he was bullying me so badly."

Her sly smile grew into a full one. "He was too busy getting tormented himself to torment you after that. I had your back. I had it then, and I had it when your jerk of a husband cheated, and we got payback by hacking his email and forwarding his boss all those horrifyingly disgusting emails he wrote to his assistant and got him fired for sleeping with a subordinate."

Her eyes glistened and mine lit up too, remembering his total and utter devastation when I'd left him, and then he'd lost his job and his side chick all in one fell swoop. And he'd thought he'd accidentally sent the emails to the whole staff and never once figured out it had been us.

I slung an arm around her shoulder. "You had my back, and I had yours. Best friends for life."

"And afterlife," she noted, gesturing to the celestial world around us.

Best friends for afterlife we were. We'd met in a foster home when we were only three years old, and the two of us had been closer than sisters ever since. We'd become each other's family growing up as we navigated a world without our own. We chose each other as family, creating a bond stronger than if we'd merely been blood relatives. Both notorious pranksters, we'd had our share of mishaps, but I'd loved every minute of our unpredictable lives causing mischief and sharing endless laughter over all the trouble we got ourselves into.

A warm breeze, always the perfect temperature, rippled

across the water. I closed my eyes and leaned back on my hands, my toes drifting in the cool pond while the sun warmed my face.

Another perfect moment. Dying at ninety-one in my nursing home had its perks, apparently. Millie had gone first, and I'd held her hand when she'd left, my grief so profound that my heart gave out only a few hours later. They called it a heart attack. I called I a broken heart. We'd been best friends for almost nine decades, and now here we were, together again, forever and ever, enjoying nothing but bliss.

Wonderful, beautiful, incredibly *boring* bliss.

At first, Heaven had been exhilarating, a non-stop adventure of discovery and wish fulfillment. But as the days wore on, the luster began to fade. Everything was perfect, yes, but that perfection came at the cost of challenge, of risk, of the very imperfections that had made life on Earth so thrilling.

"I guess I miss the unknown." I sighed, looking out at the still water. "Half the fun of doing things is not knowing if you're going to succeed. Like when we tried surfing the other day, the waves were perfectly calibrated. No wipeouts, no fear, no fun. Every painting we do turns out perfect, just like always. Where's the challenge in that? I picked up a violin last week and even though I'd never touched one in my life, I was playing like I deserved a spot at the head of a symphony. I wanted to go cliff diving back on Earth for the rush, but here, there's no rush when you know you're completely safe. No adrenaline, no thrill. That was the whole point."

"I suppose you're right," Millie said quietly, her smile fading a little. "Not much risk of dying when you're already dead. But, at least we have each other."

That simple statement soothed me as I recognized that even though I didn't seem cut out for this endless perfection business, at least the one thing I never wanted to change was getting to spend eternity with Millie.

I gazed at my friend's face, so familiar and yet so different from the one I'd known as a child. Despite the decades that had weathered us both, turning our once-brown hair to grey, her eyes sparkled with the same mischievous gleam I remembered from my earliest memories.

When we landed in Heaven, they explained we'd look like we did at our happiest. Some folks turned back into their twenty-something selves, but Millie and I only rewound a couple of decades. Apparently, our seventies were peak happiness—free from husbands and jobs, just the two of us in our little house, gardening by day and binge-watching by night.

We sat in comfortable silence for a moment, but I could feel the restlessness building inside me again. I looked around at the peaceful spot away from all the other souls that we'd chosen for our morning routine. In Heaven, things worked similar to Earth. We had homes, and each home was constructed to the exact specifications of our deepest desires. Some people had mansions, others had cabins on a lake, and others, like Millie and me, had a little stone house surrounded with gardens that we shared together, since being together is what made us happiest. An exact replica of the house we'd been so happy in on Earth decades ago.

We lived in our homes and could venture around Heaven, simply blinking ourselves to any place we'd like. There were cities filled with people and music, jungles for those who liked to explore, oceans to sail on, mountains to climb, horses to ride, and basically any of our heart's desires could be fulfilled with just a simple thought.

Well, almost all of them. Heaven never served up the kind of challenge that made life worth living. "You know, does this endless perfection ever get…" I paused, looking around to make sure no soul or angel was around to hear me. "Boring to you?"

She finished chewing her bite of cake. "You mean Heaven?"

I nodded. "Yeah. Like, I really miss all the trouble you and I used to get up to, but you can't do that kind of stuff up here. It's Heaven. Letting the air out of someone's tires because they cut you off in traffic isn't a thing. There's no traffic. And no one to cut you off. No one to piss us off so we can get our well-earned revenge on them. It's just perfect all the time, and I guess I kinda miss the thrill of our shenanigans. Our little adventures we used to go on."

She nodded. "You know, I miss it too. I don't want to complain because Heaven is, well, Heavenly, but yeah. I wouldn't mind getting into a little bit of trouble again. Some M&M Mischief as we called it when we were kids." She grinned her mischievous smile I'd seen more times than I could count, but then it fell. "But we can't, can we? I don't think that's a thing in Heaven. I think our prankster days are done. We only gave people a hard time because they deserved it. No one up here deserves it, so we'd be the jerks if we just went around causing trouble for them."

My frown deepened. "Well, I guess it's just you and me living for eternity in Heavenly bliss."

She blinked and a margarita appeared in her hand. "We may not be able to get our kicks causing trouble anymore, but at least we can do this."

She handed me the drink and I laughed. A moment later, another margarita appeared in her hand. We clinked them together then went back to our peaceful morning by the pond.

After several tranquil hours together, we strolled back toward our house. Our joints no longer ached, and our bunions no longer throbbed. With our walkers a thing of the past, we enjoyed spending much of our time walking around just enjoying the sights of Heaven. When we reached the little village square, familiar souls greeted us.

"Beautiful day!" Arthur called from a swing set.

"It always is," I replied with a wave, unable to keep a hint of weariness from my voice.

"Hi, ladies!" Edna said, and I looked over to see her and several of her friends sitting at a sidewalk café indulging in a pizza overflowing with toppings.

"Hi!" We waved back, then continued greeting our fellow Heavenly inhabitants as we continued our stroll back to our little stone house.

As we continued on, a commotion caught our attention. Nick, a soul we'd met shortly after arriving, was embracing Natalie.

"You're back!" Natalie squealed. "How was it on Earth? Did you help many souls?"

"It was wonderful," Nick beamed. "I helped so many people cross over."

I stopped abruptly, causing Millie to bump into me. "Earth? Did he say he was on Earth?"

Without waiting for Millie's response, I dragged her over to the pair. "Sorry to interrupt," I said, "but did you say you were on Earth? How is that possible?"

Nick's smile faded slightly. "Oh, I was there as a Crossing Guard. We help confused souls transition to the afterlife."

"Like the person who helped us cross over when we died?" Millie asked, her eyes wide. "I remember just staring at my corpse watching Mabel sobbing over me trying to get back in to go back to her. It was awful. But then someone showed up and explained to me about Heaven, and I was able to let go."

"Yes. Those are Crossing Guards," Nick said. "And I was recently on assignment to be one for a month. I just got back."

My curiosity piqued. "So, you get to spend a month on Earth, and in exchange, you help souls cross over?"

"Yes, exactly," he said. "We go down in shifts, and when a person dies and doesn't immediately ascend, as a Crossing Guard, we get a little notification that there is a stuck soul, and we blink over to help them. It's very fulfilling."

Natalie smiled a wistful smile. "Being a Crossing Guard is a wonderful gift to give the newly departed. I've done it twice. It's an important task to make sure delayed souls don't get stuck on Earth and end up haunting people or something."

My eyebrow arched. "You can… haunt people? That's a thing?"

Nick's brow furrowed. "Well, yes. It's a thing. A *bad* thing obviously. Most souls either head north or south, but some refuse to let go and remain on the Earthly plane. Unfinished business. Fear of where they are going. There's lots of reasons, but it's obviously frowned upon to linger, so our jobs as Crossing Guards are to make sure those souls move on quickly."

"Mmmhmm. I see." I pursed my lips together, my mind reeling with ideas. "So, just to clarify, if you're a Crossing Guard in ghostly form, could you, I don't know, say, haunt someone while you were down there?"

He scrunched his brow further. "Haunt someone? Why on Earth would I want to haunt someone?"

I waved my hand. "No, no. I'm not saying you would, or that anyone should, of course, but just... could you?"

He shrugged, still looking perplexed by my question. "I, uh... I guess? I mean, it's not easy, or even possible for most ghosts on Earth to manipulate the living world, but I suppose it's possible since we're in ghost form down there, and there are ghosts who have figured out how to manipulate the world around them. Moving things, making noises, even appearing as apparitions. So, yes. I suppose that would be possible." Then he lifted an eyebrow. "But not recommended."

"No, no, of course not." I chuckled, wafting my hand. "I was just curious. My curiosity is always getting the best of me. So, how does one become a Crossing Guard?"

Nick appraised me with a wary eye then finally answered, "You need to apply at the Office of Celestial Affairs. They're quite selective."

Millie shot me a look, but I stayed her with my eyes. "Okay, well, welcome back, Nick. I'm sure we'll see you around now. And good job on helping all those stuck souls. Huzzah to you."

"Thanks," he said, but his suspicious eyes still watched me with concern as I grabbed Millie's hand and shuffled her off behind me.

Once we turned the corner, I spun around, my insides bubbling with excitement as I gripped her shoulders. "We both said we're bored up here and we miss playing tricks on people. What if we sign up to be Crossing Guards and then... we go haunt people!"

Her eyes went big. "What? You're joking!"

I practically bounced in my skin. "No! It would be hilarious! There are a few people who pissed us off in life we never got around to paying back, so what if we paid them a friendly little visit and… haunted them! Oh, Millie! It would be hilarious!"

Fear flickered in her eyes. "I don't know, Mabel. Don't you think we could get in trouble?"

I waved a hand at her. "We won't do anything bad. Just have a few laughs at their expense. And we can spend some time on Earth watching people do bad stuff for a bit to break the monotony of this constant perfection. Like living in a real-world television show! Oh, Millie! It would be a blast!"

She chewed on her lip. "What if we get in trouble for doing that and get sent to…" she leaned closer, pointing at her toes as she whispered, "the bad place? They never explained to us how they know who is good and who is bad. Maybe we'll get in trouble, and they won't let us back up! I mean, I'm bored too, but I don't want to go to…" she whispered again, "the bad place."

"Psht," I said, shrugging off her worry as I'd always done when we were alive. "We'll be fine. We're not going to kill anyone. Just go down to Earth, have a little fun like the old days, and, I guess, help a few souls while we're there. It's a win win!"

Worry deepened the familiar creases on her face as she stared at me, and then after glancing around at the picture-perfect world around us, she quirked a half smile. "It would be kinda fun to see what's going on down on Earth and maybe check in on a few of those people still remaining on our naughty list."

I slung an arm around her shoulder. "Exactly! Let's do this, Millie. You with me?"

She looked up at me, then with a soft shake of her head,

she laughed and said, "I was with you for ninety years in life, and you know I'm with you in death. I'm in."

"Yes!" I pumped a fist in the air and hurried us back to our house to make a plan to join the Crossing Guards and get ourselves back to Earth for a little well-earned M&M Mischief.

# Millie and Mabel's Afterlife Adventures: Chapter Two

## MILLIE

We stood in front of the looming marble doors of the Office of Celestial Affairs, my hand pressed tight to my chest as if to keep my heart from leaping out. Funny thing about being dead: you still feel like you've got a body. My chest still thumped when I was nervous, my breath still sped up when I was scared, and I even got butterflies in my stomach. All three were happening right now as I braced for the trouble ahead.

"I think I'm having a heart attack," I whispered. "They're going to know our plans are dubious, and a trapdoor is going to open up and drop us straight to the bad place!"

Mabel peered down at me from behind her dark-rimmed glasses, all five-eleven of her towering over my five-three. "You can't have a heart attack, Millie. Our hearts may still beat for whatever reason Heaven keeps them going, but you're already dead."

I bumped her with an elbow. "You don't know that! We

never did fully read the welcome manual. Maybe we can die again and like, *poof* out of existence for good!"

Mabel chuckled, her sharp, intelligent eyes sparkling with mischief. "Relax, Millie. We're here to ask a few questions, fill out an application, and maybe, just maybe, get a little excitement back in our afterlives. Nothing to worry about."

I bit my lip, glancing around at the grand entrance. The Office of Celestial Affairs was as majestic as the rest of Heaven, with towering columns, sparkling fountains, and angels flitting about, their wings shimmering in the sunlight. Despite the tranquility, my nerves refused to settle.

"We don't have to do this if you don't want to," Mabel said, knowing full well that I was ready to pass out from worry. "I know I'm always the one pushing us out of our comfort zones and coming up with hair-brained plans, but as always, the choice is yours. If you want to go home and enjoy eternity with nothing but sunshine and perfection, I'll understand, and we'll turn around now. But if you want to shake things up with me a bit and get into a little mischief like old times, I really think we can pull this off."

"And you don't think we're going to go to the bad place if we get caught?"

"If we get caught, I'll take the blame and you'll be innocent. I won't let you go to the bad place."

I frowned. "But if you get sent to the bad place without me, then I'll be alone here in eternity worrying about you… living a life without you. That's worse than any fate. I'd rather be in the bad place together."

Mabel's face softened with my words. "Aw. I would rather be in the bad place with you than alone in Heaven too. But we'll be fine, Millie. I promise. We always land on our feet. Let's just go in and find out more about this whole

Crossing Guard business, and then we can decide what's next together. How does that sound?"

"Alright. Let's do this." I sighed, trying to steady my breathing as I straightened my pink hat.

I'd spent an hour choosing an outfit I thought would be appropriate for a meeting with angels. My Sunday best pink skirt suit and a strand of lovely pearls and matching earrings I'd blinked into existence. If we were going to deceive heavenly bureaucrats, I figured I should at least look respectable doing it. Mabel, on the other hand, had made no such effort to impress and wore her usual slacks and button-down cardigan, looking like she was heading to the library rather than a celestial con job.

Mabel gave me a reassuring pat on the back as we pushed through the grand doors and stepped into the building. My pangs of anxiety quickened as we approached the reception desk.

An angel with flowing golden hair and a serene smile greeted us. "Welcome to the Office of Celestial Affairs. How can I assist you today?"

Mabel stepped forward with that unwavering confidence she'd had all our lives. "Hi, we're interested in becoming Crossing Guards. We heard we could apply here."

Her smile widened. "Of course. It's a noble duty. Please take a seat, and someone will be with you shortly."

We thanked her and found a pair of plush chairs near a window overlooking more of Heaven's beauty, the lush landscape stretching as far as the eye could see. As we waited, my mind raced with a thousand thoughts. What if they saw through us? What if they knew our true intentions?

Mabel seemed unfazed, casually crossing her arms and

reclining against the seat. "You need to relax, Millie. Think of this as our next great adventure."

My body vibrated as I bounced my leg, then I forced it to remain still, trying to absorb some of her calm. "I know, but I can't help but worry. We're not the best candidates for this job. We're not exactly saints."

She smirked. "I don't think being a saint is in the job description. And hey, we were good enough to get into Heaven somehow, so we can't be all that bad. You know, we were pretty good people as a matter of fact."

I snorted. "Yeah, says the woman who took the tires off that guy's car and left it on blocks in his driveway."

She poked a finger at me and whispered, "Quiet! We don't want the angels to hear! And hey. He had it coming. He was speeding down the street so fast every day he almost killed that little boy and his dog. I was just teaching him a lesson. Justice." She lifted her chin higher.

"I suppose. You're right. Our mischief was always well-intentioned. It's not like we ever bullied anyone who didn't deserve it."

Her shoulders straightened, making her seem taller than she already was. "Exactly. We were like… Robin Hood. We stood up for the little guy."

"Well, you did most of the standing up and going toe to toe with people. I just worked behind the scenes," I admitted, since it was usually Mabel who caused the most trouble since I was always too chicken to get caught.

"You did your fair share of shenanigans too."

"Yeah, but mine were sneaky. No one ever knew it was me. You were the brave one who would look people right in the eye while you stood up to them. Like that time you—"

She lifted her hand to stop me midsentence then jutted her chin toward the angel behind the reception desk. Out of the corner of her mouth, she whispered, "We probably shouldn't be talking about all the bad things we've done in front of a literal angel."

I slid my fingers across my lips like a zipper and nodded.

We sat in silence for a long while, then an angel with a clipboard came down the hallway and approached us. "Millie and Mabel? Follow me, please."

We exchanged a quick glance and stood up, following the angel down a corridor lined with intricate tapestries depicting scenes from various afterlives. The angel led us to a spacious office, where another angel, this one quite handsome with a chiseled jaw, bright blue eyes and ebony hair, sat behind a large, ornate desk.

"Welcome," the angel said, gesturing for us to sit. "I'm Kafziel. I understand you're interested in becoming Crossing Guards?"

Mabel nodded enthusiastically. "Yes, we are. We want to help souls transition smoothly. It sounds like a very fulfilling role."

Kafziel's piercing eyes seemed to look straight through us, and I squirmed in my seat. "It is indeed a vital task. Tell me, why do you want to become Crossing Guards?"

Mabel launched into her rehearsed speech. "We're so grateful to be here in Heaven and we want to help in any way we can. We've spent our entire lives, and now our afterlives, helping each other as well as other people in need. We've seen how much a guiding hand can mean to someone. We want to extend that help to others."

I nodded along, adding, "We want to give back and make sure no soul feels lost or scared. I remember how I felt in those moments after I passed. I just stood there beside my body trying so hard to get back in it. I didn't want to leave Mabel, and even though I felt the pull to leave my mortal life, I couldn't make myself do it. But then the kindest man, Abe, showed up and told me all about Heaven and that Mabel would meet me here when it was her time. He helped me let go and transition, and I want to help someone else the same way."

The words tumbling out of my mouth weren't entirely untrue. I *did* want to help souls cross over. Abe had done that for me. But I left out the part about what we planned to do between those beautiful moments of helping those souls.

Haunting people.

Kafziel studied us for a moment, then pushed up from his desk and walked out without a word.

"They know." I trembled in my chair, whispering so loudly I may as well have been screaming.

"Shhhh," Mabel hushed. "They don't know! He's just… I don't know what the heck he's doing but they don't know. We were perfect."

"They are *angels!* They can probably read our minds, and he knows we're full of crap! Oh my God. We're going to Hell."

"We're not going to Hell," she argued back. "Just stay calm. If you act like you're guilty, they'll think you're guilty."

"I *am* guilty! You and I both know we only want to go to Earth to shake things up a bit and haunt people, and we're using this Crossing Guard thing as a cover! We're guilty and they know we're guilty and we're going to Hell. Where we probably belong!"

She reached out and took my hand, calming me down with the simple touch. "Hey, hey, hey," she soothed. "We're fine. We haven't done anything wrong. And you know what, they would be lucky to have us as Crossing Guards. We're kind, we're understanding, and what newly deceased person wouldn't want to see these mugs moments after they die." She grinned widely. "We're friendly and fun, and I bet we'd actually do a great job. And yeah, maybe we'd have a little fun between crossings, but we're good for this job. Trust me, Millie. We're gonna be fine. We've got this."

She took a big breath and nodded for me to take one with her. Together we exhaled, and I let the tension slough off my shoulders.

"You okay?"

I nodded. "Yes. Sorry. I spun out for a second there."

"You've got me to grab the wheel. Always have, always will."

She squeezed my hand and I smiled, memories of the number of times she'd calmed my easily frazzled nerves filling my mind. Mabel was always cool in any situation, and I tended to spin like a top at the slightest upheaval. It was part of why she was such a treasured person to me. Like a security blanket she could wrap me up in with just one smile.

Kafziel opened the door and walked back behind his desk, sitting down and steepling his fingers as he looked at us.

My heart pounded against my chest so hard I was certain he could hear it.

He cleared his throat. "I believe you two would make excellent Crossing Guards."

Mabel squeezed my hand tight. "You do?"

"Yes. I've reviewed your files, and I don't see anything to contradict the job description." We nodded earnestly, and Kafziel continued, "There are a few formalities. You'll need to sign these forms and undergo a brief training session. Are you prepared for that?"

"Absolutely," Mabel said, her eyes gleaming with excitement, and I nodded so hard my neck would have hurt if I could still feel pain.

He leaned back in his chair and his full lips lifted into a half smile. "Then welcome to the Crossing Guards."

The anxiety bouncing around inside me nearly burst out my skin as I smiled and said, "Thank you, Kafziel. We won't let you down."

"Good. Then follow me for processing and we'll get you assigned."

We followed him to a different room then filled out the forms, and Kafziel provided us with a detailed overview of our duties. I tried to focus on the responsibilities and the rules that applied to being Crossing Guards, but my mind kept drifting to our secret plan. Could we really pull this off without getting into serious trouble?

After several hours, we completed the paperwork and training overview. Kafziel stood up and lead us to a different room, this one a large, empty room with an ornate door marked "Earth."

"Is that how we get there?" I asked, pointing at the door.

Kafziel nodded.

"Are we going… now? Today?" Mabel's eyes got wide.

"Well, we are actually a little slow on volunteers at the moment. It's a lot to ask souls to leave the warm and wonderful world of Heaven to endure the pains and sorrows down on Earth. If you're up for it, you can start your assignment now."

I looked to Mabel for reassurance, and by the light illuminating in her expression, I knew the answer that was popping out of her mouth.

"Yes! We are ready!" she said.

He looked to me. "And you?"

With a deep breath, I gave him a nod. "I'm ready."

A stern stare passed between us. "Remember, this is a noble task, and I trust you'll take it seriously."

"We will," I answered honestly. Even if we did manage to get into a little trouble on the side, I wouldn't shirk my duties of helping souls move onto their next life.

"Normally, Crossing Guards operate individually, but we've seen in your files that you two can't be separated."

She and I looked at each other, then looked back at him giving him a confirming nod.

"So, we will only give you one beacon and the two of you will function as one. Where one goes, the other goes, and when the beacon flashes blue to alert you to a soul in need, you'll travel to them together."

"Okay, so we stay together," I said, glad for that because there was no way I was going back to Earth without Mabel.

"Here is the manual you can refer to if you have questions, and if you get in any serious trouble, you can also press your beacon and an angel will come down to assist you. Remember, it's imperative you help these souls move on to their next journey. If they refuse to go, they become lost souls and if they stay too long…"

I remembered his words in our training. "They will get reaped and cease to exist," I said, then swallowed over the lump in my throat hoping we didn't fail any of the souls that would cross our paths.

"Good luck, ladies. Your temporary shift is two weeks, and then your beacon will go off to direct you back to a door on Earth that opens to this one. At that time, we'll check in and do an evaluation to see if you are up to this task on a more permanent basis. I hope to hear only good reports."

Again, that accusatory glance passed between us, and I

could swear he knew we were up to no good, but instead of grabbing us by the hair and casting us to Hell, he just gave a sharp nod and walked over the door.

"Safe travels."

He opened the door and I squinted against the blinding white light.

Mabel bounced on her toes, her enthusiasm infectious. "This is it. Here we go. Ready, Millie?"

I took a deep breath, trying to quell the butterflies in my stomach, a potent mix of excitement and dread bubbling up inside of me. "As ready as I'll ever be."

We stood before the door, the reality of our plan sinking in. Mabel was practically glowing with excitement, while I felt a mix of fear and anticipation.

"Just think of it as our next big adventure," Mabel said, her voice filled with confidence. "What's the worst that could happen?"

I shot her a nervous glance. "You really want me to answer that?"

She laughed, and despite my fear, I couldn't help but join in. "We've got this, Millie. Together, we can handle anything."

I nodded, feeling a surge of courage. "Alright. Let's do this."

We took a deep breath, and with a final, shared look of determination, we gripped our hands tight together and stepped through, ready to embark on our newest adventure.

# Millie and Mabel's Afterlife Adventures: Chapter Three

## MABEL

Hand in hand, Millie and I stepped through the glowing doorway, the brilliant white light enveloping us. A swirling sensation overcame me as the world around us shifted and morphed.

The next thing I knew, we were standing in the midst of a bustling city street, cars whizzing by and people rushing past in a blur of motion. The sounds and smells of the urban chaos hit me like a tidal wave after the tranquil serenity of Heaven.

"Whoa..." I exhaled, looking around in awe. It had been months since I'd experienced the frenetic energy of Earth, and decades since I'd been in a big city.

Millie clutched my arm, her eyes wide. "This is... overwhelming."

"Isn't it great?" I grinned, soaking in the sights and sounds. "I'd almost forgotten what the real world felt like."

As I watched the frenzy of people rushing to and fro, I stood and absorbed everything happening around me at once. Heaven's tranquil beauty was undeniable, but there was an intensity to Earth, a vibrant energy that couldn't be replicated in the afterlife.

These people weren't just existing—they were truly living. Chasing dreams, following passions, making every second count. I envied the urgency in their steps, the determination etched on their faces. Each one was on a journey, navigating the ups and downs, the triumphs and heartbreaks that made the human experience so brilliantly messy... and utterly wonderful.

In Heaven, emotions were in a constant, unchanging state.

Happiness.

Pure, unwavering happiness.

But here, emotions flickered across expressions like a kaleidoscope. A couple holding hands radiated pure joy; a businessman barked into his phone, frustration furrowing his brow; a child's peals of laughter cut through the noises like a bright burst of sunshine. Every soul was a living, breathing masterpiece, their canvases painted in vibrant strokes of love, anger, hope, and every emotion in between.

I'd almost forgotten the raw experiences of the real world and how it felt to be truly alive. Heaven's perfection was incredible to be sure, but part of me craved the bitter to appreciate the sweet—the struggles that made the triumphs so incredibly rewarding.

As I watched a tired mother scoop her giggling toddler into an embrace, I realized what I'd been missing in my afterlife. The struggles, the heartaches... they were the balance to the eternal bliss that made you appreciate the good times… made them taste that much sweeter.

In that moment, I vowed to soak in every second of this adventure. To appreciate the chaos, the passion, the dizzying rush of the human world in a way I'd taken for granted before. This was the greatest gift—a chance to experience life anew, to let it etch itself upon my soul once more.

A car flew by close, shaking me from my nostalgic musing and nearly hitting me. I threw a fist in the air. "Watch it, buddy!"

The driver, of course, couldn't hear my protest. In fact, no one on the crowded street seemed to notice us at all.

"Hey… they can't see us!" I said, looking around at the crowd completely oblivious to our presence. "This is so weird."

Millie waved at a man on the sidewalk, and even though to me she looked like a flesh and blood human, he paid her no mind. "We're invisible! Cool!"

"I love this!" I lifted my hands in the air and started spinning around, my grin stretched wide across my face as I absorbed the wonders around me. I made another spin, and my eyes flew open as a taxicab sped straight toward us.

"Look out!" I screamed to Millie, reaching out a hand to grab her, but before we could leap out of the way, it drove right through us. I stumbled back in surprise, glancing down at my still intact body as it sped away.

"Are… are we hurt?" Millie patted herself, checking for injury.

I did the same, then looked up and smiled. "Hey! We're already dead! Nothing down here can hurt us! Heck yeah!"

Millie shuddered, her face scrunching. "That felt weird. I didn't like it. That's going to take some getting used to."

"Yeah, that was weird. But better cars can go through us than us being pavement pancakes right now." Though it didn't hurt us, I also didn't like the sensation of the car passing through me. I jutted my chin toward the sidewalk.

"Maybe let's not do that again. Come on. Let's get off the street."

"Why would they put the door to Heaven in the middle of the street?" Millie asked as she followed me.

I shrugged. "I assume Heaven's been around a lot longer than cities. That door has probably been here for millennia. Wasn't a street back then."

"Good point," Millie said as we stepped up onto the curb. "Amazing to think ghosts and Crossing Guards and all that have been living among us all this time and we were never aware."

"Nick said there are some people who can see us. I always thought those people were nuts."

She nodded. "Me too. Never believed in ghosts, yet here we are. A couple of dead gals walking around on Earth."

"Well, we know we can't get run over. That's one thing we've learned. What else can we do?" I glanced over at the newspaper dispenser beside us. Experimentally, I reached out toward it and tried to grab the handle. My otherwise solid-looking hand passed through it like smoke. I frowned. "Damn. I guess we can't interact with physical objects."

"Well, that's inconvenient," Millie grumbled.

My scowl deepened. "Yeah. That *is* inconvenient. How are we going to haunt people if they can't see us, and we can't move things?"

She shrugged. "I don't know. Maybe we're not allowed to haunt people as Crossing Guards."

My shoulders slumped. "Oh man. I really wanted to go full Casper on some people who could use a little humbling. I had my eyes set on that jerk leading Russia. What's his name? We could haunt him to the point of insanity, and then when he got locked up in the looney bin, we'd have been responsible for saving the world. Like a couple of ghostly gal superheroes."

"Oh! That's a good one! Way better than mine. I only had my sights set on Howard from our nursing home. He dug up all those beautiful flowers I planted in the garden because he didn't like the way they smelled. He killed my babies." She stuck out her lip.

My eyes flashed wide as anger reverberated in my chest that someone had been giving my Millie a hard time and I hadn't known it. "Why didn't you tell me you knew who did that? You said you had no idea. I'd have given him the business!"

"We weren't on the best terms with the nurses after we broke into the kitchen and tried making pancakes at two in the morning the week before. I knew you'd go full tilt at getting revenge and probably get us in more trouble. I figured I could get him back later, but then, well, we died."

I touched her shoulder. "Well, we may be dead, invisible, and not able to touch anything, but I bet we can find some way to torment that jerk. Let's see what else we can do as ghosts, and maybe we'll find some super power we can use to get justice! We'll practice on him and then let's go save the world by haunting that psychopath in Russia. Now, to figure out what powers we have." I pressed a finger to my chin as I started running ideas through my mind.

"Like what?" Millie asked.

"Well? I don't know. Let's play around a bit and see what we're capable of."

A man came walking past, and though he hadn't done anything to deserve a haunting, I had to try out our ghostly skills. I stuck my foot in front of him, but instead of tripping over it, he just walked right through it.

"Damn it. We can't trip people," I grumbled.

"Well, it would make sense since a taxi drove right through us."

"I had to try." I shrugged.

"Oh! Hold on. Maybe we can possess people! Like get inside of them and make them do things!"

Millie's brow furrowed in worry. "I don't want to possess anyone. That sounds terrible."

"I just want to try." I looked around and found a police officer nearby writing someone a parking ticket. "I'm just going to try hopping in him for a second."

"Mabel! What if you get stuck? I don't think you should do that!"

I just grinned and trotted over to where he was leaning forward, putting the ticket under the windshield wipers. I stepped up behind him, then with a big breath, I jumped forward into him. But instead of taking over his body and possessing him, I shrieked as I plummeted straight through him, ending up face down on the pavement under the car I'd just fallen through.

"Damn it!" I shouted from beneath it.

Millie's face appeared as she peeked down beneath it. "Are you hurt?"

Grumbling, I rose up to standing smack dab in the middle of the car's hood. "No. It doesn't seem like we feel pain in this form either because if I'd have fallen like that as an old lady human, I'd have broken a hip and been on my way to the ER."

I stepped through the car and started dusting off my clothes, but then noticed no dirt had clung to me and the whole process was in vain. "Well, that was an epic fail. We can't do *anything*!" I crossed my arms and pouted. "This whole Crossing Guard business is for the birds!"

"Well, our purpose is to help souls cross over, not haunt

people, so I'm not surprised we don't actually come equipped with haunting powers."

"I know," I admitted. "It's just that when Nick said some ghosts stay behind and can haunt, I really thought we could do it too. Maybe we can if we practice a little."

I looked over at a man passing by and leaped in front of him with one last ditch attempt to possess him. "Gah!" I screamed as I tried to dive into him. Instead, I ended up on the pavement with unaware pedestrians stepping through me.

"Oh, Mabel!" Millie shouted and hurried to help me up. "What were you thinking?"

I grumbled as a woman's shoe went through my head, then I took Millie's hand, and she lifted me to my feet.

"Possession. Not a thing," I said, once again going to dust myself off then remembering it was unnecessary.

"Your haunting skills, or lack thereof, are really something, Mabel. Maybe we should just forgo the haunting thing and just do the Crossing Guard shift then go back to Heaven and stay there," Millie said.

"Even if we can't haunt, I do still like just being down here, I guess," I admitted. "It's fun watching the humans even if we can't scare the crap out of them for funsies." An idea popped into my head, and I smirked. "Wait. If we can't haunt people, that doesn't mean there may not be other cool stuff we can do. Since we're ghosts down here, I wonder if we can…"

"If we can what?" Millie asked.

With excitement fluttering in my chest, hoping with everything I had it was possible, I bent my knees and pushed off the ground, letting out a whoop of delight as I defied gravity and floated a few feet in the air. "Check it out, Millie! We can fly!"

She gasped, her hands flying to her mouth. "Mabel, get down from there! Someone's going to see you!"

I rolled my eyes. "Who's going to see me? We're invisible, remember?"

To prove my point, I drifted over to a young woman buried in her phone, waving my hand directly in front of her face. "Boo!" I screamed at her. She didn't even flinch, continuing on her way. "See?" I called down to Millie. "Completely undetectable. Come on, Millie! Try it! This is amazing!" I did a little flip, got disoriented and had to fight to steady myself. "Okay. Baby steps. Maybe just try floating up here with me."

She pursed her lips, concern tightening her face. "In Heaven, only the angels can fly. Are you sure we're supposed to be doing this?"

"I mean, I don't think we'd be able to if we weren't allowed. Maybe as Crossing Guards, we're like temporary angels? Or maybe since we're ghosts down here, it's the ghosts who can fly? I don't know why, but I'm doing it!" I tried to fly higher but couldn't get more than ten feet off the ground. It was still exhilarating to be drifting above the people below me. I practiced going higher and lower, stopping periodically to make faces at people as I hovered upside down in front of them. I stuck my tongue out at a woman talking loudly on her phone, and for good measure, I tried, and failed, to boop her in the nose.

"Come on, Millie! You're missing all the fun! We're already dead, you can't get hurt. Lord knows I've just proved that several times. Just try it, this is amazing!"

After a moment's hesitation, she bent her knees and pushed off the ground, joining me in the air. A scream escaped her lips and then turned into a nervous giggle as she hovered uncertainly.

"I'm doing it! I'm flying!" she said, then wobbled a bit and reached over and grabbed my hand. "This is so strange."

"But fun, right?" I did a little twirl, reveling in the newfound freedom of flight.

A laugh bubbled up from her chest. "Okay, yes, it's a little fun."

We spent the next few minutes spinning, twirling, and zipping through the air, putting our new abilities to the test. At one point, Millie let out a shriek as she accidentally passed through a building, ending up on the other side of the wall.

"Jiminy Josephats. I don't recommend that," she said as she rejoined me. "It's incredibly disorienting."

"Noted," I said, though admittedly, now I wanted to try it.

As we floated above the bustling sidewalk, watching the humans scurry about, a wistful expression crossed Millie's face. "I'd almost forgotten how alive this place feels. The sights, the sounds, the smells... it's all so vibrant."

"Yeah..." I inhaled deeply, catching a whiff of exhaust fumes and street food. "It's a sensory overload after Heaven's perfection."

"Don't get me wrong, Heaven is wonderful," Millie said quickly. "But there's something about the chaos of Earth that's... invigorating."

Grab your copy…

**vinci-books.com/MillieAndMabel**

www.ingramcontent.com/pod-product-compliance
Lightning Source LLC
La Vergne TN
LVHW030918080826
845145LV00013B/2949

* 9 7 8 1 0 3 6 7 1 5 8 6 1 *